flamingo sixties classic

Len Deighton

FUNERAL IN BERLIN

Flamingo
An Imprint of HarperCollins*Publishers*

Flamingo
An imprint of HarperCollins *Publishers*
77–85 Fulham Palace Road,
Hammersmith, London w6 8jb

Flamingo is a registered trade mark of HarperCollins Publishers Ltd.

www.fireandwater.com

This Flamingo Sixties Classic edition published 2001
9 8 7 6 5 4 3 2 1

First published in Great Britain by Jonathan Cape Ltd 1964

Copyright © Len Deighton 1964

Len Deighton asserts the moral right to
be identified as the author of this work

This novel is entirely a work of fiction.
The names, characters and incidents portrayed in it
are the work of the author's imagination.
Any resemblance to actual persons, living or dead,
events or localities is entirely coincidental.

ISBN 0 00 711523 7

Set in Monotype Apollo and Optima display by
Rowland Phototypesetting Ltd
Bury St Edmunds, Suffolk

Printed and bound in Great Britain by
Omnia Books Limited, Glasgow

ALLEN W. DULLES (then director CIA):
>   'You, Mr Chairman, may have seen some of my intelli-
>   gence reports from time to time.'

MR KHRUSHCHEV:
>   'I believe we get the same reports – and probably
>   from the same people.'

MR DULLES:
>   'Maybe we should pool our efforts.'

MR KHRUSHCHEV:
>   'Yes. We should buy our intelligence data together and
>   save money. We'd have to pay the people only once.'
>
>   News Item, September 1959

>   'But what good came of it at last?'
>   Quoth little Peterkin,
>   'Why, that I cannot tell,' said he: –
>   'But 'twas a famous victory.'
>
>   SOUTHEY, After Blenheim

'If I am right the Germans will say I was a German and the
French will say I was a Jew; if I am wrong the Germans will
say I was a Jew and the French will say I was a German.'

                                            ALBERT EINSTEIN

   Most of the people who engaged in this unsavoury work
had very little interest in the cause which they were paid to
promote. They did not take their parts too seriously, and one
or the other would occasionally go over to the opposite side,
for espionage is an international and artistic profession, in
which opinions matter less than the art of perfidy.

                    DR R. LEWINSOHN, The Career of Sir Basil Zaharoff

Funeral in Berlin

Secret File No 3

1

Players move alternately – only one at a time.

Saturday, October 5th

It was one of those artificially hot days that they used to call 'Indian summer'. It was no time to be paying a call to Bina Gardens, in south-west London, if there was a time for it.

Outside the house I sought there was a bright card tied to the railings with green twine. On it in large exact capitals was penned 'Lost – Siamese cat. Answers to the name Confucius.'

Answers what? I walked up the steps where the sun was warming up a pint of Jersey and a banana-flavour yoghurt. Tucked behind the bottles a *Daily Mail* peeped its headline 'Berlin a new crisis?' There were buttons on that door-post like on a pearly king's hat but only one said 'James J. Hallam, FRSA' in a flowing copper-plate; that was the one I pressed.

'You haven't seen Confucius?'

'No,' I said.

'I only missed him last night.'

'Really,' I said, feigning warm interest.

'The bedroom window doesn't close properly,' said Hallam. He was a gaunt-faced man of about forty-five well preserved years. His dark-grey flannel suit was baggy and in the lapel of it he wore three neat discs of egg yolk, like the Legion of Honour.

3

'You will be one of Dawlish's little men,' he said.

He exposed a white palm and I walked into the cool stone hall while he closed the daylight out.

He said, 'Could you let me have a shilling – the gas will go any moment.'

I gave him one and he galloped away with it.

Hallam's room was tidy the way a cramped room has to be. He had a desk that was a sink and a cupboard that was a bed and under my feet a battered kettle on a gas ring was sending Indian signals to the bookcase. Flies were whining in great bed-spring spirals of sound, then going to the window to beat on it with their feet. Through the window there was a large section of grey brick wall; on it there were two perfect rectangles of white sunlight reflected from some high sunny place. I moved three Bartok LPs and sank into a mutilated chair. Hallam turned on the tap in the disguised sink and there was a chugging sound like a bronchial road-drill. He rinsed the cups and wiped them on a tea-cloth that depicted the changing of the guard at Buckingham Palace in primary colours. There was a clink as he set the cups into their ordained saucers.

'Don't tell me. You've come about the Semitsa business,' he said to the gas meter as he poured boiling water on to the Darjeeling. 'You like Darjeeling?'

'Darjeeling's OK,' I said. 'What I'm not so keen about is you batting that name about like that. Have you ever heard of the Official Secrets Act?'

'My dear boy, I am trussed up with the OS Act twice a year like a very old and intractable turkey.' He put half a dozen wrapped sugar pieces on the table and said, 'You won't take milk in Darjeeling': it wasn't a question. He sipped his unsweetened tea from an antique Meissen cup; around mine it said 'British Railways SR' in brown grot letters.

'So you are the man who is going to make Semitsa defect

4

from the Moscow Academy of Sciences and come to work in the west; no, don't tell me.' He waved down my protest with a limp palm. 'I'll tell you. In the last decade not one Soviet scientist has defected westward. Did you ever ask yourself why?' I unwrapped one of the sugar pieces; the paper had 'Lyons Corner House' printed on it in small blue letters.

'This fellow Semitsa. A member of the Academy. Not a party member because he doesn't *need* to be; Academy boys are the top dogs – the new elite. He probably gets about six thousand roubles[1] a month. Tax paid. On top of that he can keep any money he gets for lecturing, writing or being on TV. The lab restaurants are fabulous – *fabulous*. He has a town house and a country cottage. He has a new Zil every year and when he feels in the mood there is a special holiday resort on the Black Sea which only the Academy people use. If he dies his wife gets a gigantic pension and his children get special educational opportunities in any case. He works in the Genetics of Molecular Biology department where they use refrigerated ultra centrifuges.' Hallam waved his sugar cube at me.

'They are one of the basic tools of modern biology and they cost around ten thousand pounds each.'

He waited while that sank in.

'Semitsa has twelve of them. Electron microscopes cost around fourteen thousand pounds each, he . . .'

'OK,' I said. 'What are you trying to do, recruit me?'

'I'm trying to let you see this situation from Semitsa's point of view,' said Hallam. 'His biggest problems at this moment are likely to be whether to give his son a Zaporozhets or a Moskvich motor car for a twenty-first birthday present, and deciding which of his servants is stealing his Scotch whisky.'

---

[1] Over £2,000.

Hallam unwrapped the sugar cube and ate it with a loud crunching noise.

'What are you offering him? Have you seen those semi-detached houses they are putting the Porton people into? And as for the labs, they are little more than hardboard shacks. He'll think it's the prison camp and keep asking when he gets released,' Hallam tittered.

'OK,' I said. 'That's enough dialectical materialism for one cup of Darjeeling. Just tell me if your people at the Home Office will do your bit if we deliver him to you.'

Hallam tittered again and extended a finger like he was tapping me on the nose.

'You get him first, that's all I'm saying. We'd love to have him. He's the best enzyme man in the world today, but you just get him first.'

He popped another piece of sugar in his mouth and said, 'We'd just love him, *love* him.'

One of the flies was beating on the window trying to escape; the sound of its buzzing wings rose to a loud frantic hammering. The tiny body smashing itself against the glass made faint clicks. As the energy oozed out of it, it sank down the glass, kicking and fluttering in fury at the force that had solidified the very air. Hallam poured more tea and dug around inside one of his little cupboards. He moved a packet of Omo and a wad of travel agents' literature. The top leaflet showed people waving out of a bus which was parked in the Alhambra and said 'Suntraps of Spain' in blobby lettering. Across the side of the bus it said, 'For as little as 31 guineas.' He found a brightly coloured packet and gave a little yap of triumph.

'Custard creams,' he said.

He arranged two of them on an oval dish. 'I don't eat breakfast on Saturdays. Sometimes I go down the El Mokka for a sausage-and-chip lunch but quite often I manage with a biscuit.'

'Thanks,' I said. I took one.

'You can't trust the waiter there, though,' said Hallam.

'In what way?' I asked.

'They pad the bills,' said Hallam. 'Last week I found a shilling for bread and butter slipped in.' He picked up the final few biscuit crumbs with a moistened finger-tip.

Outside in the hall I could hear a woman's voice saying, 'If I've told you once I've told you a thousand times – no bicycles.'

I couldn't hear the man's voice properly but the woman's voice said, 'Outside – that's what we pay road taxes for.'

Hallam said, 'I *never* have bread and butter.'

I sipped my tea and nodded while Hallam opened the window for the fly.

Hallam said, 'And what's more he knows it.' Hallam gave a little laugh at the irony of life with an emphasis on the frailty of human nature.

'He knows it,' said Hallam again. Suddenly he said to me, 'You aren't sitting on my Bartoks by any chance?'

Hallam counted his records in case I had hidden a couple in my raincoat. He collected the cups and stacked them near the sink ready for washing.

He plucked back his sleeve to commune with a large wristwatch. He looked at it for a second or so before he carefully undid the grimy leather strap. The glass was scratched with a thousand tiny scratches and one or two deep ones. The green hands had come to rest at 9.15. Hallam held the watch to his ear.

'It's 11.20,' I told him.

He shushed me and his eyes rolled gently to demonstrate the expertise with which he was listening to the silent mechanism.

I could take a hint. Hallam had the door open before I had even said, 'Well I must . . .'

He walked behind me through the hall to make sure that

I didn't steal the lino. A fanlight over the entrance let a William Morris design in coloured sunlight fall across the stone floor. Fixed against one wall was a pay telephone with notices and old undelivered mail marked 'Inland Revenue' tucked behind the telephone directories. One notice said 'Miss Mortimer is away in Spain on business.' It was written in lipstick on the back of a used envelope.

At waist level the old brown wallpaper had suffered a series of horizontal white gashes. From the floor under them Hallam picked up a tin that had the words 'Acme Puncture Outfit' enmeshed in a design of scrolls, daisies and bicycle wheels. He made a clicking noise with his tongue and put the tin on top of the A–D telephone directory.

Hallam gripped the huge street door with two hands. Another notice on it said 'Slamming this at night disturbs early risers.' The *Daily Mail* and the yoghurt were still in the same position and from farther down the street I could hear the clink of milk bottles.

Hallam offered me a hand like a dead animal. 'Best enzyme man,' he said.

I nodded. 'In the world,' I said, and eased sideways through the partly open door.

'Give him this,' said Hallam. He pushed a wrapped cube of Lyons sugar into my hand.

'Semitsa?' I said very quietly.

'The milkman's horse, you silly. There. Friendly creature. And if you do see Confucius . . .'

'OK,' I said. I walked down the steps into the hot dusty sunlight.

'My goodness. I haven't paid you back for the gas-meter shilling,' said Hallam. It was a simple statement of fact; he wasn't turning his pockets out.

'Donate it to the RSPCA,' I called. Hallam nodded. I looked around but there was no sign of Confucius anywhere.

2

ROBIN JAMES HALLAM

Saturday, October 5th

After his visitor had left Hallam looked in the mirror again. He was trying to guess his age.

'Forty-two,' he said to himself.

His hair was all there, that was one good thing. A man with plenty of hair looked young. It would need a little colouring of course but then colouring his hair was something he had thought of doing for years before he had this problem of finding a new job. 'Brown,' he thought, 'a mousy brown.' So that it wouldn't be too obvious; no point in going in for one of those really bright colours because it would be spotted as phoney in two minutes. He turned his head and tried to see how much of his profile he could see in reflection. He had a lean, very aristocratic Anglo-Saxon face. The nose had sharp ridges and the cheekbones were tight under his skin. A thoroughbred. He often thought of himself as a racehorse. It was a pleasant thought and one that was easily associated with acres of green grass, horse shows, grouse-shooting, hunt balls, elegant men and bejewelled women. He liked to think of himself in that context even though his function as a thoroughbred was nearer the seat of Government. He liked that; the seat of Government. Hallam laughed at his reflection and his reflection laughed back in a friendly, dignified, handsome way. He decided to tell someone at the office but it was difficult to decide which one of them would appreciate the joke – so many of them were dullards.

Hallam walked back to the gramophone. He stroked the shiny immaculate veneer top and took pleasure in the silent way it opened; well-made – British made. He selected a record from his large collection. They were all there, all the finest composers of the twentieth century. Berg, Stravinsky, Ives. He selected a recording of a work of Schönberg. The shiny black disc was impeccable. It was as hygienic and dustfree as as as . . . why wasn't there anything as clean as his records? He put it on the gramophone and applied the pick-up head to the merest brim of the record. He did this skilfully. There was a faint hissing noise, then the room was suddenly full of rich sounds: 'Variations for wind band'. He liked it. He sat well back in his chair, fidgeting his back to find the exact position of maximum comfort like a cat. 'Like a cat,' he thought and he was pleased with that thought. He listened to the plaited threads of the instrumental sounds and decided that when the music stopped he would have a cigarette. 'After both sides,' he thought: 'after I've played both sides I will have a cigarette.' He rested back in the chair again, pleased with the self-imposed discipline.

He thought of himself as a monk-like person. Once, in the toilet at the office, he had heard one of the junior clerks refer to him as an 'old hermit'. He had liked that. He looked around at his cell-like room. Every item there had been carefully chosen. He was a man who understood quality in the old-fashioned sense of the word. How he despised those people who have a fancy modern oven and then only heat frozen super-market food in it. All he had was a gas ring but it was what you cooked on it that counted. Fresh country eggs and bacon, there was nothing in the world to beat that. Cooked carefully, cooked in butter even though he wasn't a man given to extravagance. Few women understood how to cook eggs and bacon. Or anything else. He remembered a housekeeper he had had at one time, she always broke the yolks of the eggs and had tiny black burnt specks on the whites. She didn't clean the pan properly. It was as simple as that. She didn't clean the pan properly. The times he had told her. He walked across to the wash-basin and looked in the mirror. 'Mrs Henderson,' he mouthed the words, 'you simply must clean the pan with paper – not with water – thoroughly before you fry eggs and bacon.' He gave a pleasant smile. It wasn't a nervous smile, on the other hand it wasn't the sort of smile that encouraged argument. It was in fact exactly the right sort of smile for this situation. He rather prided himself on his ability to provide the right sort of smile for every occasion.

The music was still playing but he decided to have a cigarette anyway, he certainly wasn't going to become a slave to his own machine. What he decided to do was to compromise. He could have a cigarette but it would be one of the Bachelor brand – the cheap ones that he kept in the large cigarette box for visitors. He rather prided himself on his ability to compromise. He went across to the cigarette box. There were four in there. He decided not to take one of those. Four was about right. Yes. He got a Player's No. 3 from a box of twenty that he kept in the cutlery drawer. 'Thirty-nine,' he thought suddenly. 'That's what I shall give as my age.'

The sound ended abruptly. Hallam took the record and washed it and dressed it and put it to bed with tender devotion. He remembered the girl who had given him the record. That red-haired girl he met at the awful Saddle Room. A pleasant girl in a way. American, volatile, rather incoherent in her speech mannerisms, but then Hallam supposed that there were no proper schooling facilities in America. He felt sorry for the girl. No he didn't. He didn't

feel sorry for any girls, they were all ... carnivorous.
What's more some of them were none too clean. He thought
about this man that Dawlish had just sent along to see him;
he wouldn't be at all surprised if he had been to school in
America. Hallam picked up the Siamese cat.

'Where is your little brother?' he asked her. If only they
could talk. They were more intelligent than many humans.
The cat stretched its legs and the long claws sank into the
shoulder of Hallam's suit and dragged at it with a tearing
sound.

'Secret Service man?' thought Hallam. He laughed out
loud and the cat looked up in surprise.

'Upstart,' said Hallam.

He put a finger against the cat's ear. The cat purred. An
upstart from Burnley – a supercilious, anti-public-school
technician who thought he was an administrator.

'We must do our duty,' said Hallam quietly to himself.
It was the duty of men in Government; they mustn't be
too influenced by the personalities of Government servants.
He preferred to think of the Secret Service man as a Government servant rather like the man with the wart who did
the savings bank accounts at the Post Office. He said
'Government servant' aloud and thought of all the ways
he could work the phrase into the next conversation he
had with that man.

Hallam put the Player's No. 3 into his real ebony cigarette holder. He lit it while watching himself in the mirror.
He parted his hair a little more towards the centre. He
might as well lunch at the coffee bar. They did a very fine
egg and chips there. The waiter was Italian and Hallam
always ordered in Italian. Not very trustworthy the
Italians, Hallam decided, it's all a matter of breeding. He
sorted out his change and put ninepence in his ticket
pocket for a tip. He gave a final look round before leaving.
Fang was asleep. The ashtray that his visitor had used

was brimming with cigarette ends. Foreign, coarse, cheap, inferior cigarettes.

Hallam picked up the ashtray with a shudder and tipped the contents into the little bin where the tea-leaves went. He felt in many ways the type of cigarette that man smoked typified him. So did the man's clothes, they were mass-produced, off-the-peg clothes. Hallam decided he did not like the man that Dawlish had sent to see him. He didn't like him at all.

3

Where pieces are used to protect other pieces, there
will be high casualty rate. Better by far to assign only
pawns to supporting roles.

Saturday, October 5th

'Best enzyme man in the world,' I said.

I heard Dawlish cough.

'Best what?' he said.

'Enzyme man,' I said, 'and Hallam would just *love*
him.'

'Good,' said Dawlish. I flipped the switch of my squawk
box and turned back to the documents on my desk.

'Edmond Dorf,' I read.

I riffed through the battered British passport.

'You are always saying that foreign names are more con-
vincingly English,' said my secretary.

'But not Dorf,' I said, 'especially not *Edmond* Dorf. I
don't *feel* like an Edmond Dorf.'

'Now don't go metaphysical on me,' said Jean, 'Whom
do you feel like?'

I liked that 'whom' – you've got to pay real money these
days to get a secretary that could say that.

'Eh?' I said.

'What sort of name do you feel like?' said Jean very
slowly and patiently. It was a danger signal.

'Flint McCrae,' I said.

'Act your age,' said Jean and she picked up the Semitsa file and walked towards the door.

'I'm not being horrible Edmond Dorf,' I said a little louder.

'You don't have to shout,' said Jean, 'and I'm afraid the travel vouchers and tickets are ordered. Berlin has been told to expect Edmond Dorf. If you want it changed now you must do it yourself unless I leave the Semitsa work.'

Jean was my secretary, really it was her job to do as I told her.

'OK,' I said.

She said, 'Let me be the first to congratulate you on a wise decision, Mr Dorf,' and left the room quickly.

Dawlish was my boss. He was around fifty, slim and meticulous like a well-bred boa-constrictor. He moved with languid English grace across the room from his desk and stood staring out into the jungle of Charlotte Street.

'They thought one wasn't serious at first,' he said to the window.

'Uh huh,' I said; I didn't want to appear too interested.

'They thought I was joking – even the wife thought I wouldn't go through with it.' He turned away from the window and fixed me with a mocking gaze. 'But now I've done it and I don't intend to kill them off.'

'Is that what they want you to do?' I said. I wished I had been listening more closely.

'Yes,' he said, 'and I'm not going to do it.' He walked across to me in the big leather armchair like Perry Mason appealing to the jury. 'I like weeds. It's as simple as that. Some people like one sort of plants and some people like others. I like weeds.'

'They are easy to cultivate,' I said.

'Not really,' said Dawlish sharply. 'The most powerful ones tend to strangle the others. I've got hedge parsley,

comfrey, meadow cranesbill, primroses . . . it's just like a
country lane, not a damned by-pass. One has wild birds
and butterflies. It's something to walk in; not one of these
things with flower-beds, laid out like a cemetery.'

'I agree,' I said. I agreed.

Dawlish sat down at his antique desk and arranged some
typewritten sheets with file cards that his secretary had
brought from the IBM machine. He aligned all the paper-
work in geometrical patterns with his pencils and stapling
machine and then began to polish his spectacles.

'And thistles,' said Dawlish.

'Pardon?' I said.

'I've got a lot of thistles,' said Dawlish, 'because they
attract butterflies. Later we'll have tortoise-shells, red
admirals, yellow brimstones, perhaps even commas. Fabulous. The weed-killers are destroying life in the country –
it's a disgrace.' He picked up one of the folders and began
to read it. He nodded once or twice and then put it down.

'I rely on you to be discreet,' he said.

'That sounds like a change of policy,' I said. Dawlish
sprinkled a cold smile over me. He wore the sort of spectacles that customs men tap for hollow noises. He rested
them on his large ears and then tucked a handkerchief as
big as a bedsheet into his cuff. It was a signal that we were
what Dawlish called 'on parade.'

Dawlish said, 'Johnnie Vulkan.' Then he rubbed the
palms of his hands together.

I knew the sort of thing Dawlish was going to complain
about now. We had other people in Berlin, of course, but
Vulkan was the one we always used; he was efficient,
understood what we needed, he knew the Berlin layout
and, most important, he was noisy enough to draw attention away from our residential boys whom we preferred
to let lie fallow as long as possible.

Dawlish was saying '. . . can't expect any of our people

to be saints . . .' I remembered Vulkan. He could deliver a bomb or a baby and smile as he did it.

'. . . no orthodox way of collecting information and there never can be . . .' Vulkan may have had a mixed political background but he knew Berlin. He knew every cellar, bandstand, bank account, brothel and abortionist from Potsdam to Pankow. Dawlish sniffed loudly and rubbed his hands again.

'Even earning additional payments need not be out of the question but unless he gives us full details of these associations he will no longer enjoy the protection of this department.'

'Protection,' I said. 'What sort of protection have we ever offered him? The only protection he ever had from us was old-fashioned money. People like Vulkan are in danger – physical danger – every moment of every day. The only weapon they have is money. If Vulkan is always asking for more, it's worth considering the motives.'

'Men like Vulkan don't have motives,' said Dawlish. 'Don't misunderstand me. Vulkan is working for us – however remotely – and one will work like the very deuce to see that he is looked after, but don't move this discussion into the sublime world of philosophy. Our friend Vulkan changes his motive every time he comes through that East Berlin checkpoint. When men become double agents it's just a matter of time before they lose their grip on reality. They begin to drown in a sea of confusion. Any piece of information they can snatch at will keep them afloat and alive for a few more hours.'

'You want to write Vulkan off?'

'Not at all,' said Dawlish, 'but one does want to keep him in a cul-de-sac. A fellow working against us can be very useful if we have him in a nice sterile test-tube.'

'You are being a bit complacent,' I said. Dawlish raised an eyebrow.

'Vulkan is good,' I said. 'Look at his record. 1948: his blockade prediction was with this department eleven weeks before FOIU[1] and fifteen weeks before Ross had heard anything. He can't do that if you are selecting his drinking companions.'

'Wait now . . .' said Dawlish.

'Let me finish, sir,' I insisted. 'The point I'm making is, that the moment Vulkan feels we are putting him on ice he'll shop around for another job. Ross at the War Office or O'Brien at the FO will whip him into the Olympia Stadion[2] and that's the last we will see of him. Certainly they will all tut-tut and agree with you at the Combined Intelligence Meetings but they'll go behind your back and employ him.'

Dawlish touched his finger-tips together and looked at me sardonically.

'You think I am too old for this job, don't you?'

I said nothing.

'If we decide not to continue with Vulkan's contract there is no question of leaving him available for the highest bidder.'

I didn't think old Dawlish could make me shiver.

---

[1] Foreign Office Intelligence Unit.
[2] West Berlin HQ. MI6 use the offices.

4

The Berlin Defence is a classic defence by means of
counter-attack.

Sunday, October 6th

The parade ground of Europe has always been that vast
area of scrub and lonely villages that stretches eastward
from the Elbe – some say as far as the Urals. But halfway
between the Elbe and the Oder, sitting at attention upon
Brandenburg, is Prussia's major town – Berlin.

From two thousand feet the Soviet Army War Memorial
in Treptower Park is the first thing you notice. It's in the
Russian sector. In a space like a dozen football pitches a cast
of a Red Army soldier makes the Statue of Liberty look like
it's standing in a hole. Over Marx-Engels Platz the plane
banked steeply south towards Tempelhof and the thin veins
of water shone in the bright sunshine. The Spree flows
through Berlin as a spilt pail of water flows through a building site. The river and its canals are lean and hungry and
they slink furtively under roads that do not acknowledge
them by even the smallest hump. Nowhere does a grand
bridge and a wide flow of water divide the city into two
halves. Instead it is bricked-up buildings and sections of
breeze block that bisect the city, ending suddenly and
unpredictably like the lava flow of a cold-water Pompeii.

Johnnie Vulkan brought a friend and a black Cadillac
to meet me at Tempelhof.

'Major Bailis, US Army,' said Johnnie. I shook hands with a tall leathery American who was buttoned deep into a white Aquascutum trench coat. He offered me a cigar while the baggage was being checked.

'It's good to have you with us,' said the major and Johnnie said the same.

'Thanks,' I said. 'This is a town where one needs friends.'

'We've put you into the Frühling,' the major said. 'It's small, comfortable, unobtrusive and very, very Berlin.'

'Fine,' I said; it sounded OK.

Johnnie moved quickly through the traffic in the sleek Cadillac. Cutting across the city from west to east is a ten-lane highway that successive generations have named 'Unter den Linden' and 'Strasse des 17. Juni' and once was a gigantic path leading through the Brandenburger Tor to the royal palace.

'We just call it Big Street,' said the American as Johnnie moved into the fast lane. In the distance the statue on the Tor glinted gold in the afternoon sun, beyond it in the Soviet sector a flat concrete plain named Marx-Engels Platz stood where communist demolition teams had razed the Schloss Hohenzollern.

We turned towards the Hilton.

Just a little way down the street beyond the shell of the Gedächtniskirche with its slick modern tower – like a tricky sort of hi-fi speaker cabinet – apeing the old broken one is Kranzlers, a café that spreads itself across the Kurfürstendamm pavement. We ordered coffee and the US army major sat on the far side of the table and spent ten minutes tying the laces of his shoes. Across in the 'Quick Café' two girls with silver hair were eating Bockwurst.

I looked at Johnnie Vulkan. Growing older seemed to agree with him. He didn't look a day over forty, his hair was like a tailored Brillo pad and his face tanned. He wore a well-cut Berlin suit of English pinhead worsted. He leaned back in his chair and pointed a finger lazily towards me. His hand was so sunburned that his nails seemed pale pink. He said, 'Before we start, let's get one thing clear. No one here needs help; you are superfluous to requirements as far as I am concerned. Just remember that; stay out of the way and everything will be OK. Get in the way and . . .' He shrugged his shoulders. 'This is a dangerous town.' He kept his hand pointing into my face and gave a flash of a smile.

I looked at him for a moment. I looked at his smile and at his hand.

'Next time you point a finger at someone, Johnnie,' I said, 'remember that three of your fingers are pointing back at you.' He lowered his hand as though it had become heavy.

'Stok is our contact,' he said quietly.

I was surprised. Stok was a Red Army colonel in State Security.[1]

'It's official then?' I asked. 'An official exchange.'

Vulkan chuckled and glanced at the major.

'It's more what you might call extra-curricular. Official but extra-curricular,' he said again, loud enough for the American to hear. The American laughed and went back to his shoelace.

'The way we hear it, there is a lot of extra-curricular activity here in Berlin.'

'Dawlish been complaining?' Vulkan asked, captiously.

'Hinting.'

'Well, you tell him I'll have to have more than my present lousy two thousand a month if it's exclusive service he's after.'

'You tell him,' I said. 'He's on the phone.'

---

[1] KGB (see Appendix 4).

'Look,' said Vulkan, his solid gold wristwatch peeping out from the pristine cuff. 'Dawlish has no idea of the situation here. My contact with Stok is . . .' Vulkan made a movement with his cupped hand to indicate a superlative.

'Stok is one thousand times brighter than Dawlish and he runs *his* show from on the spot, not from an office desk hundreds of miles away. If I can bring Semitsa over the wire it will be because I personally know some important people in this town. People I can rely on and who can rely on me. All Dawlish has to do is collect the kudos and leave me alone.'

'What I think Dawlish needs to know,' I said, 'is what Colonel Stok will require in return if he delivers Semitsa – what you call – over the wire.'

'Almost certainly cash.'

'I had a premonition it would be.'

'Wait a minute, wait a minute,' said Vulkan, loud enough to bring the American out of his reverie. 'Major Bailis is the official US Army observer for this transaction. I don't have to put up with dirty talk like that.'

The American took off his sun-glasses and said, 'Yes, siree. That's the size of it.' Then he put his glasses back on again.

I said, 'Just to make quite sure that you don't promise anything we wouldn't like: make sure I'm there at your next meeting with comrade Colonel Stok, eh?'

'Difficult,' said Johnnie.

'But you'll manage it,' I said, 'because that's what we pay you for.'

'Oh yes,' said Vulkan.

5

When a player offers a piece for exchange or sacrifice
then surely he has in mind a subsequent manœuvre
which will end to his advantage.

Monday, October 7th

Brassieres and beer; whiskies and worsteds; great words
carved out of coloured electricity and plastered along the
walls of the Ku-damm. This was the theatre-in-the-round
of western prosperity: a great, gobbling, yelling, laughing
stage crowded with fat ladies and dwarfs, marionettes on
strings, fire-eaters, strong men and lots of escapologists.
'Today I joined the cast,' I thought. 'Now they've got an
illusionist.' Beneath me the city lay in huge patches of light
and vast pools of darkness where rubble and grass fought
gently for control of the universe.

Inside my room the phone rang. Vulkan's voice was calm
and unhurried.

'Do you know the Warschau restaurant?'

'Stalin Allee,' I said; it was a well-known bourse for
information pedlars.

'They call it Karl Marx Allee now,' said Vulkan sardonically. 'Have your car facing west in the car park across
the Allee. Don't get out of your car, flash your lights. I'll
be ready to go at 9.20. OK?'

'OK,' I said.

*　　*　　*

I followed the line of the canal from the Berlin Hilton to Hallesches Tor U-Bahnstation, then turned north on to Friedrichstrasse. The control point is a few blocks north. I flipped a passport to the American soldier and an insurance card to the West German policeman, then in bottom gear I moved across the tram tracks of Zimmerstrasse that bump you into a world where 'communist' is not a dirty word.

It was a warm evening and a couple of dozen transients sat under the blue neon light in the checkpoint hut; stacked neatly on tables were piles of booklets and leaflets with titles like 'Science of the GDR in the service of Peace', 'Art for the People' and 'Historic Task of the GDR and the future of Germany'.

'Herr Dorf.' A very young frontier policeman held my passport and riffed the corners. 'How much money are you carrying?'

I spread the few Westmarks and English pounds on the desk. He counted them and endorsed my papers.

'Cameras or transistor radio?'

At the other end of the corridor a boy in a leather jacket with 'Rhodesia' painted on it shouted, 'How much longer do we have to wait here?'

I heard a Grepo say to him, 'You'll have to take your turn, sir – we didn't send for you, you know.'

'Just the car radio,' I said.

The Grepo nodded.

He said, 'The only thing we don't allow is East German currency.' He gave me my passport,[1] smiled and saluted. I walked down the long hut. The Rhodesian was saying, 'I know my rights,' and rapping on the counter but everyone else was staring straight ahead.

---

[1] To catch people with stolen passports, or people who spend nights in the East, the passports are often marked with a tiny pencil spot on some pre-arranged page.

I walked across to the parking bay. I drove around the concrete blocks, a Vopo gave a perfunctory glance at my passport and a soldier swung the red-and-white striped barrier skywards. I drove forward into East Berlin. There were crowds of people at Friedrichstrasse station. People coming home from work, going to work or just hanging around waiting for something to happen. I turned right at Unter den Linden – where the lime trees had been early victims of Nazidom; the old Bismarck Chancellery was a cobweb of rusty ruins facing the memorial building where two green-clad sentries with white gloves were goose-stepping like Bismarck was expected back. I drove around the white plain of Marx-Engels Platz and, at the large slab-sided department store at Alexanderplatz, took the road that leads to Karl Marx Allee.

I recognized the car park and pulled into it. Karl Marx Allee was still the same as when it had been Stalin Allee. Miles of workers' flats and state shops housed in seven-storey Russian-style architecture, thirty-foot-wide pavements and huge grassy spaces and cycle tracks like the M1.

In the open-air café across the road, lights winked under the trees and a few people danced between the striped parasols while a small combo walked their baby back home with lots of percussion. 'Warschau', the lights spelled out and under them I saw Vulkan get to his feet. He waited patiently until the traffic lights were in his favour before walking towards the car park. A careful man, Johnnie; this was no time to collect a jaywalking ticket. He got into a Wartburg, pulled away eastward down Karl Marx Allee. I followed keeping one or two cars between us.

Johnnie parked outside a large granite house in Köpenick. I edged past his car and parked under a gas lamp around the corner. It was not a pretty house but it had that mood of comfort and complacency that middle-class

owners breathe into the structure of a house along with
dinner-gong echoes and cigar smoke. There was a large
garden at the back and here near the forests and the waters
of Müggelsee the air smelled clean.

There was just one name-plate on the door. It was of
neat black plastic: 'Professor Eberhard Lebowitz', engraved
in ornate Gothic lettering. Johnnie rang and a maid let us
into the hall.

'Herr Stok?' said Johnnie.

He gave her his card and she tiptoed away into the
interior.

In the dimly lit hall there stood a vast hallstand with
some tricky inlaid ivory, two clothes-brushes and a
Soviet officer's peaked hat. The ceiling was a complex pattern of intaglio leaves and the floral wallpaper looked prehensile.

The maid said, 'Will you please come this way?' and led
us into Stok's drawing-room. The wallpaper was predomi-
nantly gold and silver but there were plenty of things
hiding the wallpaper. There were aspidistras, fussy lace
curtains, shelves full of antique Meissen and a cocktail
cabinet like a small wooden version of the Kremlin. Stok
looked up from the 21-inch baroque TV. He was a big-
boned man, his hair was cropped to the skull and his
complexion was like something the dog had been playing
with. When he stood up to greet us his huge hands poked
out of a bright red silk smoking-jacket with gold-braid
frogging.

Vulkan said, 'Herr Stok; Herr Dorf,' and then he said,
'Herr Dorf; Herr Stok,' and we all nodded at each other,
then Vulkan put a paper bag down on the coffee table and
Stok drew an eight-ounce tin of Nescafé out of it, nodded,
and put it back again.

'What will you drink?' Stok asked. He had a musical
basso voice.

'Just before we move into the chat,' I said, 'can I see your identity card?'

Stok pulled his wallet out of a hip pocket, smiled archly at me and then peeled loose the stiff white card with a photo and two rubber stamps that Soviet citizens carry when abroad.

'It says that you are Captain Maylev here,' I protested as I laboriously pronounced the Cyrillic script.

The servant girl brought a tray of tiny glasses and a frosted bottle of vodka. She set the tray down. Stok paused while she withdrew.

'And your passport says that you are Edmond Dorf,' said Stok, 'but we are both victims of circumstance.'

Behind him the East German news commentator was saying in his usual slow voice, '. . . sentenced to three years for assisting in the attempt to move his family to the West.' Stok walked across to the set and clicked the switch to the West Berlin channel where a cast of fifty Teutonic minstrels sang 'See them shuffle along' in German. 'It's never a good night, Monday,' Stok said apologetically. He switched the set off. We broke the wax on the fruit-flavoured vodka and Stok and Vulkan began discussing whether twenty-four bottles of Scotch whisky were worth a couple of cameras. I sat around and drank vodka until they had ironed out some sort of agreement. Then Stok said, 'Has Dorf got power to negotiate?' – just like I wasn't in the room.

'He's a big shot in London,' said Vulkan. 'Anything he promises will be honoured. I'll guarantee it.'

'I want lieutenant-colonel's pay,' Stok said, turning to me, 'for life.'

'Don't we all?' I said.

Vulkan was looking at the evening paper; he looked up and said, 'No, he means that he'd want the UK Government to pay him that as a salary if he comes over the wire. You could promise that, couldn't you?'

'I don't see why not,' I said. 'We'll say you've been in a few years, that's five pounds four shillings a day basic. Then there's ration allowance, six and eight a day, marriage allowance, one pound three and something a day, qualification pay five shillings a day if you get through Staff College, overseas pay fourteen and three and . . . you *would* want overseas pay?'

'You are not taking me seriously,' Stok said, a big smile across his white moon of a face. Vulkan was shifting about on his seat, tightening his tie against his Adam's apple and cracking his finger joints.

'All systems go,' I said.

'Colonel Stok puts up a very convincing case,' said Vulkan.

'So does the "find the lady" mob in Charing Cross Road,' I said, 'but they never come through with the QED.'

Stok threw back two vodkas in quick succession and stared at me earnestly. He said, 'Look, I don't favour the capitalist system. I don't ask you to believe that I do. In fact I hate your system.

'Great,' I said. 'And you are in a job where you can really do something about it.'

Stok and Vulkan exchanged glances.

'I wish you would try to understand,' said Stok. 'I am really sincere about giving you my allegiance.'

'Go on,' I said. 'I bet you say that to all the great powers.'

Vulkan said, 'I've spent a lot of time and money in setting this up. If you are so damn clever why did you bother to come to Berlin?'

'OK,' I told them. 'Act out the charade. I'll be thinking of words.'

Stok and Vulkan looked at each other and we drank and then Stok gave me one of his gold-rimmed oval cigarettes and lit it with a nickel-silver sputnik.

'For a long time I have been thinking of moving west,'

said Stok. 'It's not a matter of politics. I am just as avid a communist now as I have ever been, but a man gets old. He looks for comfort, for security in possessions.' Stok cupped his big boxing-glove hand and looked down at it. 'A man wants to scoop up a handful of black dirt and know it's his own land, to live on, die on and give to his sons. We peasants are a weak insecure segment of socialism, Mr Dorf.' He smiled with his big brown teeth, trimmed here and there with an edge of gold. 'These comforts that you take for granted will not be a part of life in the East until long after I am dead.'

'Yes,' I said. 'We have decadence now – while we are young enough to enjoy it.'

'Semitsa,' said Stok. He waited to see what effect it would have on me. It had none.

'That's what you are really interested in. Not me. Semitsa.'

'Is he here in Berlin?' I asked.

'Slowly, Mr Dorf,' said Stok. 'Things move very slowly.'

'How do you know he wants to come west?' I asked.

'I know,' said Stok.

Vulkan interrupted, 'I told the colonel that Semitsa would be worth about forty thousand pounds to us.'

'Did you?' I said in as flat a monotone as I could manage.

Stok poured out his fruit vodka all round, downed his own and poured himself a replacement.

'It's been nice talking to you boys,' I said. 'I only wish you had something I could buy.'

'I understand you, Mr Dorf,' said Stok. 'In my country we have a saying, "a man who trades a horse for a promise ends up with tired feet."' He walked across to the eighteenth-century mahogany bureau.

I said, 'I don't want you to deviate from a course of loyalty and integrity to the Soviet Government to which I remain a friend and ally.'

Stok turned and smiled at me.

'You think I have live microphones planted here and that I might attempt to trick you.'

'You might,' I said. 'You are in the business.'

'I hope to persuade you otherwise,' said Stok. 'As to being in the business: when does a chef get ptomaine poisoning?'

'When he eats out,' I said.

Stok's laugh made the antique plates rattle. He groped around inside the big writing-desk and produced a flat metal box, brought a vast bunch of tiny keys from his pocket and from inside the box reached a thick black file. He handed it to me. It was typed in Cyrillic capitals and contained photostats of letters and transcripts of tapped phone calls.

Stok reached for another oval cigarette and tapped it unlit against the white page of typing. 'Mr Semitsa's passport westward,' he said putting a sarcastic emphasis on the 'mister'.

'Yes?' I said doubtfully.

Vulkan leaned forward to me. 'Colonel Stok is in charge of an investigation of the Minsk Biochemical labs.'

'Where Semitsa used to be,' I said. It was coming clear to me. 'This is Semitsa's file, then?'

'Yes,' said Stok, 'and everything that I need to get Semitsa a ten-year sentence.'

'Or have him do anything you say,' I said. Perhaps Stok and Vulkan were serious.

6

A bad bishop is one hampered by his own pawns.

Monday, October 7th

Going along the Unter den Linden wasn't the fastest way of getting to the checkpoint but I had to keep to the main roads in order to find my way about. I saw the 'S' signs on the Schnellstrasse and moved up to the legal 60 kph. As I came level with the old Bismarck Chancellery, black and gutted in the bright velvet moonlight, a red disc was moving laterally across the road ahead. It was a police signal. I stopped. A Volkspolizei troop carrier was parked at the roadside. A young man in uniform tucked the signal baton into the top of his boot, walked slowly across to me and saluted.

'Your papers.'

I gave him the Dorf passport and hoped that the department had gone to the trouble of getting it made up by the Foreign Office and not been content with one of the rough old print jobs that the War Office did for us.

A Skoda passed by at speed without anyone waving it down. I began to feel I was being picked on. Around at the rear of the Taunus another Vopo shone a torch on the US Army plates and probed the beam across the rear seat and floor. My passport was slapped closed and it came through the window accompanied by a neat bow and salute.

'Thank you, sir,' said the young one.

'Can I go?' I said.

'Just switch on your lights, sir.'

'They're on.'

'Main beams must be on here in East Berlin. That is the law.'

'I see.' I flicked the switch on. The troop carrier glowed in the fringe of the beam. It was just a traffic cop doing a job.

'Good night, sir.' I saw a movement among the dozen policemen on the big open bus. By now Johnnie Vulkan had also passed me. I turned left on to Friedrichstrasse and tried to catch up with him.

Johnnie Vulkan's Wartburg was some fifty yards ahead of me as I drove south on Friedrichstrasse. As I reached the red-striped barrier the sentry was handing Johnnie his passport and lifting the pole. The American sector was just a few feet away. He allowed the Wartburg through, then lowered the boom and walked round to me, hitching the automatic rifle over his shoulder, so that it clanged against his steel helmet. I had the passport handy. Beyond the barrier the low hardboard building that was the control post was a mass of red geraniums. In front of it two sentries exchanged words with Vulkan, then they all laughed. The laughter was loud in the still night. A blue-uniformed Grenz-polizist clattered down the steps and ran across to my car.

'You are wanted inside,' he said to the sentry in his shrill Saxon accent. 'On the phone.' He turned to me. 'Won't keep you a moment, sir,' in English; 'I am sorry for the delay,' but he took the sentry's automatic rifle to hold just the same.

I lit a Gauloise for myself and the Grepo, and we smoked and stared across the hundred yards that separated us from the little walled island that is West Berlin and we thought our different thoughts or maybe the same ones.

It was less than two minutes before the Vopo returned.

He said would I please get out of the car and leave the keys where they were. There were three soldiers with him. They all had automatic rifles, none of which were slung on anyone's shoulder. I got out of the car.

They walked me a few yards west on Leipziger where no one in the west sector could see us no matter how high on the ladder they were. There was a small green van parked there. On the door was a little badge and the words 'Traffic Police'. The motor was running. I sat between the German soldiers and one of them offered me a strange-tasting cigarette which I lit from the stub of my Gauloise. No one had searched me, put on handcuffs or made a formal statement. They had merely asked me to come along; no one was using coercion. I had agreed to go.

I watched the street through the rear window. By the time we had reached Alexanderplatz I had a pretty good idea of where we were headed. A couple of blocks away was Keibelstrasse: the Polizei Praesidium.

In the cobbled centre courtyard of the Praesidium I heard the sound of half a dozen marching men. Words of command were shouted and the rhythm of the boots varied. I was in a room on the first floor. It was thirty-three steps above the main entrance, where a guard in an armoured glass cubicle must press a small button to unlock the entrance gate. The aged wooden seat upon which I sat backed up against the cream-painted wall; there were two well-thumbed copies of *Neues Deutschland* lying on it. To my right a large window had the view divided into square spaces by solid-looking bars. Behind the desk was a middle-aged woman, her hair drawn tightly back into a bun. Every action on the desk brought the loud rattle of a large bunch of keys. I knew there must be a way out. None of those young fellows on late-night TV would find it any sort of dilemma.

The grey-haired woman looked up. 'Are you carrying

any sort of knife or weapon?' Her eyes glinted clearly behind the thick circular lenses.

'No,' I said.

She nodded and wrote something on a sheet of paper.

'I mustn't be late back,' I said. Which didn't seem so hilarious a thing to say at that time.

The grey-haired woman locked each drawer of her desk and then left the room, carefully fixing the door wide open to preclude my taking a short walk around the filing cabinet. I sat there for five minutes, maybe ten. The whole situation was curiously simple and matter-of-fact, like waiting for a driving-licence renewal at County Hall. When the grey-haired woman came back she had my passport in her hand. She gave it to me. She didn't smile but it seemed friendly just the same.

'Come,' she said.

I went with her down the long cream corridor to a room at the extreme western wing of the building. The décor too was like County Hall. She tapped gently on a large door and without waiting for a reply motioned me through. It was dark inside the room with just enough light filtering through the window from the courtyard to see where the desk was. From behind the desk was a sudden red glow like an infra-red flash-bulb. As my eyes grew accustomed to the dark I saw that the far side of the room was filled with a silvery sheen.

'Dorf,' said the voice of Stok. It boomed almost like an amplifier. There was a click from his desk; the yellow tungsten light came on. Stok was sitting behind his desk almost obscured by a dense cloud of cigar smoke. There was Scandinavian-style East German furniture in the room. On the table behind me there was a Hohner simple button-key accordion, piles of newspapers, and a chessboard with some of the pieces fallen over. There was a folding bed near the wall with two army blankets on it and high leather boots placed together at the head. Near the door was a tiny sink and a cupboard that might have held clothes.

'My dear Dorf,' said Stok. 'Have I caused you great inconvenience?'

He emerged from the cigar smoke in an ankle-length black leather overcoat.

'Not unless you count being scared half to death,' I said.

'Ha ha ha,' said Stok, then he exhaled another great billow of cigar smoke like a 4.6.2 pulling out of King's Cross.

'I wanted to contact you,' he spoke with the cigar held between tight lips, 'without Vulkan.'

'Another time,' I said, 'write.'

There was another tap at the door. Stok moved across the room like a wounded crow. The grey-haired one brought two lemon teas.

'There is no milk today I am afraid,' said Stok; he drew the overcoat around him.

'And so Russian tea was invented,' I said.

Stok laughed again in a perfunctory sort of way. I drank the scalding hot tea. It made me feel better, like digging your finger nails into your palm does.

'What is it?' I said.

Stok waited while the grey-haired one closed the door behind her. Then he said, 'Let's stop quarrelling, shall we?'

'You mean personally?' I said. 'Or are you speaking on behalf of the Soviet Union?'

'I mean it,' said Stok. 'We can do far better for ourselves if we co-operate than if we obstruct each other.' Stok paused and smiled with studied charm.

'This scientist Semitsa is not important to the Soviet Union. We have other younger men with newer and better ideas. Your people on the other hand will think you marvellous if you can deliver him to London.' Stok shrugged his shoulders at the idiocy of the world of politics.

'Caveat emptor?' I said.

'Not half,' said Stok in a skilful piece of idiom. 'Buyer watch out.' Stok rolled the cigar across his mouth and said, 'Buyer watch out,' a couple of times. I just drank the lemon tea and said nothing. Stok ambled across to the chessboard on the side-table, his leather coat creaking like a wind-jammer.

'Are you a chess player, English?' he said.

'I prefer games where there's a better chance to cheat,' I said.

'I agree with you,' said Stok. 'The preoccupation with rules doesn't sit well upon the creative mind.'

'Like communism?' I said.

Stok picked up a knight. 'But the pattern of chess is the pattern of your capitalist world. The world of bishops and castles and kings and knights.'

'Don't look at me,' I said. 'I'm just a pawn. I'm here in the front rank.' Stok grinned and looked down at the board.

'I'm a good player,' he said. 'Your friend Vulkan is one of the few men in Berlin who can consistently beat me.'

'That's because he is part of the pattern of our capitalist world.'

'The pattern,' said Stok, 'has been revised. The knight is the most important piece on the board. Queens have been made . . . impotent. Can you say impotent of a queen?'

'On this side of the wall *you* say what you like,' I said.

Stok nodded. 'The knights – the generals – run your western world. General Walker of the 24th Infantry Division lectured all his troops that the President of the USA was a communist.'

'You don't agree?' I asked.

'You are a fool,' boomed Stok in his Boris Godunov voice.

'I am trying to tell you that these people . . .' he waved the knight in my face, '. . . look after themselves.'

'And you are jealous?' I asked seriously.

'Perhaps I am,' said Stok. 'Perhaps that's it.' He put the knight back and he pulled the skirt of his overcoat together.

'So you are going to sell me Semitsa as a little bit of private enterprise of your own?' I said. 'If you'll forgive the workings of my bourgeois mind.'

'You live only once,' said Stok.

'I can make once do,' I said.

Stok heaped four spoonfuls of coarse sugar into his tea. He stirred it as though he was putting an extra rod into an atomic pile. 'All I want is to live the rest of my life in peace and quiet – I do not need a lot of money, just enough to buy a little tobacco and the simple peasant food that I was brought up on. I am a colonel and my conditions are excellent but I am a realist; this cannot last. Younger men in our security service look at my job with envy.' He looked at me and I nodded gently. 'With envy,' he repeated.

'You are in a key job,' I said.

'But the trouble with such jobs is that many others want them too. Some of my staff here are men with fine college diplomas, their minds are quick as mine once was; and they have the energy to work through the day and through the night too as once I had the energy to do.' He shrugged. 'This is why I decided to come to live the rest of my life in your world.'

He got up and opened one of the big wooden shutters. From the courtyard there was the beat of a heavy diesel engine and the sound of boots climbing over a tailboard. Stok thrust his hands deep in his overcoat pockets and flapped his wings.

I said, 'What about your wife and your family, will you be able to persuade them?'

Stok continued to look down into the courtyard. 'My wife died in a German air raid in 1941, my only son hasn't written to me for three and a half years. What would you do in my position, Mr Dorf? What would you do?'

I let the sound of the lorry rumble away down Keibelstrasse.

I said, 'I'd stop telling lies to old liars for a start, Stok. Do you really think I came here without dusting off your file? My newest assistant is trained better than you seem to think I am. I know everything about you from the cubic capacity of your Westinghouse refrigerator to the size your mistress takes in diaphragms.'

Stok picked up his tea and began to batter the lemon segment with the bowl of his spoon. He said, 'You've trained well.'

'Train hard, fight easy,' I said.

'You quote Marshal Suvarov.' He walked across to the chessboard and stared at it. 'In Russia we have a proverb, "Better a clever lie than the foolish truth".' He waved his teaspoon at me.

'There was nothing clever about that clumsy piece of wife-murder.'

'You're right,' said Stok cheerfully. 'You shall be my friend, English. We must trust each other.' He put his tea down on the desk top.

'I'll never need an enemy,' I said.

Stok smiled. It was like arguing with a speak-your-weight machine.

'Truthfully, English,' he said, 'I do not want to defect to the West but the offer of Semitsa is a genuine one.' He sucked the spoon.

'For money?' I asked.

'Yes,' said Stok. He tapped the fleshy palm of his left hand with the bowl of the spoon.

'Money here.' He closed his hand like a vault.

7

Knights can pass over squares controlled by enemy
forces. Knights always end their move on a square
of the opposite colour.

Tuesday, October 8th

There was plenty of activity at Checkpoint Charlie. Photo-
flashes sliced instants from eternity. The pavement shone
with water and detergent under the pressmen's feet. Way
down towards Hallesches Tor a US military ambulance
flasher sped towards the emergency ward and was all set
to change direction to the morgue.

One by one the reporters gunned their VWs and began
composing tomorrow's headlines in their minds. 'Young
Berliner killed in wall crossing' or 'Vopos Gun Down Wall-
Hopper' or 'Bloody Sidewalk Slaying at the Wall'. Or
maybe he wouldn't die.

I waved the insurance papers at the guard box and
moved gently through. It's not far to Hallesches Tor – a
district of pimps and brothels – and that's where I had to
go next.

An ill-lit doorway gave on to a steep stone staircase.
There were a dozen grey metal post-boxes in the hallway.
On one of them it said, 'Bureau for the rehabilitation of
German Prisoners of War from the East'. There were no
letters inside. I doubt if there ever had been. I walked up
the stairs and pressed a small buzzer. I had a feeling that,

even had I not pressed it, the front door would have opened.

'Yes?' said a calm young man in a dark-grey flannel suit. I used the words of greeting which London had provided.

'This way, please,' said the young man. The first room was like a dentist's waiting room. There were lots of periodicals, lots of chairs and very little else except a distinct lack of privacy. They left me there for a few moments before they took me inside. I was ushered through the door only to find another door – a steel one – facing me. The second door was locked and I stood nervously in the tiny 'cupboard' which was lit by a blinding overhead light. There was a soft whirr and then the steel door moved open.

'Welcome to the Feldherrnhügel,'[1] said the calm young man.

It was a large room lit by blue neon tubes that produced a soft hum. There was a bookcase full of files and several pull-down maps hung on the wall. Two long metal tables were crammed with phones of various colours, a TV screen, and a powerful radio receiver. Four young men sat along one table. They were like the man who had opened the door; young, pale, clean-shaven and white-shirted, they might represent the new prosperous Germany but they were also representatives of something rather older. This was a cell of the Gehlen Bureau.[2] From here men were spirited in to the DDR[3] or spirited out. These were the men that the East Germans said were Nazis and the ones that Bonn never talked of at all.

I wasn't exactly a welcome visitor but I represented a

---

[1] Feldherrnhügel: the mound upon which the commanding generals stood to direct the battle.

[2] Later the BND or Federal German Intelligence Service, but still generally referred to as the 'Gehlen Bureau'. *See* Appendix 2.

[3] Deutsche Demokratische Republik.

section of the Gehlen Organization income; they gave me coffee.

One of the identical men slid into steel-rimmed spectacles and said, 'You need us to help you out.' It had a discreet layer of insult. I sipped the Nescafé.

'Whatever you need – the answer is, yes we can do it,' the spectacled one said. He passed me a small jug of cream. 'What is it that you need done first?'

'I'm trying to decide between having Dover encircled and Stalingrad subjugated.'

Steel Spectacles and the other three men smiled, perhaps for the first time.

I fed them some Gauloises and then we got down to business.

'I need something moved,' I said.

'Very well,' said Steel Spectacles. He produced a small tape machine.

'Place of consignment's origin?'

'I'd try to arrange that to your convenience,' I said.

'Excellent.' He clicked the switch on the mike. 'Origin nul,' he said.

'To?' he asked me.

'Channel ports,' I said.

'Which one?'

'Any,' I said. He nodded again and repeated my answer into the tape recorder. We were getting on fine together.

'Size?'

'One human,' I said. No one batted an eyelid; he immediately said, 'Willing or unwilling?'

'I'm not sure yet,' I said.

'Conscious or unconscious?'

'Conscious willing or unconscious unwilling.'

'We prefer conscious,' said Spectacles before relaying it on to the tape.

The phone rang. Spectacles spoke into the mouthpiece

in a rapid series of orders, then two of the Gehlen boys slipped into dark raincoats and hurried for the door.

'A shooting at the wall,' Spectacles said to me.

'No kidding,' I said.

'Right at Checkpoint Charlie,' said Spectacles.

'One of your boys?' I asked.

'Yes, just a courier,' said Spectacles. He uncupped the phone; the caller was to wait there and phone back if he wasn't contacted in thirty minutes. He hung up.

'We are the only people who get anything done here in Berlin,' Spectacles said. The other man, blond with a large signet ring said, 'Ja.' Then Spectacles and he nodded to each other.

'Since Hitler?' I almost said, but I swallowed the words with a second cup of hot coffee. Spectacles produced a street map and clipped a piece of transparent acetate across the face of it. He began marking circles here and there across the east side of the city.

'These are the sort of places we favour as jumping-off places,' he said.

'Not too near the Sektor boundary and within a mile of the Soviet Zone. Things can heat up very quickly in this burg, especially if you grab someone hot. Sometimes we prefer to put our cargo on ice in the zone somewhere. Anywhere from Lübeck to Leipzig.' Spectacles had a smooth American accent and here and there it came through his lucid Rhineland German.

'We will need at least forty-eight hours' notice,' said Spectacles. 'But after that we will be responsible even if we take longer to actually do the movement. Do you have any questions?'

'Yes,' I said. 'What's the procedure if I want to contact your people and I am in the East?'

'You phone a Dresden number and they will give you an East Berlin number. It changes every week. The Dresden number changes sometimes too. Check with us before you go over.'

'OK but does anyone have phones going across the city of Berlin?'

'Officially one. It connects the Russian Command in Karlshorst with the Allied Command in the Stadion here in West Berlin.'

'Unofficially?'

'There *have* to be lines. The water, electricity, sewage and gas authorities all have lines to speak to their opposite number in the other half of the city. There could be an emergency but they are not officially recognized.'

'And you don't ever use these lines?'

'Very seldom.' There was a buzz. He flipped a switch on his desk. I heard the voice of the calm young man say, 'Yes. Good evening,' and another voice. 'I'm the man you were expecting from Dresden.' Spectacles clicked another switch and the TV screen flashed blue. I could see the waiting room as a short man entered it and I saw him enter the brightly lit cupboard. Spectacles swung the TV receiver around so that I couldn't see it.

'Security,' he said. 'It wouldn't give you much confidence if we let you penetrate another operation, would it?'

'You're damn right it wouldn't,' I said.

'So if that's all,' said Spectacles, closing a big ledger with a snap.

'Yes,' I said. I could take a hint.

He said, 'You will act as Vulkan's case officer[4] for this

---

[4] Case officer: In the American system of espionage (from which the Gehlen Bureau had borrowed the term) the case officer is the go-between connecting Washington to the agent in the field. He is generally empowered to vary slightly the aims and objects of the operation and always controls payment. In the case of the above operation I did not act as Vulkan's case officer in the strict sense of the term, since a case officer keeps well concealed and does not reveal himself to other units.

operation. His code name is "King". Your code name will be . . .' he looked down at his desk. '. . . Kadaver.'

'Corpse,' I said. 'That's very chummy.'

Spectacles smiled.

I thought about 'King' Vulkan when I got back to the Frühling. I was surprised that he was one of the best chess players in Berlin but he was full of surprises. I thought about my code name – Kadaver – and about *Kadavergehorsam*, which is the sort of discipline which makes a corpse jump up and salute. I poured a Teacher's and stared down at the screaming shining lights. I had begun to get the feel of the town; both sides of the wall had wide well-lit streets separated by inky lakes of darkness. Perhaps this was the only city in the world where you were safer in the dark.

8

Skilful use of knights is the mark of
the professional player.

Tuesday, October 8th

Examine closely the eyes of certain bold young men and
you'll see a frightened little man staring anxiously out.
Sometimes I saw him in Vulkan's eyes and at other times
I wasn't so sure about it. He carried himself like an advert
for hormone pills; his muscles rippled under well-cut light-
weight wool suits. His socks were silk and his shoes were
made on a personal last by a shop in Jermyn Street. Vulkan
was the new breed of European man: he spoke like an
American, ate like a German, dressed like an Italian and
paid tax like a Frenchman.

He used all the Anglo-Saxon idioms with consummate
skill and when he swore did it with calm and considered
timing and never with frustration or rage. His Cadillac
Eldorado was a part of him; it was black with real leather
upholstery, and the wooden steering wheel, map-reading
lights, hi-fi, air conditioning and radio phone were
unobtrusive, but not so unobtrusive that you could fail
to notice them. There were no woolly tigers or plastic
skeletons, no pennants or leopard-skin seat-covers in Vulkan's car. You could scrape the surface of Johnnie Vulkan
however you liked; he was gold as deep as you cared to
go.

LEN DEIGHTON

The commissionaire at the Hilton saluted and said, 'Shall I park the Strassenkreuzer, sir?' He spoke English and, although the term street-cruiser is an uncomplimentary word for American cars, Johnnie liked it. He flipped him the car keys with a practised movement of the fingers. Johnnie walked ahead of me. The tiny metal studs that he affected in his shoes made a rhythm of clicks across the marble. The discreetly shaded light fell across the carefully oiled rubber-plants and shone on the *Trinkgeld* of the girl in the newspaper stand where they sold yesterday's *Daily Mail* and *Playboy* and coloured postcards of the wall that you could send to friends and say, 'Wish you were here'. I followed Vulkan into the bar where it was too dark to read the price-list and the piano player felt his way among the black and white keys like someone had changed them all around.

'Glad you came?' Vulkan said.

I wasn't sure I was. Vulkan had changed almost as much as the city itself. Both found themselves in a permanent state of emergency and had discovered a way of living with it.

'It's great,' I said.

Johnnie sniffed at his bourbon and downed it like it was medicine. 'But you thought it would be different by now,' he said. 'You thought it would all be peacetime, eh?'

'It's too damn peacetime for my liking,' I said. 'It's too damn "sundowners on the veranda" and "those infernal drums, Carruthers". There are too many soldiers being Brahmins.'

'And too many German civilians being untouchables.'

'I was in the Lighthouse cinema in Calcutta once,' I said. 'They were showing *Four Feathers*. When the film came to that section when the beleaguered garrison could hold out no longer, across the horizon came a few dozen topees piping "Over the seas to Skye", some short-muzzle Lee

46

Enfields saying, "Cor blimey", and some gay young sahibs with punkah wallahs in attendance.'

'They put the tribesmen to flight,' said Vulkan.

'Yes,' I said, 'but in the cinema the Indian audience cheered as they did it.'

'You think we are cheering on our Allied masters?'

'You tell me,' I said and I looked around and listened to English speech and drank the sherry that cost twice the price it would fetch anywhere else this side of the wall.

'You English,' said Vulkan. 'You live out there in the middle of the cold sea surrounded by herring. How will we ever get you to understand? June the sixth, 1944, was D-Day; up till then you British had lost more people in wartime traffic accidents than you had lost in battle,[1] while we Germans had already suffered six and half million casualties on the Eastern front alone. Germany was the only occupied country that failed to produce a resistance organization. It failed to produce one because there was nothing left; in 1945 we had thirteen-year-old kids standing where you are standing now, pointing a bazooka down the Ku-damm waiting for a Joseph Stalin tank to clank out of the Grunewald. So we fraternized and we collaborated. We saluted your private soldiers, gave our houses to your non-coms and our wives to your officers. We cleared the rubble with our bare hands and didn't mind that empty lorries passed us coming back from your official brothels.'

Vulkan ordered two more drinks. A girl with too much make-up and a gold lamé dress tried to catch Vulkan's eye, but when she saw me looking took a tiny mirror from a chainmail bag and gave her eyebrows a working over.

---

[1] In the first four years of war British casualties (including POWs and missing) were 387,966. The number killed and injured in traffic accidents was 588,742.

As Vulkan turned to me he spilled his bourbon over the back of his hand.

'We Germans didn't understand our role,' he said. He licked the whisky from his hand. 'As a defeated nation we were to be forever relegated to being customers – supplied by the Anglo-American factories – but we didn't understand that. We began to build factories of our own, and we did it well because we are professionals, we Germans, we like to do everything well – even losing wars. We became prosperous and you English and Americans don't like it. There has to be a reason that lets you keep your nice cosy feeling of superiority. It's because we Germans are toadies, weaklings, automatons, masochists, collaborators or ——lickers that we are doing so well.'

'You are breaking my heart,' I said.

'Drink,' said Vulkan and downed his most recent one with lightning speed. 'You aren't the one I should be shouting at. You understand better than most, even though you hardly understand at all.'

'You are too kind,' I said.

At about 10 P.M. a bright-eyed boy that I had seen at the Gehlen Bureau flashed his cuffs at the bartender and ordered a Beefeater martini. He sipped at it and turned slowly to survey the room. He caught a sight of us and gulped at his drink.

'King,' he said quietly. 'Here's a surprise.'

It was like finding a cherry in a sweet martini; a big surprise but you raise hell if it's not there.

'I'm Helmut,' said the bright-eyed boy.

'I'm Edmond Dorf,' I said; two can play at that game.

'Do you want to speak in private?' Vulkan said.

'No,' said Helmut politely and offered his English cigarettes. 'Our latest employee is, alas, in a traffic accident.'

Vulkan produced a gold lighter.

'Fatal?' asked Vulkan.

Helmut nodded.

'When?' said Vulkan.

'Next week,' said Helmut. 'We bring him around the corner[2] next week.' I noticed Vulkan's hand flinch as he lit the cigarette.

Helmut noticed it too, he smiled. To me he said, 'The Russians are bringing your boy into the city in two weeks from next Saturday.'

'My boy?' I said.

'The scientist from the Academy of Sciences Biology Division; he will probably stay at the Adlon. Isn't that the man you want us to move?'

'No comment,' I said. It was very annoying and this boy was making the most of it. He flashed me a big smile before giving his teeth a rebore with the Beefeater martini.

'We are arranging the pipeline now,' he added. 'It would help us if you supply these documents from your own sources. You will find all the data there.' He handed me a folded slip of paper, shot his cuffs a couple of times to show me his cuff-links, then finished his martini and vanished.

Vulkan and I looked across the rubber-plants.

'Gehlens Wunderkinder,' said Vulkan. 'They're all like him.'

---

[2] Helmut used the expression 'Um die Ecke bringen', which in German means to kill.

9

In certain circumstances pawns can be converted into
the most powerful unit on the board.

Tuesday, October 8th

I put the Gehlen request for documents on the teleprinter
to London and marked it urgent.

The paper said:

Name: Louis Paul BROUM
National Status: British
Nationality of Father: French
Profession: Agricultural Biologist
Date of birth: August 3rd, 1920
Place of birth: Prague, Czechoslovakia
Residence: England
Height: 5 ft 9 ins   *Weight:* 11 st 12 lb
Colour of eyes: brown   *Colour of hair:* black
Scars: 4-inch scar inside of right ankle
Documents required.
1. British Passport issued not before beginning of current
year.
2. British Driving Licence.
3. International Driving Permit.
4. Current Insurance Policy on a motor vehicle in British Isles.
5. Motor Vehicle Registration Book (for same vehicle).
6. Diners' Club credit card (current).

10

JOHN AUGUST VULKAN

Wednesday, October 9th

'Oh boy,' thought Johnnie Vulkan *Edelfresswelle* – a great calorific abundance of everything but faith – and quite frankly it was great. There were times when he saw himself as an untidy recluse in some village in the Bavarian woods, with ash down his waistcoat and his head full of genius, but tonight he was glad he had become what he had become. Johnnie Vulkan, wealthy, attractive and a personification of *Knallhärte* – the tough, almost violent quality that post-war Germany rewarded with admiring glances. The health cures at Worishofen had tempered him to a supple resilience and that's what you needed to stay on top in this town – this was no place for an intellectual today, whatever it may have been in the 'thirties.

He was glad the Englishman had gone. One could have too much of the English. They ate fish for breakfast and always wanted to know where they gave the best rate of exchange. The whole place was reflected in the coloured mirror. The women were dressed in sleek shiny gowns and the men were wearing 1,000-mark suits. It looked like those advertisements for bourbon that one saw in *Life* magazine. He sipped his whisky and eased his foot on to the foot-rail of the bar. Anyone coming in would take him for an American. Not one of those crummy stringers who hung around writing groundless rumours with 'Our special correspondent in Berlin' on the dateline, but one of the Embassy people or one of the businessmen like the one sitting against the wall with the blonde. Johnny looked at the blonde again. Boy, oh boy! he could see what type of suspender belt *she* was wearing. He flashed her a smile. She smiled back. A fifty-mark lay, he thought, and lost interest. He called the barman and ordered another bourbon. It was a new barman.

'Bourbon,' he said. He liked to hear himself saying that. 'Plenty of ice this time,' he said. The barman brought it and said, 'The right money, please, I am short of change.' The barman said it in German. It made Vulkan annoyed.

Vulkan tapped a Philip Morris on his thumbnail and noticed how brown his skin was against the white cigarette. He put the cigarette in his mouth and snapped his fingers. The bloody fool must have been half-asleep.

Along the bar, there were a couple of tourists and a newspaper writer named Poetsch from Ohio. One of the tourists asked if Poetsch went across to the 'other side' very much.

'Not much,' Poetsch said. 'The Commies have me marked down on their black list.' He laughed modestly. Johnnie Vulkan said an obscene word loud enough for the barman to look up. The barman grinned at Johnnie and said, 'Mir kann keener.'[1]

Poetsch didn't speak German so he didn't notice.

There were lots of radio men here tonight: Americans with the blunt accents of their fathers who spoke strange Slav dialects over the jammed night air. One of them waved to Vulkan but didn't beckon him across there. That was because they considered themselves the cultural set of the city. Really they were mental lightweights equipped with

---

[1] Mir kann keener: you can't fool me (a typical Berliner comment).

a few thousand items of cocktail-time small talk. They wouldn't know a string quartet from a string vest.

The barman lit his cigarette for him.

'Thanks,' said Johnnie. He made a mental note to cultivate the barman in the near future, not for the purpose of getting information – he hadn't sunk to that peanut circuit yet – but because it made life easier in a town like this. He sipped his bourbon and tried to think of a way to appease London. Vulkan felt glad that Dawlish's boy was heading back to London. He was all right as the English go, but you never knew where you were with him. That's because the English were amateurs – and proud of it. There were some days when Johnnie wished that he was working for the Americans. He had more in common with them, he felt.

All around there was a rumble of courteous conversation. The man with nose, moustache and spectacles that looked like a one-piece novelty was an English MP. He had the managerial voice that the English upper class used for hailing taxis and foreigners.

'But *here* in the actual city of Berlin,' the Englishman was saying, 'taxes are twenty per cent *below* your West German taxes and what's more your chaps at Bonn *waive* the four per cent on transactions. With a bit of wangling they will insure your freight free and if you bring in steel you have it carted *virtually* without charge. No businessman can afford to overlook it, old chap. What line of business you in?' The Englishman brushed both ends of his moustache and sniffed loudly.

Vulkan smiled to a man from the Jewish Documentation Section. That was a job Vulkan would enjoy, but the pay was very small, he heard. The Jewish Documentation Section in Vienna collected material about war crimes to bring ex-SS men to trial. There was plenty of work about, Vulkan thought. He looked through the tobacco smoke; he could count at least five ex-SS officers in here at this moment.

LEN DEIGHTON

'Best thing that ever *happened* to the British motor car industry.' The Englishman's loud voice cut the air again.

'Your Volkswagen people felt the draught in *no* time. Ha ha. Lost a source of cheap labour and found the trade union johnnies dunning them for money. What happened? *Up* went the price of the Volkswagen. Gave our chaps a chance. Say what you like, *best* thing that ever happened to the British motor car industry, that wall.'

Johnnie fingered the British passport in his pocket. Well, the wall didn't make much difference to him. He preferred it in fact. If the communists hadn't stopped all their riff-raff streaming across here in search of jobs, then where would they have got people to work in the factories? Johnnie knew where they would have got them: from the East. Who wanted to go swimming out on the Müggelsee and have it full of Mongolians and Ukrainians? Lot of chance there would be then of restoring East Prussia, Pomerania and Silesia to Germany. Not that Vulkan gave a damn about the 'lost territories' but some of these loud-mouths, who did, shouldn't shout about the wall so much.

There was a girl from Wedding. He wondered whether it was true what they said about her chauffeur. It was a strange place for a girl like her to live, horrible low-class district. That tiny house with the TV set over the bed. He had put the Scots colonel on to her. What was it he had said afterwards about her wanting a 21-inch model with colour and remote control? Vulkan remembered how the whole bar had laughed at the time. Vulkan blew her a kiss and wrinkled his eyes in greeting. She waved a small gold-mesh evening bag at him. She was still sexy, Vulkan thought, and in spite of all his resolution found himself sending the barman across to her with a champagne cocktail. He wrote a little note to go with it. He wrote the note with a small gold propelling pencil on the back of an engraved visiting card.

54

'Take dinner with me,' he wrote. He debated whether to add a query but decided that women hate indecision. Domination was the secret of success with women.

'Will join you later,' he added, before giving it to the barman.

Two more people had joined Poetsch down at the far end of the bar; a man and a girl. The man looked English. Poetsch said, 'You saw it, did you? We call it the "wall of shame", as you know. I'd like to show it to every living person in the world.'

A man called 'Colonel Wilson' winked at Vulkan. To do this, 'Colonel Wilson' had to remove a large pair of dark glasses. Around his left eye and upper cheek there was a mesh of scars. Wilson slid a cigar along the bar to Vulkan.

'Thanks, Colonel,' Vulkan called. Wilson was an ex-corporal cook who had got his scars from spluttering fat in a mess hall in Omaha. It was a good cigar. 'Colonel' wouldn't be such a fool as to give him a cheap one. Vulkan smelled it, rolled it and then decapitated it scientifically with a small flat gold cigar-cutter that he kept in his top pocket. A gold guillotine. An amalgam of sharp steel and burnished gold. The barman lit the cigar for him.

'Always with a match,' Vulkan told him. 'A match held a quarter of an inch away from the leaf. Gas lighters never.' The barman nodded. Before Vulkan had the cigar properly alight, 'Colonel' had moved alongside him at the bar. 'Colonel Wilson' was six feet one-and-a-half inches of leathery skin encasing meaty sinew, packed dense like a well-made *Bockwurst*. His face was grey and lined: his hair trimmed to the skull. He could have made a living in Hollywood playing in the sort of film where the villains have thick lips. He ordered two bourbons.

Vulkan could hear Poetsch saying, 'Truth – I'm fond of saying – is the most potent weapon in the arsenal of freedom.' Poetsch *was* fond of saying that, Vulkan thought.

LEN DEIGHTON

He knew that 'Colonel Wilson' wanted something. He drank the bourbon quickly. 'Colonel Wilson' ordered two more. Vulkan looked at the barman and tipped his head a millimetre towards the girl from Wedding. The barman lowered his eyelids. It was one of the great things about this town, thought Vulkan, this sensitivity to signs and innuendo. He heard the English MP's voice, 'Good heavens, *no. We* have a few tricks left up our sleeve *I* can tell you.' The English MP chortled.

The British were deadly, Vulkan decided. He remembered his last visit there. The big hotel in Cromwell Road, and the rain that never stopped for a week. A nation of inventive geniuses where there are forty different types of electrical plug, none of which works efficiently. Milk is safe on the street but young girls in danger, sex indecent but homosexuality acceptable, a land as far north as Labrador with unheated houses, where hospitality is so rare that 'landlady' is a pejorative word, where the most boastful natives in the world tell foreigners that the only British shortcoming is modesty.

Vulkan winked to the girl from Wedding. She smoothed her dress slowly and touched the nape of her neck. Vulkan turned to 'Colonel Wilson' and said, 'OK, what's on your mind?'

'I want thirty-nine Praktika cameras; with the f/2 lens.'

Vulkan reached for a piece of ice from the canister on the bar. The piano-player did a fancy cadenza and stopped playing. Vulkan put his cigar in his mouth and clapped his hands. His face scowled at the ribbon of smoke. Several people joined in the applause. Vulkan said, 'Do you?' still looking at the piano-player.

'Good price and in dollars,' said Colonel Wilson. There was no reply from Vulkan.

Wilson said, 'I know that you don't do that kind of thing for a living; but this is a special favour for a friend

56

of mine. It's more of a memento – you know, a camera smuggled out of the East – these guys like that kind of thing.'

'What guys?' said Vulkan.

'Trade delegation,' said Wilson.

'Thirty-nine,' said Vulkan reflectively.

'It would be no trouble to you,' said Wilson. 'Just bring them with you when you come back with a Russian. You are the only guy I know who ever rides through Checkpoint Charlie with a Russian.' He laughed nervously.

'Thirty-nine must be the delegation of American radio and TV producers. Poetsch is running that, isn't he?'

'Aw,' said Wilson, 'don't go yelling it around. I told you in strict confidence. If you can deliver them before . . .'

'You told me nothing,' said Vulkan. 'I told *you*. I'm not a camera dealer, tell Poetsch that.'

'Leave P's name out of this.'

Vulkan gently blew smoke at Wilson, saying nothing.

'Don't cross me, Vulkan,' Colonel Wilson said. 'You don't want me spilling it to your British pal that I'm no longer a US Army major.'

'No longer,' said Vulkan gleefully, almost choking on his drink.

'I can make plenty of trouble,' said Wilson.

'And you can make a one-way trip through the wire,' said Vulkan quietly.

They stared at each other. Wilson swallowed to moisten his throat and turned back to his drink.

'OK Johnnie,' Wilson said over his shoulder. 'No hard feelings, eh, pal?'

Johnnie pretended not to hear and moved along the bar calling for another bourbon.

'Two?' said the barman.

'One will be enough,' said Johnnie.

He could see Wilson's face in the mirror; it was very

pale. He could see the girl from Wedding too, touching the hair at the nape of her neck like she didn't know she was straining her brassiere. She crossed her legs and smiled at his reflection.

'Poetsch,' Johnnie thought.

He had wanted to get something on Poetsch, if only to cut down his ranting at the bar. He could hear his voice now. Poetsch was saying, 'The very same people who made the great little TV film about the tunnel. The whole thing was paid for by the TV company, NBC. And what I'm saying, folks, is that those fifty-nine people who escaped owe their very freedom to our American system of unshackled enterprise and bold corporate drive . . .' There were a couple of favours Poetsch could do for Johnnie Vulkan. Johnnie relished the idea of telling Poetsch about them; even the girl from Wedding wasn't a better prospect than that.

The lounge was beginning to fill up now. Vulkan leaned back against the bar, tensed his muscles and relaxed. It was good to feel he knew them all and that even Americans like 'Colonel Wilson' couldn't take advantage of him. Johnnie Vulkan could pick out the tarts and the queens, the hustlers and the fairies. He knew all the heavies waiting assignment: from the nailers-up of notices to the nailers-up of Christs. He saw the girl from Wedding trying to catch his eye. Poetsch's crowd had grown too. There was that elderly English queer with the dyed hair, and a stupid little Dresdener who thought he was going to infiltrate the Gehlen Bureau – except that Johnnie had told them all about him last week. He wondered whether Helmut had been serious about having the Dresdener killed in a traffic accident. It was possible. King was right as a code name Vulkan decided; they acknowledged his stature by allotting it to him. Freudian. King Vulkan of Berlin.

He supposed the red-haired girl talking to Poetsch now

was the one Poetsch had mentioned to him; the girl from Israeli Intelligence.

'Boy, oh boy!' thought Vulkan. 'What a town this is!' and he eased his way down the bar towards them, smiling at Poetsch.

11

Zugzwang: to move a chess piece under duress.

London, Thursday, October 10th

I moved into top as I passed Parliament Square. The night was young and it had nothing much to do. Tiny moons moved across St James's Park playing tiddly-winks with the shiny leaves, and the speedometer moved up to nudge sixty. The radio-telephone called me back to earth. It was the Charlotte Street Control Room: 'Message for you oboe ten from Northern Car Hire.[1] Do you read me? Over.'

'Loud and clear. Let's have it.'

'Message from Mr D. You are to contact Mr Hallam at Betty's Club. Is that roger? Oboe ten. Over.'

'Only too roger.'

'Observe your r/t procedure, oboe ten. Your customer will ask you for change of ten shillings. You will have four half-crowns ready for him. Is that roger? Over.'

'What are you talking about? What's Hallam want ten bob for?'

'Oboe ten. Observe procedure please. I am giving you your introduction formality for this customer. Is that roger? Over.'

'I don't know what you are talking about,' I said. 'Phone me at home later on. On the landline. OK?'

[1] Our radio procedure is designed to make an eavesdropper think we are a taxi service. For this same reason our car pool uses radio-equipped taxi-cabs with the flags always set at 'hired'.

The Scots operator's nerve broke before I got to Hyde Park Corner.

'For Christ's sake. Oboe ten. You know what the Home Office people are like. He wants you to give him four half-dollars so that he knows who you are.'

'What do you mean "so that he knows who I am"? I saw Hallam only the other day. Who the hell is he going to think I am if I don't give him four half-crowns – James Bond?'

'*Please* just give him the half-crowns, oboe ten.'

'I don't know how many make ten bob,' I said, but the operator didn't come back on the air again. Inside the car the radio shone with a faint green spot of light. I turned the volume and filled the car with big band sound as a volley of raindrops spattered across the windscreen.

Betty's was one of the small set of London clubs that have been going over twenty years on a mixed membership, face up to the financial crisis of imminent closure once a year but never get around to pasting the corners of the wallpaper back into place. Next to the magazine rack, a brown-haired man was slugging shillings into a one-armed bandit without letting go of his Tuborg lager. The crash of the machine punctuated some gentle Sinatra. Without looking at me he sensed my approach, but he continued to watch the spinning oranges and pineapples.

'Got change of ten bob?' he said. Before I could reply, the fruit machine gave three neat clicks and then a shudder as shillings showered into the metal tray.

'Looks like you won't be needing change now,' I said.

He turned suddenly and grasped my cuff. His watery brown eyes stared into mine for a long time before he said, 'Don't you believe it, dear. I still do.' It was Hallam, the man from Bina Gardens, but his hair was now a rich brown colour. He scooped up the shillings and showered them into his already sagging pockets.

'First-rate for the gas meter,' he said. I held four half-crowns extended towards him while he spent five minutes trying to pry apart two ten-shilling notes that were only one. Reluctantly he gave it to me. Then he took his time fitting the base of a Player's No 3 into a four-inch holder. I flicked a Swan Vesta alight with my thumbnail and he nosed his fag down into the fire and flame. He was well alight before he spoke.

'Stok and the Gehlen boys are both being helpful?'

'Both being very helpful,' I said. 'Did you ever find Confucius?'

'Yes,' said Hallam. 'The fickle creature came back to me Tuesday morning, very early. So dirty; heaven knows where he had been. So independent the Siamese. I really should buy a collar for him but it seems so cruel.' Somehow he got four syllables into 'cruel'.

'Yes,' I said.

I had a street map of Berlin in my pocket. I moved a couple of ashtrays and a vase of plastic tulips and spread it across the table.

'Stok will bring Semitsa into East Berlin somewhere within this rectangle.' I drew a very light pencil mark just north of Alexanderplatz.

'He will tell me where later. If I don't like it, I can fix somewhere else in the same district.' Hallam had his Tuborg wrapped around his face but I knew he was taking in every word.

'Why don't you make the Russkies bring him down to Marienborn and hand him over the West German frontier?' he asked.

'Not possible,' I said.

He nodded.

'Outside Stok's district. How foolish of me. Very well then. You have Semitsa − or you think you have him − here.' He stabbed the street map.

'Now,' I said, 'from there the Gehlen boys will post him special delivery to West Berlin.'

'Then what?' asked Hallam.

'If I know anything about the Gehlen boys they will delay the transfer at least twenty-four hours so that they can pump Semitsa for anything that might be useful to them. Then using the documents that your Home Office people are going to provide we bring him to London as a naturalized British subject returning home.'

'How will the Gehlen people move him across the wall?' said Hallam.

'You know better than to ask that and so do I,' I said. 'If I ask, they'll just tell me a lot of reasonably creative lies.'

'Did you give me my change?' he said.

'Yes I did,' I said, 'four half-crowns.'

Hallam opened his wallet and counted his paper money.

'The Home Office won't release the documents until one of our own people actually sees Semitsa in the flesh in West Berlin.' I could see the slack red lining of his watery eyes. He swung his chin from side to side to emphasize the negative and the jaw opened to repeat the decision.

'You see why . . .' he began.

I reached out and with my finger-tips gently closed Hallam's mouth. 'You wouldn't want to see Semitsa's flesh,' I said. 'You don't like *flesh*, do you, Hallam? It isn't nice.'

His face flushed like dipped litmus. I went across to the bar, bought two XO brandies and set one in front of Hallam. His face was still red.

'Just have the papers ready, love,' I said. 'I'll manage.'

Hallam poured the brandy down his throat and his eyes watered more than ever as he nodded agreement.

12

Every piece has its mode of attack but only a pawn
will attack en passant. Similarly only a pawn can be
captured in this manner.

Thursday, October 10th

When I left Hallam I drifted north. The Saddle Room was
rocking until the spurs jingled and a girl with a back-
combed bouffon of red hair was twisting with obsessive
grace on a table top which put her ten inches above floor
level, not allowing for the back-combing. Her feet knocked
the glasses to the floor with rhythmic abandon. No one
seemed to mind. I walked as far as the stairs and peered
into the smoke and noise. Two girls with large but tight
sweaters narcissistically twisted back to back. I poured two
or three double whiskies into the back of my throat,
watched the floor and tried to forget what a crummy trick
I had pulled on Hallam.

It was still raining outside. The doorman and I looked
around for a taxi. I found one, gave the doorman a florin
and climbed in.

'I saw it first.'

'What?' I said.

'I saw it first,' said the girl with the back-combed bouffon. She said it slowly and patiently. She was about five
foot ten, light in complexion, nervous of movement,
dressed with skilful simplicity. She had a rather wide, full

mouth and eyes like a trapped doe. Now she kneaded her face around while querulously telling me yet again that she'd seen the cab before I had.

'I'm going towards Chelsea,' she said, opening the door. I looked around. The bad weather had driven cabs into hiding. 'OK,' I said, 'hop in. We'll do your journey first.'

The cab pulled into a tight lock and my new friend eased her back-combing on to the leatherwork with a sigh.

'Cigarette?' she said and flicked the corner of a pack of Camels with a skill that I can never master. I took one and brought a loose Swan Vesta match from my pocket. I dug my thumbnail into the head and ignited it. She was impressed and stared into my eyes as I lit the cigarette. I took it pretty calmly, just like I didn't have a couple of milligrammes of flaming phosphorus under the nail and coming through the pain threshold like a rusty scalpel.

'Are you in Advertising?' she said. She had a soft American accent.

'Yes,' I said, 'I'm an account executive with J. Walter Thompson.'

'You don't look like any of the Thompson people I know.'

'That's true,' I said. 'I'm the vanguard of the button-down shirt mob.' She gave a polite little laugh. 'Where in Chelsea?' the driver called. She told him. 'It's a party,' she said to me.

'Is that why you have that bottle of Guinness in your pocket?' I asked.

She tapped it to make sure it was still there. 'Ghoul,' she said smiling. 'That's to wash my hair in.'

'In Guinness?' I said.

'If you want body,' she said patting her hair.

'I want body,' I said. 'Believe me, I do.'

'My name is Samantha Steel,' she said politely. 'People call me Sam.'

13

Roman Decoy: a piece offered as bait to save a
hazardous situation.

London, Friday, October 11th

Charlotte Street runs north from Oxford Street and there
are few who will blame it. By mid-morning they are writing
out the menus, straining yesterday's fat, dusting the plastic
flowers and the waiters are putting their moustaches on
with eyebrow pencils.

I waved to Wally who runs the delicatessen across the
road before turning into the doorway marked, among other
things, 'Ex-Officers' Employment Bureau', by a smooth
polished brass plate. In the hall the same floral wallpaper
had moved ever nearer autumn. The first-floor landing
smelled of acetone and from behind a doorway marked
'Acme Films Cutting Rooms', I could hear the gentle purr
of a movie projector. The next floor pretended to be a
theatrical tailor so that we could buy, alter or make any
kind of uniform we needed. This is where Alice sat. Alice
was the cross between librarian and concierge. Anyone
who thought they could do anything in that building without having Alice's approval should just try doing it.

'You are late, sir,' Alice said. She was thumping the lid
into a caterer's-size Nescafé tin.

'Right as always, Alice,' I said. 'I don't know what we'd
do without you.' I climbed towards my office. From the

dispatch department came the mournful trombone solo of 'Angels Guard Thee' as the CWS Brass Band played their part in the dispatch department's ceaseless record recital. Jean was waiting on the stairs. 'Coming in late,' she said.

'It's one of the B-flat cornets,' I explained, 'clipping the notes.'

'I mean *you* are coming in late.' She put my old raincoat on a wooden hanger that had the words 'stolen from typing pool' burned into the surface.

'How do you like it?' Jean said, 'the office.'

I looked around at the balding carpet, Jean's teak desk and the gleaming new IBM typewriter, and then I saw it. There was a large spiky indoor plant on the window sill.

'It's lovely,' I said. The leaves were long and prickly, the bright green giving way to a dull yellow at the thorny edge. All it did as far as I could see was block just a little more of the already inadequate grey London daylight. 'Lovely,' I said again.

'Mother-in-law's Tongue,' said Jean, 'that's what it's called.'

'Don't stretch my credulity too far,' I said.

'That's what Dawlish said when he saw your expense sheet for last month.'

I unlocked my 'In' tray. Jean had already sifted most of it. The worst was the political reading matter. Long fools-cap translations of excerpts from *L'Unità*, *Party Information*[1] and two other information sheets had been waiting there for nearly a week. It was a job no one else could do for you.

'It was that bill at The Ivy,' said Jean. I signed the two information sheets as read and put them into the 'Out' tray. It was the only way to fight it down.

---

[1] A Peking publication for Party Executives.

'I told you he would notice that it was my birthday,' Jean said.

'Stop gnawing your knuckles,' I said. 'I can handle Grannie.'

'Ha ha,' said Jean. 'Well, don't fire him.'

'I'll make the jokes,' I said. 'What have you done about this Paul Louis Broum business?'

'I've passed the request for documents to Home Office. I then sent Interpol a blue[2] with instructions for a Bertillon if they find anything. No reply so far. Grannie wants you to go down to Acme Films at ten fifteen when they will screen all the film we have of Red Army people who work for the Karlshorst Security Control Area. Dawlish himself would like you to see him after that at eleven o'clock. You have no lunch appointments. I will order some sandwiches from Wally's if you wish. Hallam at the Home Office phoned and wanted to see you. I said you would call to see him between ten and ten thirty tomorrow morning. You are confirmed on tomorrow evening's flight to Berlin and I have checked with your hotel there. All OK.'

I said, 'You wonderful creature.'

Jean put a dozen letters on my desk, her arm brushed my shoulder and I caught the faint drifting perfume of Arpège.

'I can't make it tonight,' I said.

'The top three should be ready for the eleven o'clock collection. The requisitions don't matter.'

'I was looking forward to it,' I said, 'but there's this damn business with the Steel girl.' Jean walked towards the door. She stood there for a moment looking at me. I

<hr>

[2] Blue is a code request for information. Other codes include Red for a criminal arrested and ready for extradition. Black for an unidentified corpse. Bertillon is a speaking-portrait system. There is also a synoptic index with a colour tag for each sixth of the face.

detected the faint angry flush in her cheek only because I knew her so well. The severity of her straight-style dress emphasized her feminine stance.

'I am Circe,' she said. 'All who drink of my cup turn into swine.' She turned to go. 'You are no exception.' She threw the word over her shoulder like spilled salt.

'Be reasonable, Jean,' I said, but she had gone.

Dawlish had the only office with two windows in the building. You didn't need dark glasses there but on the other hand you didn't need a flashlight either. Dawlish was always buying pieces of antique furniture. Every now and again he would say he had business to attend to and everyone would know that he was coming back with a writing-desk or an aspidistra-stand from Portobello Road.

So Dawlish's office was like a junkshop. There was an antique umbrella stand and an antique desk under a green-shaded Victorian lamp. Across one wall stood a bookcase with glass doors; inside was a shiny leather set of Dickens with only *Martin Chuzzlewit* missing. Dawlish got the set for twenty-five shillings. *Martin Chuzzlewit* wasn't one of Dickens's best as Dawlish was always saying. On the other wall, where the big IBM machine stood, there were two cases of butterflies – one had a cracked glass – and photographs of various Civil Service cricket teams in which the granular wrinkled face of Dawlish could be recognized.

On October 1st the coal fires were lighted. A freezing September or a scorching October made no difference. A small cardboard box marked 'OMO', bulging with coal eggs, stood in coal dust in the hearth. I pulled the leather armchair nearer to the flickering fire. This tiny fireplace had been built when Britain's fleet steamed the world on coal and when diplomacy largely consisted of sending them somewhere.

Dawlish read my report. He pinched the bridge of his

nose and without looking up said, 'I notice everyone's getting at you again.'

Alice brought coffee, set it down on Dawlish's desk and left without a word.

'Yes,' I said.

Dawlish passed me a cracked cup with pink flowers around the rim. 'Tell me about Stok,' he said. 'Ginger biscuit?'

I shook my head. 'I'm getting too fat,' I said. 'Stok is just doing a job.'

Dawlish was holding his cup and saucer at eye level.

'Not bad for one-and-six each,' he said. 'They are German porcelain: quite old.'

I watched the little islands of Nescafé powder spin ever smaller in the swirl of hot water.

'Don't you think they are beautiful?' Dawlish said.

'They aren't exactly the Portland vase but they're OK for Nescafé.'

'Is Stok good at his job?'

'I think he is,' I replied. 'Much too good to think that I'd go for that clumsy cover story about his wife being dead. Either he wanted me to discover the lie so that I'd be more likely to believe his subsequent story –' Dawlish brought his coffee across to the chair near the fire and sat down. 'Or?' he said. He took his pipe to pieces and blew loudly through each component.

'Or he thought I wasn't bright enough to . . .' Dawlish was looking at me with a particularly stupid expression.

'Very funny,' I said.

Dawlish assembled his pipe.

'And this description that the Gehlen people want on the document.' He looked at the flimsy green teleprinter message. 'What's wrong with Broum as a cover name for Semitsa?'

'Nothing except that I don't like being pushed around.

I don't mind them mentioning one or two things they want – I understand that they are preparing other documents – but this sheet they've given us is almost a biography.'

'You are just piqued personally.' Dawlish produced a two-pound bag of sugar.

'Perhaps you're right,' I said. 'I don't like the Gehlen mob treating me like an employee.'

'But what would be their purpose in wanting such documents? Not to sell them, they have plenty of money.'

I shrugged and put three spoonfuls of sugar into my coffee.

'That's how you put on weight,' said Dawlish.

'That's right,' I said.

'And the girl?' said Dawlish. 'What have you found out about the girl, Samantha Steel?'

'It's probably a phoney name anyway but there are no green or white cards at the Yard.[3] Nor anything at Central Register.[4] She's American; I've put a teleprinter request through to Washington.'

'What a performance,' said Dawlish. 'You never think of the expense. It'll all end up like that other girl. In the end you found she had a press agent just dying to send biography and pictures to anyone who asked for them.'

'This girl followed me,' I said. 'It was clumsy and it was obvious; we can't just ignore it.'

'You are quite sure?'

'Quite sure,' I said.

'Umm,' said Dawlish grudgingly. 'Well, you may be right; we can't be too careful. Check on her.'

'I already am,' I said patiently.

---

[3] In Scotland Yard's CRO files, a green card indicates a suspected person with no criminal record. White cards are used for ordinary criminal records.

[4] Central Register is the Government's intelligence file on suspected persons and for those of national importance – trade union officials, scientists, directors of large companies, etc.

'And see her again,' said Dawlish.

'Don't worry about that,' I said. 'I may as well get something out of this job, if it's only entertainment.'

'Did you check on Mr Vulkan's playmate?' asked Dawlish.

'Yes,' I grinned. 'There is no Major Bailis. US Army Records said the description fitted a civilian layabout named Wilson. He was there just to impress me, I suppose. He's a character, that Vulkan.'

'He's a rogue,' said Dawlish. He grabbed his bag of sugar and got up. 'Well, this won't do. Everything else OK?'

'My electric fire doesn't work,' I said. 'I'm freezing downstairs and Jean said you were unhappy about my expenses. Was I too extravagant?'

'Being extravagant is just a state of mind, my boy,' he said, 'and so is being cold. Just see what you can do about both.'

I was a bit relieved. 'What I'd like is an interest-free loan of eight hundred quid to buy a new car,' I said.

Dawlish gently packed tobacco into the bowl of his pipe with a match. He put the pipe into his mouth before looking up at me.

'Yes,' he finally said. He lit the pipe with great care.

'Yes I want it or yes I can have it?' I said.

'Yes, everything they say about you is true,' said Dawlish. 'Go away and let me work.'

'What about the decision on Stok's forty thousand pounds?' I said.

'Ah,' said Dawlish. 'That's what has been giving you ideas above your station.' He let go with a great puff of smoke.

'We might lose him,' I said. Dawlish prodded the match into the pipe bowl.

I added, 'The Egyptian Intelligence people will buy Semitsa like a shot if they get wind of it.'

'That's what's worrying me,' said Dawlish, showing no trace of worry whatsoever. 'The Egyptians collect German scientists, don't they?'

'Yes.'

'Our Zürich people had better watch MECO[5] – that's who will be handling the deal if there is one.'

'Yes,' I said again.

'Very well,' said Dawlilsh. 'Keep an ear to the ground. If you send Jean up with a War Office Armoury chit I'll give you a signature for a pistol.'

'Thank you, sir,' I said. It was unprecedented. If Dawlish thought I needed a gun, I was living on borrowed time.

'For God's sake be circumspect with it. It's a hell of a responsibility for me.'

'I'll bear you in mind if anyone starts shooting at me,' I said. 'I'll take it over to HQ and bump off Hallam tomorrow morning for a start.'

'Hallam.' Dawlish looked up suddenly. 'Leave Hallam alone,' he said. 'You haven't been threatening him, have you?'

'I leaned on him a tiny bit,' I admitted. 'We nearly had HQ running this whole project.'

'Don't do anything like that,' said Dawlish. He took out a large white handkerchief and polished his spectacles. 'I don't care what else you do; but treat Hallam with kid gloves.'

'I think he'd go more for green velvet with sequins,' I said, but Dawlish just puffed smoke.

I went downstairs and tried to get the Ministry of Works fire going. Chico came in.

---

[5] MECO: Mechanical Corporation, 155 Birmendorferstrasse, Zürich. An agency which buys jet planes, missiles and talent on behalf of the Egyptian Government.

'I've got a file from AEASD.'

'What?' I said.

'Atomic Energy Authority, Security Department,' Chico said.

'That's better,' I said. 'You've been watching those spy films on TV again. So what?'

'What do I do with it?'

'Pass it on somewhere,' I said.

'It's marked immediate.'

'Then pass it on immediately.' Chico smiled sheepishly, tucked the file under his arm and walked across to the window. He really only wanted to kill time till lunch. Chico was a delicate bloom from an old family tree. He had too much forehead and not enough chin to be handsome and he carried himself in that sort of crouch that Englishmen adopt to avoid humiliating their more stunted brethren. He looked round my office furtively.

'Is it true about the old man's garden?'

'Is what true?' I grunted without looking up, although I guessed what was coming.

'One of the chaps across at the War House said that Grannie grows weeds.' Jean came in to get something from the filing cabinet; she waited for my reply.

I said, 'Mr Dawlish has achieved considerable status as an amateur botanist. He's written a number of books including *Forest Marsh and Moor Plants* and *The Dehiscent Capsule of the Pennycress in the Seeding Cycle*. Has become something of a specialist on meadow and hedgerow flowers. What do you expect him to grow in his garden? Tomatoes?'

'No sir,' said Chico. 'Golly, I didn't know he was an expert on weeds.'

'Hedgerow flowers we usually say. And don't call Mr Dawlish "Grannie".'

'Yes, hedgerow flowers. Those friends of mine didn't know that.'

'One of these days, Chico,' I said, 'you are going to face up to the fact that those friends of yours in what you persist in calling the War House know nothing about everything. They are as ignorant as you are. You should do something about it. Go down to the library and read a book.'

'Do you have any particular book in mind, sir?'

'Start at A or the shelf nearest the door and see what you can learn by Christmas.'

'You're joking, sir.'

'I never joke, Chico. The truth is quite adequately hilarious.' Jean found the file and left the office without saying anything, which is generally a bad sign in one way or another.

Chico came round the desk. 'What are you marking?' he said.

'Confidential,' I said. 'If you've got no work to do, fix the electric fire. The plug has gone wrong.'

'Yes sir. I'm rather good at that sort of thing.'

He picked up the fire and unscrewed the plug with a sixpence. I went back to *It pays to increase your word power*.

'What does "sibling" mean, Chico?' I asked.

'No idea, sir.' He'd spent three years at Cambridge, getting his gown tangled in bicycle chains and he couldn't do the *Daily Telegraph* crossword without cheating. There was silence until he began to tell me the plot of a film he'd seen the night before. I made a note of the title.

Chico gave me the plug. 'I've lost the very tiny screw under your desk, sir,' Chico said.

'Beat it, Chico,' I said. 'I need the oxygen.'

He made for the door. 'And take your bloody file with you,' I said. 'You're not passing it on to me.'

The outside phone rang. It was a clear GPO line without gimmicks that we have listed as the 'Ex-Officers' Employment Bureau'.

'It's Sam,' said the caller.

'Not Sam, Sam the . . .'

'Samantha,' she said. 'Samantha Steel.'

'Hello, how are you?'

'You should know,' she said.

'Just as great without eyebrows,' I said.

'That's what the milkman said this morning.'

'A man of fine judgement.'

'Are you coming over?'

'Yes, I'll come across and get you right away.'

'Come across, you ghoul, but don't count on anything.'

14

J'adoube: a word used to indicate that a player intends
to touch a piece but not move it.

Friday, October 11th

Samantha lived in the sort of road where driving schools
teach people to turn round. Beyond the Sickertian back-
waters of Camden Town there is a salient of quiet houses
where once lived the mistresses of Victorian businessmen
who couldn't get one in Hampstead.

The ivy-encrusted fortress was set well back into the
garden, and a modern sign, 'Heathview House – service
flats', looked odd tacked to the Gothic entrance. Statuary
in the garden glowered motionless through the shrubbery
like jungle-trained guerrillas. I pushed open the turquoise
front door and stepped in. Stained glass printed great-
shapes of thin sunlight across the marble floor like someone
had been hurling bottles of ink around. Whoever had
divided the house into flats was making enough money
out of it to put framed prints and fresh flowers in the hall.
A tall Gothic tracery window, rich with a tortuous pattern
of huge yellow flowers, illuminated the staircase. The light
held the dusty air in suspension and I climbed the stairs
like a fly fighting its way out of amber.

The door at the top of the stairs bore a typewritten card:
'S. Steel.' I pressed the bell-push and heard a noise like
someone had walked into a xylophone.

Samantha Steel came to the door wearing a bathrobe and a towel around the head.

'Who are you?' she said. 'The Fuller Brush man?'

'I'm from American Express,' I said. 'It's OK to drink the local water.'

'I was in the tub,' she said.

'Maybe I can help.'

'Yes,' she said. 'Go and build two drinks and give one to me.'

I walked into the lounge. It was about thirty foot of ankle-high carpeting from silk wall to silk wall. The cocktail cabinet was in the corner. I opened it and was socked in the head by a pink neon. I groped inside the cabinet among a platoon of bottles, mixed a martini and slammed ice into it.

The bathroom was all mosaics and radiant heating. A low marble table held three dozen bottles of lotion and salts and above that there was a huge pink mirror and a complexity of stainless steel shower fittings.

The bathtub was made of some sort of black stone. Samantha was in it. She was wearing half a dozen bracelets and a string of pearls.

'Don't stand there. Gimme the drink,' said Sam. Five feet ten inches isn't very tall, but when it's horizontal in a black bath it takes you a devil of a time to look at it.

I said, 'Do you always wear your accessories in the bath?'

She grinned. 'Accessories always – jewellery sometimes.' She sipped the drink. 'The hell you put in it?'

'Vermouth and gin,' I said.

'It's filthy,' she said. 'Pour it away and do it again.'

I brought her a much stronger mix. She downed it in one gulp and climbed from the bath dripping and dancing across the carpeting, gleaming with silver, diamonds and wet skin. She began to dry herself in a brisk, sexless sort of way.

'Put some music on,' she yelled, draping a huge red

bath towel around herself. I opened the gramophone and switched it on. The pickup arm moved across the black shiny disc and Claire Austin sang 'I'm Through With Love' like she meant it and the backing was all a backing could be. Sam had picked up her cigarettes and I was ready to give her a light.

'Down, ghoul. None of that, buddy boy.'

'I was just going to light your cigarette,' I said.

'I'll manage,' she said. She flicked the corner of the Camels pack, put the cigarette in her mouth and lit it. She inhaled the smoke with a cheek-sunken concentration and blew a great warm happy cloud of smoke across the room. Her eyes were enormous and they studied me carefully as I sat on the sofa. The room was furnished with the sort of expensive, impersonal taste that landlords save for wealthy foreign transients. There were lots of satin-shaded tablelamps and glass ashtrays as big as hand basins. Sam walked across to the sofa where I sat.

'You are the best thing that ever happened to me in this crummy town,' she said. 'Where were you hiding?'

'I was waiting outside the Overseas League,' I said. 'But you never showed up.'

She sat down next to me. Her skin was warm and damp and her body smelled of fresh talcum powder and Pepsodent.

'You can kiss me,' she said. Her head lolled back on the sofa and her eyes closed. I did it without hurry.

She got to her feet. 'I'm not a crumpled five-pound note,' she said. 'I don't need smoothing out.'

She walked across to the cocktail cabinet stroking her upper arms and using her elbows to keep the towel in place. She poured herself a drink and turned round to face me with a charming, big, dentifrice-ad smile. She said, 'There's a new kind of tranquillizer on the market; it doesn't soothe you . . .'

'It makes you enjoy being tense,' I finished sourly. She nodded and tipped her drink into her face.

'This isn't the ladies' bridge club,' I said. 'Any time that entertaining me becomes a strain just let me know.' She nodded again and gave me a long hard look. The player was still emitting the silk-and-sandpaper voice of Claire Austin.

'Stop pouting and put some clothes on,' I said. She came across and kneeled on the sofa. Her forehead was large and under it her milky grey eyes studied each part of my face in turn. When she smiled her face wrinkled far too much, but now when she spoke her voice was fresh and childlike and there was none of the hardness left.

'If you say so,' she said. I kissed her very gently on the lips.

'I say so,' I said. 'Get dressed and we'll take a ride into the English countryside.'

'After that?' she said.

'A concert or a theatre.'

'After that?'

'Dinner.'

'After that?'

'We'll see,' I said. She smiled wickedly. Then as suddenly her mood changed. 'I'd like a concert best,' she said. 'At the Royal Festival Hall it's . . .'

'Charles Ives and Alban Berg,' I finished.

'And Schönberg,' she said. 'They are playing Schönberg's "Variations for wind band". It's my very favourite. Do let's go. I'll wear my flame chiffon dress. Can we?'

'Certainly,' I said. 'It will be easy to get tickets; no one seems to like modern . . .' She kissed me again and a strand of hair was mixed into our kiss. As she pulled her head back from me her eyes were shiny – not with soft dewy tear-drops but wet as though she had bathed her eyes – and long strands of hair were gummed across her cheeks.

I waited for her to say something that would match the soft vulnerability of her damp smudged face. She said nothing. I had a feeling that she had never said anything without first considering the consequences. Or perhaps once she had.

She pushed my chest away roughly and yelled, 'My neutralizer.'

'What?' I said. She broke away from my embrace.

'My neutralizer,' she said again. 'My home perm, I should have put it on ten minutes ago. Now it'll be all frizzy.'

She disappeared into the bathroom, unwrapping the towel from her hair and leaving a long stream of monosyllabic Anglo-Saxon four-letter words. I removed a long silky hair from my mouth and poured myself another drink. The hair had been dyed but what was unusual about that?

15

Even a pawn can make a 'double attack'.

Friday, October 11th

Damp leaves shone underfoot like a million newly struck pennies. Ferns had shrivelled to intricate bronze abstract sculptures and shiny leaves were suspended magically in space from invisible twigs.

The pub wasn't yet in sight and we stood for a moment in the churchyard listening to the whining and rustling and looking at the gravestones which shone in the failing light. Samantha read the large curlicue lettering aloud.

> Praises on stones are titles vainly lent.
> A man's good name is his best monument.
> Thomas Merrick. Died August 15, 1849.

She moved through the soft light like a wraith. 'Here's a crazy one,' she called.

> Here lies the dust of Billy Paine.
> Whole undisturbed may he remain.
> On this date that he was slain.
> Many a kind thought died in Paine.

From underfoot the sweet smell of damp grass rose like perfume. Birds were still singing in the trees that stood across the major surgery of sunset like massed artery forceps. Sam insisted upon looking into the tiny church. The door opened with a vibratory screech. A small hand-lettered notice pinned to the door read: 'All brass rubbing suspended until further notice.' Inside the semi-precious light of the stained glass softly dusted the smooth, worn pews, and a complex of brass candlesticks glinted like a medieval oil refinery. Sam held my hand very tightly.

'You are the best thing that ever happened to me,' she said as though she meant it.

The pub was crowded when we got there. Men in rough-knit cardigans were lying at attention in the best armchairs and making a big thing about being local residents.

'I say, Mabel,' one of them shouted to the barmaid, 'how's about another noggin of the usual all round?' A man with a paisley scarf tucked inside an open-necked shirt was saying, 'He's the best damn photographer in the country but he's a thousand guineas a shot.'

A man with suede chukka boots said, 'Our deep-frozen fish-fingers nearly beat him. I said, "Make the beastly things out of plaster, old boy; we'll get the piping-hot effect by burning incense." We did too. Ha, ha! Put the sales up six and three-quarter per cent and he got some kind of Art Director's award.' He laughed a deep, manly laugh and sloshed down some beer.

Sam hadn't let go of my hand. We walked across to the bar and sat on the high stools where girls with camel coats and cowboy boots and black tights were drinking Pimm's Number 1 and exchanging West End hairdressers.

'Two large bitters,' I said. Through the window the moon was yellow like a low-power bulb in a blue velvet room.

'Do you ever imagine what it would be like to be on the moon?' Sam said.

'Nearly all the time,' I said.

'Serious,' she squeezed my hand, 'serious, ghoul.'

'What would it be like?' I asked.

'Spooky but wonderful,' she said.

'Like you,' I said and meant it.

Sam picked up her bitter and pulled a face at me. Outside there was the brutal noise of a sports car starting. It scattered a little gravel against the window and broke wind into the damp night air.

Sam was right about the Schönberg 'Variations for wind band'. I'd wanted to go on account of the Charles Ives 'Three places in New England', because I liked the crazy military band sequence, but the Schönberg was something else again. Everyone likes to convert people to something they like. Sam was no exception. She was being laughing and loving and little-girlish. I was a sucker for erudite little girls. We had dinner in Kensington in a poky little two-room place where the menu is as big as a newspaper and everything that can be flambé is flambé.

We moved through the powdered shoulders and borrowed evening suits and Sam felt out of place because she didn't have elbow-length gloves with jewelled bangles over.

'Don't worry,' I said. 'You've got a great face.'

She poked her tongue out at me.

'Don't be sexy,' I said and the waiter heard me and Sam blushed like a beetroot, which surprised me.

We both liked the same things. We both liked oysters without melon. 'I like oysters without dressing,' Sam said.

I raised my eyebrow at the waiter but Sam saw me and gave me a vicious kick in the ankle. The steak was OK and I was strong-willed enough not to hit the sweet-trolley too hard. We'd finished coffee by half past midnight and as we drove home I parked the car near the Serpentine in the Park. Sam said that if we were on the moon we could see which half of the world was sleeping.

'And we'd be the only people who could still see the sun,' I said.

'I would love that.' It began to rain as I restarted the car.

'Come and explain why at my place,' I suggested.

'My place,' she said. 'I still haven't got my eyebrows.'

'Tomorrow I'll buy a complete range of eyebrow pencils and keep them in my flat,' I promised. She held my arm tight.

I rang the chimes at Sam's front door. 'Don't do that,' Sam said. 'I have quiet neighbours.' She opened the door with a flourish and flipped the light switch.

It wasn't hard to recognize the signs. Burglars open chests beginning with the bottom drawer, so that they don't have to waste time shutting each to get at the next. Sam stood looking at the mess – clothes everywhere and wine spilled across the rug. She trapped her lower lip under her teeth and flung it forward in a heartfelt monosyllabic obscenity.

'Shall I phone the police?' I asked.

'The police,' said Sam scornfully. 'You mean that your police in England won't trample around the place like idiots, ask a million questions and end up doing sweet FA?'

'They will,' I said. 'But they are very nicely spoken.'

Sam said she would like to be alone.

'Whatever you wish,' I said, for I knew how she felt.

When I got back to my flat I phoned Sam. She didn't seem nervous or too distressed.

'She seems OK,' I said to Austin Butterworth, after replacing the receiver.

'Good,' he said. Austin was sitting well back in my most comfortable armchair supping my favourite whisky and being as modest as hell. 'Run of the mill job,' he was saying, 'french windows with slide bolts – child's play.

People are so silly. You should see my place, that's really well protected against burglars.'

'Is it?' I said.

'Of course,' said Ossie, 'you have to pay to have the best protection but it beats me why people are so mean. *After* – that's when they get properly equipped, *after* they've been done.'

'Yes,' I said.

'I made a lot of mess,' said Ossie.

'I noticed,' I said.

'Modus operandi,' said Ossie mysteriously. 'Sometimes I'm neat, sometimes I'm messy. It keeps the Yard puzzled.'

'I'll bet it does.'

'Mind you,' said Ossie, 'thanks for the old one-two on the door bell. I'd quite forgotten how the time was. I had to scarper when I heard you at the door.' He tugged at his nose and gave a little smile.

'What did you make of it?'

'Well,' said Ossie cautiously. 'Unmarried girl living alone. Lots of men friends. Gets three hundred dollars per week from Chase Manhattan Bank, New York.'

I nodded.

'United Nations Plaza Branch,' said Ossie. He was proud of being thorough.

'US passport in name of Samantha Steel. Israeli passport in name of Hanna Stahl showing same girl but with blonde hair. Quite a lot of jewellery – expensive stuff, no rubbish. Real mink coat. Real. *I* could get a thousand quid for it. So legit, it would be worth three or four.'

'Would it?' I said. I poured more refreshment and Ossie removed his boots and a pair of scarlet socks which he arranged in the fireplace.

'I don't say she's a whore,' said Ossie, 'but she's got a good standard of living.' His socks were steaming in the heat of the fire. 'Educated,' said Ossie.

'Yes?' I said.

'All kinds of books – psychology, poetry, all sorts of stuff.'

I went and made coffee while Ossie dried his feet. Outside the weather was terrible; the rain trickled constantly against the windows and there was a hollow drumming sound as torrents of it roared along the guttering and spilled over in great sheets that crashed on to the concrete of the back garden. By the time I returned with the coffee, Ossie had unpacked his little Gladstone bag. There were a couple of tiny jemmies and a Stillson wrench and a lot of lock-picking devices that Ossie had made himself. There were two yellow dusters, a pair of carpet slippers and a Polaroid Automatic 100 camera.

'Like this,' said Ossie. He held the set of Polaroid photos for me. Only one of them was of interest: a view of a box-room showing a bench with a monocular microscope – a professional-looking job with revolving objectives and some chemical gear – mounted specimens and test tubes. It was the titles of the books on the bench that I wanted to see.

'It's no good,' I said. 'I can't read the titles even with a glass. Don't you remember any of them?'

'I told you,' said Ossie. 'I was going to write some of the titles down when I heard you bash the door bell. I can go back – it's easy.'

'No, don't do that. Just try and remember one title.'

We sat there, with me looking at Ossie's funny bulbous old face and Ossie's bright little eyes gazing in the fire and trying to recollect the brief glimpse of the books.

'For instance,' I prompted, 'did any one of them say "enzyme"?'

'Luvaduck,' said Ossie, his face glowing with a huge smile of content. 'That's it, you've said it, "enzymes", they nearly all were about enzymes.'

LEN DEIGHTON

He couldn't remember the full titles but I knew he wouldn't make them up. He was one of the best B & E[1] men we had and one of our most reliable retainers.

'How did you know?' said Ossie.

'I just guessed,' I said. 'She just seemed the sort of girl who would be interested in enzymes.'

[1] B & E: Breaking and entering.

16

Every pawn is a potential queen.

Whitehall, Saturday, October 12th

'Wonderful at coronations.'

'I'll bet,' I said.

'You can see them for miles. I was here for the Victory procession too. Quite lovely.'

'We'd better start . . .'

'Would you like to come up here on Armistice Sunday?' Hallam asked. 'It's a most impressive sight.'

'Yes,' I said. 'Now about . . .'

'A moment,' said Hallam. He went across to the desk and spoke into his bright-green telephone.

'We'd like a nice cup of creamy coffee, Phyllis. Will you tell Mrs Meynard? The nice china, Phyllis, I have a visitor.'

Hallam's office was on the top floor. There was a great view along Whitehall, and under us the Cenotaph was dotted with lines of starlings. The office was well furnished, as Whitehall offices go; it had rush matting over the Ministry of Works lino and there were blue curtains, two Cézanne prints and a basketwork chair that had gone to seed. Hallam sorted through his files to find two manilla dossiers and a booklet. The booklet was a Ministry of Agriculture publication called *Chemicals for the Gardener*. Hallam opened one of the dossiers. It said 'Special Import

Licences' in a Roman typeface and under that, neatly biro'd, was the name 'Mr Semitsa'.

'We call all official requests for false documents "import licences",' Hallam explained. He tapped the other dossier with a sharp bony finger. 'And this is a report from –' he read, 'Advisory Committee on Poisonous Substances.'

'You are the most poisonous man I know,' I said cheerfully.

'You're being naughty,' said Hallam, 'I thought we'd agreed to get along nicely together. It will be to the advantage of both of us in the long run, you know.' He smiled what he thought was a winning smile. He was dressed in Home Office uniform today – black jacket, pin-stripe trousers, stiff white collar and an Old Mill Hillian tie.

'Gehlen's people told me that Semitsa should come into Berlin two weeks from today,' I said.

'Oh, we know all about that,' said Hallam airily.

'How?' I asked.

'Oh, you people from Charlotte Street. You're all secrecy and bad manners. Grannie Dawlish is the worst of all.' I nodded.

'We call him Grannie Dawlish here, you know.'

'You just did,' I said.

'Semitsa isn't a secret agent, my dear chap. He is giving a talk at Humboldt University on "Synthetic Insecticides – the development of resistance in Pests to DDT". He gives the talk on Tuesday the 29th, so he'll arrive some time the previous week-end. I got all that from ADN.[1] It isn't secret. What's more, I would wager you he'll stay at the Hotel Adlon.'

'Now you *are* guessing,' I said.

'Not at all,' said Hallam. 'That's where Humboldt usually put their top-rank guest lecturers.' He produced his ciga-

---

[1] ADN: East German official news agency.

rette holder. 'Can you let me have a cigarette?' he asked.
I brought out a pack of Gauloises, tore the corner and
offered them.

'French?' Hallam said. 'They're rather coarse, aren't
they?' As he was lighting it there was a tap at the door.
An aged crone in a floral apron limped painfully across the
carpet.

'Put it down there, Mrs Meynard, that's lovely: and
chocolate digestives too. My goodness, we don't deserve
it.' Hallam moved a large jug of cut flowers to make room
for the coffee tray.

The aged crone smiled a big smile and locked an errant
forelock into a curler in embarrassment.

'How's your back today, Mrs Meynard?' Hallam asked.

'I think it will rain, sir,' she said.

'Never wrong, our Mrs Meynard,' Hallam said to me
proudly.

'Really?' I said. 'She should be on the Air Ministry roof.'

Mrs Meynard grinned, picked up three cups and saucers
from the window sill and said to Hallam, 'You owe me two
weeks' coffee money, Mr Hallam sir.'

'*Two* weeks?' asked Hallam. 'Are you sure?'

'Yes, sir,' said Mrs Meynard very shortly.

Hallam produced a small leather purse, undid the flap
with great care and shook coins into his hand like they
were segments of the Dead Sea Scrolls.

'*Two*?' said Hallam, hoping for a final reprieve.

'Sir,' said Mrs Meynard, nodding firmly.

He sorted through the money like he didn't want the
light to get at it, gave Mrs Meynard two half-crowns and
said 'Keep the change', rather grandly.

'There'll be another shilling,' said Mrs M. 'You're forget-
ting the three lots of biscuits.' Hallam gave her the money
and she left, but Hallam was gazing at the door for a long
time. He felt quite certain that he had paid her last week.

'For Christ's sake, Hallam,' I said. 'Let's get down to it. Why do we want to mess about bringing an insecticide expert here?'

'Please keep still,' Hallam said. 'Isn't that chair comfortable?' He poured out the coffee from a fine Dresden china pot and passed me a cup that didn't sell for one and six in Portobello Road.

'It isn't so comfortable that I want to sit here all week trying to get you to answer two or three simple questions.'

'Biscuits?' he said.

'No thanks,' I said shortly.

Hallam wrinkled his nose. 'Go on,' he said. 'They're chocolate.' As Hallam stretched his sleeve, I noticed the large gold Jaeger-le-Coultre wristwatch.

'New watch?' I said.

Hallam stroked the sleeve over his watch. 'I saved up for it,' he said. 'It is nice, isn't it?'

'You are a man, Hallam,' I said – I watched his face, as I paused – 'of the most impeccable taste.' His eyes shone with delight as he busily arranged papers on his desk.

He said, 'I don't know if I'm allowed to tell you all this – it's very secret.' It was Hallam having a little joke. I gave him a nod and a smile.

'You know that this Semitsa chap is an enzyme specialist. Is that too strong for you?'

'No,' I said. 'Go on talking.'

Hallam clasped his thin hands behind his head and swung gently from side to side in his swivel chair. As the light from the window moved across his features, I could see the handsome ground plan of his bombed-out face. Now the powdery skin, sun-lamped to a pale nicotine colour, was supported only by his cheek-bones, like a tent when the guy ropes are slackened.

'Do you know what DDT is?' Hallam asked.

'Tell me.'

'It's one of a group we call chlorinated hydrocarbons. These tend to persist in the soil. They all persist in body fats too. *You* probably have one-twentieth of a gram of DDT in your body fat right now.'

'Is that bad?'

'It may well be,' said Hallam, 'but many Americans have five times as much as that. Frankly, some of our people here are a little alarmed. Anyway, the other group that Semitsa has done so much on is called the organophosphorus group. They don't persist – they break down very quickly.'

'That's nice,' I said.

'Yes,' said Hallam. He sipped a little coffee and then settled the cup into the saucer like he was landing a damaged helicopter.

'Where does Semitsa's knowledge of enzymes come in?' I asked.

'Good question,' said Hallam. 'That's the important part. You see, two of this last group – Parathion and Malathion – work by depressing the production of an enzyme named cholinesterase. This kills the insect. The great advantage Parathion and Malathion have over DDT is that at present insects haven't been able to develop resistance to them the way they have to DDT.' He drank a little coffee.

'And that's important?'

'Very important,' said Hallam. 'Semitsa's research doesn't sound very *dramatic*, but agriculture is the keystone of our island heritage.' He smiled a big supercilious porcelain smile. 'Emerald isle and all that.' He popped a piece of sugar into his mouth.

'And that's what you sent for me for?' I said.

'Not in even the slightest way, my dear boy. You brought up that little subject, didn't you now?' He crunched the sugar into oblivion.

I nodded. Hallam said, 'It's a political matter we want

to talk about.' He put an elastic band around the Semitsa
file and tripped carefully through the filing cabinet with his
finger-tips until sliding it down into its rightful position.

'Colonel Stok. That's what I want to talk to *you* about . . .'
He sniffed loudly and tapped his long cigarette holder on
the inkstand.

'Can you let me have another one of those French cigarettes. They are rather . . .' He searched for a word.
'. . . exotic.'

'Don't develop a taste for them,' I said. 'When this pack's
gone, you'll be buying your own.' Hallam smiled and lit
up.

'Stok,' I said.

'Ah yes,' said Hallam. 'We are rather interested in Stok.'

'Grannie' Dawlish, I thought. That was pretty good,
coming from Hallam.

Hallam looked up and raised a bony finger. '"War is a
continuation of politics . . ." You know what Clausewitz
tells us.'

'Yes,' I said. 'I'll have to have a word with Clausewitz.
He keeps saying the same thing over and over.'

'Now now,' said Hallam. He waggled the bony finger.

He picked up a slip of paper from his desk, read it
through quickly, then said, 'We need to know to what
extent Chekists[2] like Stok are happy with the idea of the
Party being in complete control of the land. Also whether
in five years' time the Army expect to have regained an
elite position. As you know there is this constant change
of balance in their influence.' Hallam moved his flat palms
up and down like scale pans.

'A love-hate relationship,' I said.

'Beautifully put,' said Hallam. 'Well, our political fore-
cast people are rather keen on this sort of information.

[2] See Appendix 4: Soviet Security System.

They say that when the Army people are feeling confident we can expect the cold war to blow hot. When the Party are firmly in the saddle, we get lessening of tension.' Hallam made a little movement of the fingers, as though brushing a fly away from his hand. 'They like all that sort of thing downstairs.' He obviously thought them eccentric.

'So you don't believe that Stok will defect,' I said.

Hallam raised his chin and looked down his long nose at me. 'You've rumbled that already, surely. You aren't a complete fool.' He rubbed a finger along his nose. 'So why take me for one?' He rearranged the dossiers. 'Stok's an interesting case, you know; a real Old Guard Bolshie. He was with Antonov-Ovseyenko in the storming of the Winter Palace in '17; you understand what that means in Russia.'

'It means you are an expendable hero,' I said.

'I say, that's rather good,' said Hallam. He took out a gold propelling pencil. 'In an absolute nutshell. I'll write that down. "Expendable hero", that's what Stok is all right.' He popped another piece of sugar into his mouth and began to write.

17

A knight can be used to simultaneously threaten two
widely spaced units. (This is called a 'fork'.) If one of
these threats is against a king the other piece must
inevitably be lost.

Saturday, October 12th

The grey stones of the Cenotaph shone in the hard wintry
sunlight as I surrendered my Home Office pass and stepped
into Whitehall. In Horse Guards Avenue and right along
to the Thames Embankment, hollow tourist buses were
parked and double-parked.

The red-cloaked Horse Guards sat motionless clutching
their sabres and thinking of metal polish and sex. In Trafal-
gar Square pigeons were enmeshed in the poisonous diesel
gauze.

A cab responded to my wave by carving abruptly
through the traffic.

I said: 'Henekey's, Portobello Road.'

'Portobello Road,' said the cab driver, 'where the beat-
niks go?'

'Sounds like it,' I said. The driver jammed the flag down
and pulled abruptly back into the traffic. A man in a Mini
shouted, 'You stupid bastard!' at my driver and I nodded
agreement.

Henekey's is a great barn of a place, bare enough not to
be spoiled by the odd half-glass of best bitter being spilled

across the floor; cashmere, suede, straw, leather and imitation leather jostle, jabber and posture with careful narcissism. I bought a double Teacher's and edged through the crowd.

A girl with Edwardian hair and science-fiction breasts produced a Copenhagen teapot from a huge straw basket. '. . . I said you're a bloody old robber . . .' she was saying to a man with a long beard and a waisted denim jacket, who said, 'Academic training is the final refuge of the untalented.' The girl put the teapot away, fluttered her big sooty eyes and said, 'I wish you'd told the silly old — that.' She retied the belt of her leather coat and took a packet of Woodbines from the man's jacket pocket.

'I'll throttle him,' she said. 'He is the biggest . . .' she described the man in Chatterleyan terms while the unacademic man held a pint glass of stout to his lips and studied his reflection with loving skill.

I sipped my drink and watched the door. There was still no sign of Sam. Behind me the man with the denim and beard was saying '. . . I'll tell you who I feel like when I smoke it. I feel like Hercules, Jason, Odysseus, Galahad, Cyrano, D'Artagnan and Tarzan with a football-pool cheque in my pocket.' The sooty-eyed girl laughed and tapped her straw bag to be sure the teapot was still there. The bearded man looked at me and said, 'You waiting for Samantha Steel?'

'Could be,' I said.

'Yeah,' he said, studying my clothes and face carefully. 'He said you'd look a bit square.'

'I'm as square as a cube root,' I said. The sooty girl had a high-pitched giggle.

'Here's an oblong for you,' said the bearded man. He gave me an envelope. Inside was a sheet of paper with 'Dear Mr Kadaver, All the papers must be at our Berlin office by Monday a.m. or we can't guarantee delivery.' There was a signature that I couldn't decipher.

'What did he look like, the man who gave you this?' I asked.

'Like Martin Bormann,' said the bearded man. He laughed briefly and plucked the paper from my hand. 'I said I'd destroy this for him because we don't want it getting in the wrong hands.'

'What is it?' said the sooty girl.

'— off,' said the bearded man. 'This is business.' He folded the sheet of paper and tucked it into his denim pocket. 'Here's your tart now,' he said affably to me. Samantha was twisting her head trying to see me across the room.

Samantha said 'Hello David' to the bearded man and 'Hello Hettie' to the sooty girl who was studying Sam's leather boots too carefully even to notice. Then she said 'Hello' to about a dozen other poets, painters, writers, art directors (with organizations known only by their initials), and occasionally a model or a photographer. No one was introduced as a secret agent; not even David.

18

Mate: a word from Old French meaning to overpower
or overcome.

Saturday, October 12th

Sam drove me back to her place in a white Sunbeam Alpine.
The flat was tidied and the small rug upon which the wine
had spilled had been taken away for cleaning. She clattered
around in the kitchen and I could hear the whirr of an
electric can-opener. I wandered into Samantha's bedroom.
The dressing-table was crowded with pint-size bottles of
Lanvin, Millot and Givenchy, torn pieces of cotton wool,
gold hair-brushes, cleansing cream, half a cup of cold
coffee, witch hazel, skin food, hand lotion, roll-on
deodorant, scissors, tweezers, six different nail polishes,
seven bright bottles of eye make-up from green to mauve,
a capsule containing silver paint and a large bowl full of
beads and bracelets. In a silver frame there was a photo of
a blond man in very small knitted swimming-trunks. I
picked up the frame. The photo was a little too small
and slid down to reveal the top of another man's head.
The photo underneath was a studio portrait, well lit and
carefully printed; it leaned into the frame at a forty-five-
degree angle, like film stars like to lean. In bold loopy
writing it said: 'To Samantha with immortal love. Johnnie
Vulkan.'

Long, slim hands gripped my chest from behind and I

LEN DEIGHTON

felt the soft, fragrant shapes of Sam press herself tightly
against me.

'What are you doing in my bedroom?' she said.

'Looking at photos of your lovers,' I said.

'Poor Johnnie Vulkan,' she said. 'He's still madly in love
with me. Does it make you insanely jealous?'

'Insanely,' I said.

We stood there very close, watching our reflection in
the dressing-table mirror.

On the bed there was a selection of toys. There was a
huge moth-eaten teddy bear, a black velvet cat with a
damaged ear and a small cross-eyed alligator.

'Aren't you getting a little too old for cuddly toys?' I
asked.

'No,' she said.

I said, 'Who needs cuddly toys?'

'Don't do that,' she said then, 'Men use women as cuddly
toys, women use babies as cuddly toys and babies use
cuddly toys as cuddly toys.'

'Really?' I said.

'Now now,' said Sam and ran a finger-nail up my spine
muscle. Her voice became a whisper. 'There are four stages
of a love affair. First there is the stage of being in love and
liking it.' Her voice was muffled by my shoulder. 'That's
this stage.'

'How long's it likely to last?'

'Not long enough,' said Sam. 'The other stages soon
follow.'

'What stages?' I said.

'There's being in love and *not* liking it,' said Sam. 'That's
the second one. Then there is *not* being in love and not
liking *that*. And finally there is not being in love and liking
that – you are over it then – cured.'

'Sounds great,' I said.

'You have to be make-believe tough,' Samantha said.

'I'm serious and it makes me sort of sad. If people in love synchronized their movements through those stages . . .' She snuggled deeper into my shoulder. 'We'll stay at the first stage for ever. No matter what calls us away, we'll stay up here on the moon. OK?'

'OK.'

'No. I'm serious.'

'Looks like we're first here on the moon,' I said.

Sam said, 'Just think of all those poor dopes down on earth who can't see that great sun.'

'It's really frying us,' I said.

'Stay still,' said Sam. 'Don't do that. I have a can of corn on the stove; it will burn.'

'Corn,' I said, 'is expendable.'

19

One can escape from check by removing hostile pieces
or interposing oneself.

Berlin, Saturday, October 12th

I gave the doorman at the Frühling my bags and stepped out
in search of supper. It was late, the animals in the zoo had
settled down but next door in the Hilton they were just
becoming fully awake. Near by the Kaiser Wilhelm Memorial
Church bells clanged gently and around it came a white V W
bus, its hoo-haw siren moaning and its blue light flashing a
priority. Cars halted as the bus bearing the words 'Military
Police US Army' roared past, its fan whining.

Maison de France is on the corner of Uhlandstrasse not far
away. I was hungry. It was a good night for walking but the
pressure was rising and rain was in the air. The neon signs
gloated brightly across the beleaguered city. On the Ku-
damm the pavement cafés had closed their glass sides tight
and turned on the infra-red heating. In the glass cases diners
moved like carnivorous insects. Here the well-dressed *Insulaner*[1] ate, argued, bartered and sat over one coffee for hours
until the waiters made their annoyance too evident. Outside,
the glittering kiosks sold magazines and hot meat snacks to
the strollers, while double-decker cream buses clattered up
and down, and nippy VWs roared and whined around the

---

[1] *Insulaner*: islanders — Berliners' name for themselves.

corners past the open-topped Mercedes that drove lazily past, their drivers hailing and shouting to people they recognized and to quite a few that they didn't.

Knots of pedestrians paraded at the traffic crossings and at the given signal marched obediently forward. Young men in dark woollen shirts parked and played jazz on their car radios and waited patiently while their white-haired girl friends adjusted their make-up and decided which club they would like to go to next.

Two men were eating *Shashlik* at a corner kiosk and listening to a football match over a transistor radio. I crossed half of the wide street; down the centre of it, brightly coloured cars were parked in a vast row that reached as far as the Grunewald. High above I could see the lights of the Maison de France restaurant.

I heard footsteps behind. It was one of the men from the kiosk. I was between two parked cars. I turned and let the weight of my back fall upon the nearest car, flattening the palms of my hands against the cold metal. He was a bald-headed man in a short overcoat. He was so close behind me that he almost collided with me when I stopped. I leaned well back and kicked at him as hard as I could. He screamed. I smelled the rich meaty *Shashlik* as he stumbled forward out of balance. I groped towards the scream and felt the wooden *Shashlik* skewer drive into the side of my left hand. The man's bald head smashed against the window of the other car. The safety glass shattered into milky opacity and I read the words 'Protected by Pinkertons – Chicago Motor Club' on a bright paper transfer.

He held his head in his hand and began lowering it to the ground like a slow-motion film of a touchdown. He whimpered softly.

From the kiosk the second man came running, shouting a torrent of German in the ever-comical accent of Saxony. As he began to cross the roadway towards me there was

another 'hoo-haw' of police sirens and a V W saloon with
blue flasher and spotlight full on came roaring down the
wide street. The Saxon stepped back on to the pavement,
but when the police car had flashed past he ran towards
me. I drew out the 9-mm FN automatic pistol[2] that the
War Office Armoury had made such a fuss about and used
my left hand to slam the slide back and put a cartridge
into the breech. An edge of pain travelled along my palm
and I felt the sticky wetness of blood. I was crouched very
low by the time the Saxon got to the rear of the car. Just
inches to the left of my elbow, the whimpering man said,
'But we have a message for you.' He rocked gently with
the pain and blood ran down the bald head like earphones.

'Bist du verrückt, Engländer?'

I wasn't mad I told him as long as he kept his distance.
The Saxon called again from the rear of the Buick. They
had a message for me 'from the Colonel'. In that town I
knew several colonels but it was easy to guess who they
meant.

The man sitting on the ground whimpered and, as a
car's headlights rolled past, I saw his face was very white.
The blood moved down the side of his head. It glued his
fingers together and moved slowly to form new patterns
like a kaleidoscope. Little puddles of it formed in the
wrinkles of his shiny ears and splashed on his knitted tie
like tomato soup.

I took the written address from the Saxon with apologies.
These were no B-picture heavies, just two elderly messengers. I left them there in the middle of the Ku-damm, the
Saxon and his half-conscious friend. They would never
find a taxi on a Saturday night, especially now that rain
had begun.

[2] The Browning FN automatic has now replaced the .38 revolver as
standard issue.

20

Enemy territory is that area of the board within one-
move range of opposing forces.

Saturday, October 12th

I washed the gash that the wooden skewer had made in
my hand and bound it with Elastoplast but it began to
bleed again before I reached the check post at Friedrichstrasse. Inside there was a good-natured argument going
on. A red-faced man waving an Irish passport said,
'. . . neutral and we have always stayed neutral.'

The Grepo said, 'Not only does your Government not
recognize the Deutsche Demokratische Republik but the
USSR has been waiting forty-five years for your Government to recognize *them.*'

They returned my passport after only a perfunctory
glance. I could have taken an M-60 tank through, let alone
my 9-mm FN pistol.

As I stepped out into the rain I heard the Irishman say,
'Marry in haste, repent at leisure – that's what we always
say.'

Karlshorst is the Russian part of East Berlin; the Komman-
datura is here and most of the Russians reside here. The
address the Saxon had given me was a narrow street to
the south of the district. The rain beat down in earnest
and there were no pedestrians anywhere. The lightning lit
up the whole sky in flashes and it was by the light of one

of them that I saw the street name. It was a cobbled alley, on each side of which were tiny narrow-fronted shops. The wooden shutters were shiny in the rain and number twelve was even more deserted-looking than the others.

I put my pistol in my jacket and pulled the Elastoplast tighter. The blood was seeping under the adhesive part and making smudge marks on my cuff. I knocked at the door. Everywhere the windows were dark and the only light came from the gas lamps in the street. As I knocked again the door creaked slowly open. I pulled a flashlight from my pocket and shone it around the cracked plaster walls. I found the switch but it gave no light.

To my left a well-oiled door opened on to a large room. In the centre of the room the two huge gleaming discs of a bandsaw reflected back the light of my torch. In the corner was a tall chain mortiser. Around the base of each machine the floor was reinforced with concrete, and rusty bolts held the carefully oiled machines in true. Across one wall, planks were stacked and the aroma of cut wood clung to the water vapour on the damp night air. There was no one there. I opened a cupboard and pointed the gun at a broom and a tin of polish. Ahead of me the main corridor ended in a narrow twisting staircase. I held the torch well to one side of my movements and eased the first pressure on the automatic. The torch was slimy with blood and a droplet flicked in the lamp beam before soaking softly into the sawdust. The stairs creaked. I tested each step with part of my weight as I moved down. The wooden steps were thick with sawdust and the cellar floor crackled under foot with a deep autumnal carpet of shavings.

I moved the light slowly across the wall. I could smell the sweet, sappy scent of freshly cut wood. In Prussian orderliness the framesaws, London hammers, try squares, pad saws, chisels, rasps and shining bottles of stains and polishes were arranged geometrically in their rightful place above the veneering press. Five long joiners' benches were arranged in the centre of the cellar. Upon them were rusty pots of fish-glue and thin slivers of veneer.

The end of the cellar was kept clear. There was a tiny ring with an enormous kettle used for bending the veneer. Six cracked cups were draining upside down on a tea-cloth; on one of them it said 'A present from Dresden'.

A handful of countersunk screws and a heavy screwdriver on the heavy table at the end marked where the metal fittings joined the woodwork. Directly overhead was a trapdoor and a hoist, as they were altogether too big for the staircase; there were six of them leaning against the wall, shining and polished lovingly and ready for use.

These coffins were very elaborate. Their lids were as deep as the base and around them was the embossed scrollwork of leaves and flowers that culminated in six vast metal handles. I tapped each of the great cases; one two three four five six. The last one wasn't hollow, and before the sound of my rapping had ceased to echo around the walls the lid fell away from it and hit the floor with an echoing crash. I flashed the torch into the silken cavity and levelled my gun. The torch beam fell upon the shape of a uniformed man crammed tightly into the straight-sided casket. Before I had studied the face the medals and gold wire insignia told me it was Stok.

He giggled. 'I frightened you, English, admit it, I frightened you.'

'You frightened me so much that I nearly gave you six extra navels,' I said. I put the pistol into my pocket and helped extricate the broad shoulders of Stok from the coffin.

'You'd better come to England to die,' I said. 'Our coffins widen out at the shoulders.'

'Yes?' Stok dusted the sawdust from his summer uniform and found a peaked cap under the nearest joiner's bench. He switched four neon lights into action.

'What's the joke, Stok?' I said.

Stok slapped the coffin with the flat of his hand. 'It's for Semitsa,' he said. 'Look.' He pointed to the inside of the coffin. Holes had been bored through the intricate embossed patterns of the lid.

Stok slapped the coffin again. 'One of the few real quality places left this is; quality.' He rapped the side. 'Elm wood,' he said, 'soundly constructed of twenty-millimetre seasoned timber. Waterproofed, waxed and upholstered with satin-covered calico. Side sheets, robe and shroud. Robust electro-brassed handles, inscribed or written name-plate, brass closing-screws, lid ornament, end-rings, silk cords and tassels.'

'Yes,' I said. Stok walloped me on the back playfully and laughed.

'Two hundred marks,' he said, 'but don't worry. It will come out of my forty thousand pounds.' Stok smiled again. His face was carved of pink sandstone, his features worn smooth by a millennium of pilgrims' hands. He opened a blouse pocket and produced a buff-coloured form.

'This is a form by means of which relatives claim the body of a deceased person. Sign here.' Stok jabbed the form with a finger like a Lyons sausage – slightly overdone.

I brought out my fountain pen but hesitated to use it.

'Give your hotel as your address and sign it "Dorf". Why are you so cautious, you English? You will only be Dorf for a few more days.'

'It's those days I'm worrying about,' I said. Stok laughed and I signed the paper for him.

'You've cut your hand, English,' Stok said.

'Opening oysters,' I said.

'So,' said Stok.

'It's a real decadent life we live over there,' I told him. Stok nodded.

He said, 'We will pass Semitsa, in this, through Checkpoint Charlie in three weeks' time; 5 P.M., Monday, November the fourth. Now what about the arrangements for the money?' Stok produced a packet of Dukat cigarettes. I took one and lit up.

'When your Government has positively agreed the payment of the money you will signal so by having Victor Sylvester play "There's a small Hotel" on his Overseas Service programme of the BBC. If the deal's not on, he doesn't play it. OK?'

'You're too damned wholesale, Stok. It would do you good to face some of my difficulties for a week. I'm not sure that I can do that.'

'Not sure if you can make this man Sylvester play "There's a small Hotel"?' said Stok incredulously.

'Not sure if I can stop him,' I said.

'Your capitalism,' said Stok. He nodded sagely. 'How can it ever work?' He removed a woodshaving from his sleeve. 'There is a village in Africa where the tribesmen stand in the deep crocodile-infested water, fishing. They send the fish they catch for barter to the next village where the main industry is manufacturing wooden legs.' Stok laughed loudly until I had to join in.

'That's capitalism,' said Stok. He tapped my arm.

'I heard a very good joke the other day.' He was speaking very softly now as though there was a chance of us being overheard. 'Ulbricht is going about incognito testing his own popularity by asking people if they like Ulbricht. One man he asks says, "Come with me." He takes Ulbricht on a train and a bus until they are deep in the Saxon hills near the Czechoslovak border. They walk in the country until they are many kilometres from the nearest house and then they finally stop. This man looks all around and whispers to Ulbricht, "I personally," the man says, "don't mind him at all."' Stok roared with laughter again. 'I don't mind him at all,' said Stok again, pointing at his own chest and laughing hysterically.

'Look, Stok,' I said.

'Alexeyevitch,' said Stok.

'Look, Alexeyevitch,' I said. 'I don't have to come over here to find out the truth about capitalism.'

'Do you not?' said Stok. 'Perhaps you'll find you do.'

'Why, what's the next revelation?' I said. 'More pranks in coffins?' I finished the cigarette in silence.

Stok's eyes went suddenly narrow. He prodded my chest viciously.

'We know how mature you are, and how sophisticated you are. Otherwise you wouldn't choose to work with bandits like Vulkan and criminals like Gehlen. You make me sick, English.'

I took out my cigarettes. Hallam hadn't left me with many but I offered Stok one. The yellow match flame reflected in his eyes as he lit them. He began to speak quietly again.

'They are making a fool of you, English,' Stok said. 'They all have their roles to play except you. You are expendable.'

'There goes that word again,' I said. 'Someone was saying the same thing about you only the other day.'

'I *am* expendable, English, but not until the game is over. You are expendable the moment Gehlen gets the documents for Semitsa.' He looked at me closely. 'What do you think the Gehlen organization is, English? You think it's something to do fetch-and-carry jobs for your Government?'

'They will do most things; for money,' I said.

'For real money, yes,' said Stok. He eased his bottom on to the bench and became very confidential. 'You know how much twenty-one billion dollars is, English? It's what the US Government spent on armaments in one year. Do you know who gets it, English? The General Dynamics Corporation got one and a quarter billion; and just four other corporations got about a billion each. That's real money, isn't it?'

I said nothing.

Stok said, 'Over eighty per cent of the twenty-one billion dollars is spent without the big businesses doing any competitive bidding. Are you following me?'

'I'm way ahead,' I said. 'But what's it to do with you?'

'Tension here in Berlin is a lot to do with me – it's my job. Your military men are pushing that tension as hard as they can go. I'm trying to reduce the tension in every way I can.'

'You don't reduce it,' I said. 'You play a tune on it like a gipsy minstrel.'

Stok sighed histrionically.

'Look, my friend. Next year, lots of your military friends will be retiring into big capitalist businesses that make armaments. Most of them have signed the contracts already . . .'

'Wait a minute,' I said.

'I won't wait a minute,' said Stok. 'We know what's happening. We spend a lot of trouble and money finding out. The type of job your generals retire into depends upon how many big orders for armaments they place. A state of tension makes it easy to order guns. Gehlen provides the tension – it increases the demand – just like an advertising agency. That's the kind of people who are twisting you around their fingers.'

'Vulkan said . . .'

'Don't tell me anything Vulkan said.' Stok spat the words out like bloody teeth. 'He's a filthy little Fascist.' Stok moved near to me and began to speak quietly as though he was sorry he had got excited.

'I know Vulkan is a brilliant man and I know he's clever

at political debate but believe me, English, he is at heart a Fascist.'

I began to see what a clever con-man Johnnie Vulkan was. It was no part of my job to tell Stok that Vulkan had a brain like a whale's throat – huge but straining out only shrimp-size thoughts. I said, 'Then why do you deal with him?'

'Because he's helping me make a fool of the Gehlen organization.'

'And of me?'

'Yes and of you, English. Try and find your friend Vulkan this night. Ask your friends at the US State Department. Ask your friends at Gehlen's office. Ask everyone you know, English, and when you come to a dead end come to the Friedrichstrasse Kontrollpunkt or anywhere on the East Berlin phone system and phone me in my office. I'll tell you where he is and I'll be the only one to tell you the truth.'

'We have a deodorant ad that uses the same pitch,' I said.

'Try it then,' said Stok.

'I might,' I said. I walked across the room without looking back and went upstairs to my car. I saw Stok's big shiny Volga parked a little way farther down the street and beyond it two T-54 tanks and an infantry carrier. On my way to Friedrichstrasse I passed a banner that read 'Learning from the Soviet union means learning to triumph.' I was beginning to see what they meant.

I phoned everyone I knew that night to check on Vulkan. I phoned everyone from the Berlin Documents Centre to Onkel Toms Hütte U-bahn Station. Everywhere the reply was the same. Vulkan wasn't there, they didn't know where he was and no one knew when he was expected. Some of the sources *really* didn't know, who can say which.

I looked through the glass panel of the telephone booth at the grey hardboard and potted plants of the East German control hut.

'It's the African fisherman speaking,' I said into the phone.

'Who are you calling?' said the girl, to whom strange names came as no surprise.

'It's either an artificial-limb manufacturer or a crocodile,' I said. 'I can't remember which.'

I heard the girl repeat that, then I heard Stok's booming laugh as he came to the phone.

'Hendaye-plage,' said Stok, 'near the Spanish border.'

'Stay tuned to Victor Sylvester,' I said and rang off. The Grepo who had given me the East German coin for the phone waved me good night as I turned around and travelled the ten yards back into the Western Sector where the signs were more likely to say 'komm gut heim'.

21

The king may well be moved to a well-protected spot
away from danger.

Hendaye-plage, France, Monday, October 14th

The road along the plage was marbled with drifting sand.
The sun was bright but lifeless as it lowered itself wearily
behind the mauve hills. For miles the lonely beach wandered with just one dog for company until the cold wind
became too much even for playful dogs. The casinos and
hotels were shuttered and stained with the dribbling rust
of early winter rain.

From one glass-encased restaurant on the Boulevard de
la Mer came the doleful clack of a typewriter. I passed the
padlocked kiosk where the torn sign said 'laces' and went
through the glass door. A young girl in a pink smock
looked up from the accounts.

She brought me coffee and I stared out at the grey con-
fluence of sky and sea, growing pink in the light of the
setting sun. For another six months the sea would go on
practising for summer, coming in each day to smooth out
the sand like some fussy old chambermaid making the bed.

'Do you have any guests?' I asked wearily.

'Yes.' The girl's smile was gentle and faintly mocking.
'A Monsieur King and his wife.'

22

Checkmate remains the ultimate aim of every player.

Monday, October 14th

In the long dining-room a dozen tables were carefully arranged, even though only three guests were expected to dine. Across the bar were Cinzano ashtrays and shiny equipment for making 'le cocktail': strainers, shakers, fruit-knife and swizzle-sticks. Behind the bar were rows of bottles, undisturbed since last summer. The tile floor reflected the cold evening air and from the ceiling I heard the chambermaid thumping pillows as my bed was made up for me.

The girl in the pink smock had put away the typewriter and changed into a black dress. 'What would you like to drink?' she asked. I poured two Suzes into my face in rapid succession while we agreed how few people came there in the winter. From the kitchen I heard the crinkle of boiling fat and the swish of things being dropped into it. Yesterday they arrived, who knew how long they were staying; she joined me in a second Suze, the third one I took up to my room. When I came down for dinner the other guests had arrived back.

Vulkan had a cashmere overcoat over his lightweight Savile Row suit – his tie was Dior and his shirt creamy silk.

'Hello, Mr King,' I said. 'Introduce your friend.'

'This is Samantha,' said Johnnie Vulkan.

Samantha said 'Hello'.

23

King's Gambit is an opening in which his own side's
pawns are sacrificed.

Monday, October 14th

Dinner was eaten quietly: codfish in the Basque style. Then
Johnnie said, 'Do you have to follow me?'

I said, 'I came on business – there's been some difficulty.'

'Difficulty?' said Vulkan. His jaws ceased to chew the
codfish.

'Have you swallowed a bone?' I asked.

'No,' said Vulkan. 'What difficulty?'

'Nothing much,' I said. 'But Gehlen keeps asking for the
documents . . .'

'Why haven't you let them have them?'

'London's spelled the name wrongly,' I said. 'They
spelled it BROOM when it should be . . .'

'I know what it should be,' Vulkan said very loudly,
then quietly added, 'The stupid, stupid, stupid bastards.'

'It matters then,' I said.

'It certainly does.'

'I had it correct when I sent it,' I said.

'I know, I know,' said Vulkan in a preoccupied way. 'I
might have guessed it would all go wrong.'

The waitress came from the kitchen; she saw Vulkan's
plate with only half the fish eaten.

'Didn't you like it?' she said. 'Shall I bring you something else?'

'No,' said Vulkan.

'There is *entrecôte* or *ris de veau*.'

'*Ris de veau*,' said Samantha.

'*Ris de veau*,' I said.

'*Ris de veau*,' said Vulkan, but his mind was far away.

We sat in the bar for the coffee and brandy. Samantha had an English newspaper and she gave me a sheet of it. Finally Vulkan leaned across from his chair.

'Can you wire London and ask them to do another set?'

'Certainly Johnnie, anything you say. You know that.'

Vulkan slapped me on the knee.

'That's what we'll do then.' He smiled a big smile. 'Trust London to mess it all up after we do all this work.'

I shrugged. 'When you've worked directly for London as long as I have, you see their good points and their bad ones. You end up just being glad you aren't on piecework; and start striking heavily into the expenses.' I downed the last of my brandy.

'You are right,' said Vulkan. He shouted for the waitress and ordered three treble brandies, just to show how well he understood the point I had made.

'What about the cash for Stok?' Vulkan said. 'He'll want cash you know.'

'No kidding,' I said. 'I was going to try using my Diners' Club card on him.'

Vulkan laughed lightly and rubbed his hands.

'You see,' said Vulkan. 'This trip to Hendaye is to do with the Semitsa deal.'

'I don't want to . . .'

Vulkan waved his hand. 'I don't have to keep it secret. It's just that in the past I have found it best to compartmentalize my contracts. It's something I learned in the War.'

'The War,' I said. 'What did you do in the War, Johnnie?' I asked.

'What everyone did, I suppose,' said Johnnie. 'I did as I was told.'

I said, 'Some people were told to do some pretty fantastic things.'

'I did plenty of things I'm not proud of,' said Johnnie. 'I was a guard in a concentration camp at one time.'

'Really,' said Samantha. 'You never told me that.'

'There's no point in denying it,' Johnnie said. 'A man has to live with the things he does. I suppose everyone has skeletons in the cupboard. I never did anything terrible. I never tortured anyone or killed anyone and I never saw any atrocities take place, but I was part of the system. Unless there had been men like me going on duty in the control towers and sitting up there in the freezing cold wind drinking bad coffee and stamping about trying to keep warm – unless there had been little men like me, there couldn't have been all the rest of it. I'm ashamed of the part I played but so, if he is honest, is the factory worker and the policeman and the railway guard, they were all bits of the system too. We should all have overthrown the system, shouldn't we?'

Johnnie looked at me provocatively. I said nothing but Samantha said, 'Yes, you should. You shouldn't have had to wait until those generals messed around. The whole nation should have recoiled with shock at the things that were done to Jewish shopkeepers in the 'thirties.'

'Yeah,' said Johnnie in a low growl. 'That's what I keep on hearing, how we should have overthrown Hitler. That's because all the stupid people who say so don't know what they are talking about. What do you mean "overthrow" – you mean that one morning I come on guard duty and shoot the sergeant?'

Samantha was getting the brunt of Johnnie's wrath. 'Perhaps it would have been a start,' she said quietly.

FUNERAL IN BERLIN

'Yeah,' said Johnnie. 'Great start. The sergeant had a
wife and six kids. He was an old-time Social Democrat. He
hated all Nazis and was crippled with frostbite that he had
caught in Smolensk in 1942.'

'Someone else then,' said Samantha.

'Sure,' said Johnnie sarcastically. 'At random, eh?' and
he laughed a laugh that told you that even if he went on
talking all night you would never understand what it was
like to be inside a concentration camp, especially as a
guard.

'I was glad I was in the camp,' said Johnnie viciously.
'Glad, do you hear? Because if I hadn't been with the
concentration camp unit I would have been in the fighting
line on the Eastern Front. It was a good job in the camp.
A plum job. Everyone wanted that job. Do you think that
the whole of Germany was queuing up to fight Bolshevism?
That's what you Americans would like to believe, eh? Well
they weren't – except for the crackpots in the SS. Everyone
with an ounce of intelligence was trying to get a job a long
way from the fighting line even if he couldn't eat his lunch
for the stink of the cremation ovens.'

Samantha pressed the palms of her hands over her ears
and Johnnie laughed another of his laughs. It was more
eloquent than anything he could say.

24

A skewer is an attack along a straight line. As the first
piece avoids capture it exposes the second, real target
to the full force of the attack.

Monday, October 14th – Tuesday, October 15th

We all went to bed at half past eleven: or I suppose it
would be more correct to say that *none* of us went to bed
at half past eleven, although we all said good night and
went through the motions. I put on my sheepskin-lined
raincoat and stood out on the plage with the wind screaming around me like demented seagulls.

'It just has to be,' I was thinking at 1.15 A.M. The yeasty
smell of the ocean had moved closer on the evening tide.

At 2 A.M. I was thinking the same thing but it was 2.30
A.M. before anything happened. Along the front came
two bright headlamps. The fact that they were not yellow
helped me guess that they were from across the border. It
was a white Citroën DS 19. The tyres shot the final inch
with a crunch as it halted on the sandy road. The chauffeur
jumped out smartly and opened the rear door as Vulkan
came down the steps. The light above the rear seat showed
the other passenger to be a white-haired man of about fifty,
but without binoculars it wasn't possible to discern more.
Vulkan got in hurriedly and I saw him look back up at
my bedroom window. The chauffeur closed the door
quietly, got in, and they drove away.

I went back to the hotel wondering who in Spain was chic enough to afford a Citroën with San Sebastian number plates and a chauffeur who would wear sun-glasses at 2.30 A.M.

I closed the hotel door silently. I stepped into a small room at the foot of the stairs that held the toilet, a bucket, two mops, four packs of Omo, three raincoats, two umbrellas and a pay phone. I had two phone calls to make; the first call was to suggest the Gare St Jean as a meeting place; the second call was to spread the description of the San Sebastian number plates among people who would really care. There is no point in just wondering about the things that puzzle us.

I finished the phone calls without switching on the electric light.

From overhead I heard stiletto heels move quickly across the room. I left the phone off the hook to avoid making any sound and moved across the porch silently in my rubber shoes.

I walked out along the moonlit sea front. The phosphorescent breakers crumbled into shimmering lace-work and the moon was an overturned can of white paint that had spilled its contents across the sea. As I looked back towards the hotel, the front door shot a long trapezium of yellow light across the sandy path. A girl's figure made a brief shadow-graph in the light, then hurried along the sea front.

Samantha was fully dressed. Ear-rings to eye-shadow proclaimed that she had not been to bed.

'Johnnie's gone,' she said.

'Gone where?' I asked.

She buttoned her neck deeper into the big coat. 'Just gone,' she said. 'He said he was going downstairs. Then I heard a car drive away.'

We both stood looking at each other for a long time.

'I'm cold,' she said, 'and I'm frightened.'

I began to walk back towards the hotel.

'Johnnie's car is still there,' said Samantha. She hurried to catch me up and walked alongside me. 'What he said last night – was that all true?'

'All true,' I said.

'But what, wise guy? I can hear the sneer.'

'No sneer,' I said. 'People seldom report facts wrong. What they distort is their relationship to the facts. It's possible to describe the charge of the Light Brigade whether you were on the leading charger or at the other end of the valley brewing up tea.'

'You're so sharp,' said Sam.

'Now who's sneering?'

'Look. Vulkan's a bright boy, whether you like him or not. He's written an analysis of Bartok's string quartets which will shatter the music world when it's published.'

'Look,' I said. 'If you want to buy a subscription to Vulkan's fantasy-of-the-month club, go ahead, but I've been inoculated against moonshine.' I was walking quickly and Samantha had to make a hop, skip and jump every few steps to keep alongside. She grabbed my arm.

'Is that the same moon that we were voted lunar candidates of?' she asked softly. 'Didn't we get elected after all?'

'We did,' I said, 'but I'm demanding a recount.' I pulled my arm free and opened the glass door. The dining-tables with their shiny plates and conical napkins were bright yellow in the dim light. Sam overtook me on the stairs and, fumbling in her handbag, produced the key by the time we reached her room. She swung the door open. On the bed was a grey leather travelling case and there was another at the side of the wardrobe. One was empty. I reached for the other. There was a small packet of Kleenex and a shoe-horn inside. There were clothes inside the wardrobe and I quickly examined them, prodding and twisting the shoulder padding and listening for the crackle of paper in the seams.

On the dressing-table there were bottles of Cologne, nail varnish, mascara, face-powder, shampoo, suede-cleaning brushes, packets of cotton wool, sun-glasses and cigarettes. I held the open case under them and swept them into it with my elbow. From the dressing-table drawers I shovelled up handfuls of Samantha's underwear, transparent packets of nylons, flat-heeled shoes with gold straps and a cardboard box containing two diamond rings, a silver bangle, a jewelled wristwatch and some assorted cheap beads. I stretched out my hand towards her without looking up.

'Handbag,' I said. 'Purse.'

She still had it in her hand and now she opened it and studied the contents carefully. She removed two cigarettes, lit them and passed one lighted Camel and the shiny patent leather handbag to me.

I riffed quickly through it. I removed a green American passport in the name of Samantha Steel and twenty-two very new crisp 100 NF notes. I put the notes and the passport into my pocket.

'I thought we had something special,' said Samantha. She looked shorter than five foot ten now. She was All-American innocent, lost and betrayed in big bad Europe.

'We still have it,' I said. 'But this is business – let's not mix it with pleasure.'

'I've had all the business I need for a century,' said Samantha. 'When do I see the pleasure?'

'I'll see what I can do,' I said. I grinned and got a faint movement at the corner of her mouth.

'I'd like you to know . . .'

'Save it, Sam,' I said. 'I'm giving you a twenty-four carat deal when all I have to do, as far as my office is concerned, is lift the phone.'

She nodded and unzipped the side of her dress. She

removed the dress unhurriedly like a Girl Guide at a medical. Her eyes were waterlogged. 'It's the smoke,' she said. 'I should never smoke when I'm tired. It wrecks my eye make-up.' She smiled amd planted three inches of unsmoked Camel into the Cinzano ashtray. She walked across the room in her black underwear, oblivious of my eyes. She carefully selected a red-striped wool dress from the wardrobe. 'It does things for me, red,' she said.

'That's right,' I said.

She held the dress high above her head. 'I may as well look my best.' The dress dropped over her head like a candle-snuffer. Then suddenly she fought against the enveloping fabric in a sudden panic of constricted elbows until her hair shook itself nervously into the light again.

'Stay here,' I said. 'I'm going to my room and I'll fix both the bills.'

'You're a goddam cool ghoul,' she said in neither admiration nor bitterness. She stared at her reflection while mauling her face around.

I had no baggage in my room. I waited downstairs to see if Samantha was taking the thing sensibly.

I stepped out on to the porch and looked down the road. There was no sign of any movement except for the patter of sand that the sea wind was driving into the doorway. I finished my cigarette on the porch while the freezing night air was purging the last heaviness of the wine from my head. I stared towards the headland that stretched along the western horizon; only a few yards beyond it was Spain. The crippled, stunted trees along the plage pointed there.

The cases went on to the back of the Mercedes 220 SE. I put the heater on and we both sat quietly listening to the noise of the fan. I started up and the car bumped down over the kerb. The plage was dark and, apart from the howl of the wind, silent. It wasn't until we turned on to the main road that I switched on the lights. The speedometer changed colour as I put the accelerator down and chased after the long horns of yellow light.

'Looks like you got the booby prize,' said Samantha.

'Looks like it,' I agreed.

'You really wanted Johnnie, didn't you?'

'If you say so,' I said.

'You are determined to be discreet, aren't you?'

'Perhaps,' I said. Then Sam snorted with bad temper and fished out her Camels.

'Cigar lighter is the first one after the radio,' I said, 'but don't be mad if your eye make-up runs.' We drove in silence for a long time. Then Samantha said, 'You're cuter than Vulkan.' She leaned across and gave me a perfunctory kiss on the ear lobe. 'Personally,' she went on, 'I think you are a doll. Vulkan on the other hand . . .' She was speaking slowly and quietly as though working out her attitude as she told me, 'Vulkan is a thorough-going, dyed-in-the-wool, black-hearted, London-shrunk, copper-bottomed bastard.' She didn't raise her voice even slightly. 'But Vulkan is a genius. Vulkan has a mind like a diamond while you have a mind like glass.'

'Commercial diamond versus hand-cut crystal glass,' I said. 'So I am typecast as the loser?'

'It's a one-horse race,' said Samantha with finality.

The greatest tribute you can pay to a secret agent is to take him for a moron. All he has to do is to make sure he doesn't act too exactly like one. That was my concern now.

It's about two hundred kilometres along the N10 to Bordeaux, but it's a good road and in the early hours only the odd market truck, decked with a multitude of lights, and the slower long-distance stuff from San Sebastian across the frontier shared the road with us. Samantha slept for at least half the journey, which took about three and a half hours; there was no need to burn up any road-speed records nor to get the man I was going to see out of bed.

After Bayonne there is just good, sealed, wide road all the way through the great sullen Landes to Bordeaux. As far as the horizon the seedlings parade, the saplings posture, regiments of stumps march and countermarch. Oceans of standing timber await the executioner's axe and the occasional scoured black desert of destruction marks the passage of a terrible fire. Behind Sam's head the graticule of trees glowed with a fiery foliage, like a badly printed colour photo with the red block out of register.

Twig after twig shone red with the hoar frost of dawn until the sun's corona mixed gold with lead and by some inverse alchemy made clear blue morning. I doused the headlights in the outer periphery of Bordeaux's suburbs. We began to see lonely cyclists moving with the stiff precise arrogance that early risers acquire. The end walls of houses held gigantic faded advertisements for aperitifs, and a cat's-cradle of wires caged the cobbled streets. I drove to the Gare St Jean and parked in front of it. The town had its head under a blanket of cloud.

I parked beyond the bus shelter. The cyclopean eye of the Gothic railway station showed 7 A.M. and outside the Hotel Faisan the cane chairs leaned drunkenly against the Formica tables. Workmen were darting into the Bar Brasserie and downing a glass of something warming on their way to work. The roar and clang of a slow-moving dustcart could be heard from close by and an old woman in black was slopping pails of water across the pavement and scrubbing at it with a broom.

'Wake up,' I said, and almost before she was awake Sam was opening a small compact and watching herself dab colours and lotions on her skin.

Two black-clad police motor-cyclists who had been talking outside the Hotel Faisan pulled on their white gauntlets, eased their black leather belts, tugged down the hem of their jackets and in choreographic unison leaned lovingly across their machines, stabbed at the kick-starters and with a graceful *jeté* and *plié* moved forward. Gathering speed they leaned into the curve of the road and sped away past the vibrating wooden doors and shutters, leaving a trail of exhaust smoke in the cold air. Samantha shivered.

'Can we have coffee?' she said. I nodded.

The tiny bar was crowded. A dozen men in *bleu de travail* were drinking, talking and breathing garlic fumes and Gauloise smoke into the limited air space. Two of the men made room for us and someone near the door made a joke about him making a pass at the foreign girl. I asked for two coffees with milk in English. You can never despise the conversation of men who work in shipping, if eavesdropping is your stock-in-trade.

'It's not too late,' I said to Samantha. 'Even now.'

'To work for you?' she said. I nodded. She said,

> 'On this date that he was slain
> Many a kind thought dies in Paine.'

I said, 'Stone cold dead in the graveyard.'

'I like the work I do already.' She was fencing around, not sure how much I knew. It was a woman's game and she began to enjoy it. 'I couldn't possibly give that up now,' she said.

'No one will suggest you do,' I said archly.

Samantha gave a snort of rage that made conversation there cease for thirty seconds. 'You are a cynical swine,' she said.

I smiled and drank my coffee quietly. The sky was even darker. She smoked the usual half-inch of Camel before dropping it on to the floor and giving it the stiletto-heel treatment. 'You can scram now,' I said. I gave her her passport.

'Give me my money, buddy boy.'

'That's not part of the deal,' I said. 'You've got your baggage. Don't look a gift horse in the mouth, peach blossom. Take off.'

'I don't understand,' Samantha said. 'You bring me all this way before saying it.'

'DST[1] offices are not open in the middle of the night, but . . .' I looked at my watch. '. . . my boyo will be in his office in seventeen minutes time.'

'You sadist.'

'You've got me all wrong,' I said. 'You've committed no crime against France. They are only going to treat you as an undesirable alien, stamp "nul" on your passport and heave you on to the first ship or plane pointing towards the North American continent. I could have had you picked up in London. They would give you a much tougher time.'

Samantha described me in one pithy indelicate word.

'Flattery will get you nowhere,' I said. But Sam just repeated the same word in a paucity of invention.

'Phone some friends – reversing the charges,' I said. 'You must have someone in the vicinity who will give you a helping hand.' I leaned towards her and smiled gently. 'But don't put your pretty little head into this operation any more because Helena Rubinstein doesn't make anything that will stick a head back on to shoulders.'

Samantha walked behind me to the car. I reached her baggage out of the rear seat and put it on the ground. The engine was still warm and the Bosch fuel injector forced me across the station yard in violent acceleration.

In the driving mirror I saw Samantha standing alone. Her big military-style greatcoat of olive mohair was buttoned high against the cold, and grey knitted socks came to just below the knee.

[1] See Appendix 5.

As I steered towards the Cours de la Marne two middle-aged men in belted raincoats came out of the Hotel Faisan and walked towards Samantha.

25

Corridor mate: when a king can only move along an expected route, he can be trapped by closing the corridor.

Tuesday, October 15th

She was an elderly woman dressed in the black dress that was obligatory in a French Government office. She wheeled an aged art-nouveau trolley in front of her. On the trolley were two dozen cups and saucers, metal filters, some spoons, an earthenware pot with a lid, a gas bottle and a huge stainless steel drum inside which the clear blue gas-flame could be glimpsed. As she carefully removed the lid from the earthenware jar, a strong smell of dark roasted coffee climbed out. She measured the expensive grains into the filters and placing one on each of our cups poured scalding water on to it. She placed two wrapped sugars alongside each cup and wheeled the tinkling clanking juggernaut through the door.

'I don't *know* that she works for West German Intelligence but what else can you suggest?' I asked him.

Grenade opened the lid of his filter and grimaced at the pain. 'Every day I burn my fingers.' He dropped a sugar cube into his coffee, looked up and said, 'I know your "plausible voice of the simple man" and I know that you are just using us for your own ends.'

'So forget her,' I said. 'Forget I ever said anything about Vulkan, the girl or Louis Paul Broum.'

Grenade wrote something on his notepad.

'And, as you well know, I can't do that; no more than you could if we were sitting in *your* office with the roles reversed. Tell me.' He lifted the lid again. 'It's ready now. Why did you take so much trouble with this girl and yet let the man go free?'

Through the french windows the sky was almost black. I looked around at Grenade's office: the brown-stained wainscoting, the plaster walls discoloured in patches near the ceiling and the old-fashioned metal radiators under which a rash of cream-coloured pimples proclaimed the haste of a clumsy painter. On the wall a pendulum paced the glass confines of its cage.

'We still need the man,' I said. On Grenade's desk was a wrought-metal device like a toy merry-go-round; the 'riders' were shiny bulbous rubber stamps. Grenade spun the merry-go-round. He laughed a soft little laugh. 'Ask me,' he said. 'I can't bear the suspense.'

'Well naturally,' I said, 'we would like you to let him move freely at least for the next week or so, but I'd like you to take a look at him, tell me what he's carrying, then let him go.'

Grenade shook his head and smiled; the first drops of rain smacked the window. 'It's not undeserved, you know, this reputation you Englishmen have gained.'

'You can have the girl,' I said indignantly. 'She'll show you the whole network if you play her right. All I want . . .'

Grenade waved a long bony hand at me. 'It's a bargain if you answer me one question.' He didn't wait to see if I agreed. 'But the truth now, don't try to deceive me or I shall be angry.' It had begun to rain steadily and a complex rivulet of water was moving under the french window.

'You'll have the truth or silence,' I said. The radiator made a noise like a machine gun. Grenade stretched out a long thin elegant leg and, steadying his hands on the desk, gave it a powerful kick. The noise stopped. Still looking at the painted metal radiator, Grenade said, 'How did you know that we had Vulkan under surveillance?'

'I knew that STASI[1] knew where the girl was. In fact, they deliberately leaked the information to us. It seemed probable that if they had had a consort watch[2] on this girl you would be watching the watchers and the watched.' Grenade gave me a deep bow of mock dignity and mock gratitude. A fierce gust of wind made the glass of the french window move in its frame.

'If they had told me that the girl was in Paris, I wouldn't have jumped to any such conclusion. But Hendaye; if you dropped an "h" in your paternoster they'd know out as far as the three-mile limit.'

Grenade kicked the central heating again and said, 'Sounds all right.'

I polished my spectacles and tried to look like the respectable type of Englishman. I wondered how much of it Grenade swallowed. It wasn't too far from the truth but then no lie worth the name ever was. I had got the tip from East Germany even though it was from Red Army Command Security and not from STASI. He had said that Hendaye was the place, although he had talked of the man, not the girl. What about the girl? Working for West German Security certainly made it hang together better as far as Grenade was concerned. As for the girl, she had to start looking out for herself one day.

Grenade got up from his desk and walked across to a roll-front cabinet. Out of it he slid a drawer of a card file index. He took one card back to his desk. He read the card

[1] East German Intelligence Security Service.
[2] Consort watch: knowing where someone is (eg by bribing a concierge) but not necessarily watching them all the time.

through and flipped it to scan the back. 'Right then,' he said. 'We'll do that for you.' Like a man promising delivery on a vacuum cleaner.

I stood up abruptly and resting the flat of my palm upon his desk I leaned my face close to him. I noticed a small scar on his forehead and the way hair grew from only one nostril. 'You'll be thanking me for doing you a favour the next time you are in London,' I said softly.

Grenade languidly spun the merry-go-round, selected a rubber stamp and printed the word 'Nul' on the back of my hand. 'Don't press your luck,' he said, then he offered his thin hand across the desk and shook my hand firmly. 'Take care,' he said, 'it's a nasty vicious city.'

'I'll only be in Berlin a few more days,' I said.

'I meant London,' he said drily. He rang a small bell on his desk and a slight young man with a haircut *en brosse* and rimless spectacles opened the door.

'Albert will take you down,' said Grenade. 'It will save all sorts of complications at the door. We have gone terribly secret since the last time you were here.' Grenade smiled again.

I followed Albert down the staircase that curved around the inside of the huge stair-well. Halfway down I heard Grenade's voice. I looked up the great vertical tunnel into the glare of an overhead skylight. Grenade was leaning over the balcony. He looked minute in this great stone building, full of carefully penned archives and aged bureaucrats scratching quietly in a silence broken only by the clink of nib against inkwell. Grenade called again, almost whispering the words, 'As a liar, my friend, you are incorrigible.' The perspective of the great curves of balustrade repeated themselves as far as infinity, like the echoes of Grenade's whisper. I saw his head prise a way through one of the smallest rings and smile.

'The word,' I said, 'is professional.' I started again down

the staircase of this Caligarian cabinet. I knew that it would take ages to get that marking ink off my hand. I rubbed it self-consciously.

26

The skilled player memorizes and uses the classic
sequences of the games of masters.

Tuesday, October 15th

Bordeaux occupies a special semantic importance in the
minds of all Frenchmen (as Munich does to Britons). In
1871, in 1914 and in 1940 Bordeaux was the city to which
the French Government fled, yelling 'Stand firm!' over their
shoulder. Each large hotel knew the influx of folding chairs
and filing cabinets, typewriters and armed sentries. As I
drove past them I remembered June 1940; Bordeaux was
the halfway house between Verdun and Vichy.

I pressed the accelerator; at this stage of the game, speed
had acquired an importance. I moved the Mercedes Benz
220 SE through the gear box. The steering was sensitive
at high speeds and the hydraulic damper on it made the
controls quietly accurate. Most of the traffic was slow stuff
setting out from Bordeaux and after half an hour the road
was mine. I kept the speedometer at 150 kph for long
stretches and told myself over and over it wasn't a morning
wasted.

I passed the Casino on Hendaye-plage and eased down
the Boulevard de la Mer as unobtrusively as I knew how.
I bumped up the kerb and parked in the exact position I
had been before. Vulkan's Cadillac Eldorado was in the same
position too. There was no sign of movement anywhere

135

even at 10.40 A.M. I pushed open the front door. From the kitchen there was the noise of a kettle being filled. I went up to my room. The 'Do not disturb' notice was still on the door-knob. I turned the key and pushed the door gently open, standing a little behind the door-frame. I went through everything they taught me at Guildford but there was no need — Vulkan was still miles away. I poured myself a stiff whisky from a bottle in my case. I set the alarm mechanism on my wristwatch for dinner time and went to bed. There was nothing more I could do for the time being. It was just a matter of letting matters simmer. When something came to the boil I would hear the rising steam.

27

Any move that attacks a hostile king is known as check.

Tuesday, October 15th

The hammering on my door came at 6.30 P.M. Johnnie Vulkan was standing there looking angry and sad.

'Come in,' I said. I turned round to find him still glaring. I glared back but since my eyes were slits he didn't detect it.

'I've been to the police station,' he said. His cashmere overcoat was slung over his shoulders and the sleeves hung limp like broken limbs.

'Really?' I said like a man trying to make polite conversation. 'Why?'

'I've been given the third degree,' he said. He ran a hand through his grey hair and looked around my room for hidden policemen.

'Why?' I said. 'You must have done something to irritate them.' I began to dress.

'Irritate them!' he spoke loudly. 'I work for your Government for one thing.'

'Well, surely you didn't tell them that,' I yawned. 'Are you sitting on my tie?'

'Of course not,' said Johnnie. 'I didn't tell them anything.' He was getting angry. 'They've been asking me all sorts of questions' – he looked at his huge gold wristwatch – 'for four hours.'

'You must be gasping.' I poured him a drink of whisky.

'I'm not,' he said, which was odd, because he downed the Scotch like a man dying of thirst. 'I'm not hanging around here,' he said. 'I'm going back to Berlin.'

'Just as you say,' I said. 'I'm trying to help.'

He gave me a spiteful look. I said, 'Come along, Johnnie. Either tell me what it's all about or don't tell me at all, but you can't expect me to believe that the police took you to the station because they didn't like the way you parted your hair.'

Vulkan sat on the bed. I poured him another drink and my wristwatch alarm sounded. 'I came down here to consult a man. I went to see him last night. He lives in Spain.'

I tried to look like a man who is just listening to someone else's trouble to be polite. 'This man,' Johnnie went on, 'I was in the army with him.'

'In the concentration camp?' I said.

'Yes. He was the camp doctor. I've known him for years. The French have got their knife into him, I suppose. When he was driving me back here, they refused him entry at the frontier and hauled me out of the car.'

'Oh,' I said like a man to whom it is suddenly made clear. 'You have been across into Spain and they stopped you at the border.'

'Yes,' said Johnnie.

'Well,' I said. 'I shouldn't worry about it. It's just a routine check.'

They sounded a little bell downstairs to tell us that the dinner was cooked. I finished dressing hurriedly and Vulkan drank a lot of whisky. Dinner wasn't any too jolly because Vulkan was miserable as sin. One of the policemen had told him that Samantha had been asked to leave the country because her papers weren't in order. 'What papers?' Vulkan kept asking and I really couldn't tell him.

'Everything has gone wrong on this job,' said Johnnie

after the coffee had arrived. He stretched his legs and studied the toes of his expensive Oxford shoes. 'I *try* to keep everyone happy . . .' He made a surrender motion with the palms of his hands.

'Try to make everyone happy,' I said, 'and you'll wind up a rich mediocrity; but you'll never get anything done that is worth doing.'

Johnnie stared at me for a long time, fixing me with his eyes until I began to think he had gone off his trolley.

'You are right,' he said finally. He went back to studying the toes of his shoes and he said 'You are right' two or three more times. I poured him coffee. He thanked me, still in this abstract mood, then he said, 'London will be mad at me now?'

'Why?' I asked.

'Well,' he said. He moved his arm like he was trying to throw his hand away. 'Messing about down here on my own affairs instead of being in Berlin when you needed to know about the name on the document. Sometimes I feel I'm not cut out for this life. I should be writing music, not having a one-man war with London. London could murder me.'

'London has no personality,' I said. 'Believe me, I know them very well. They're just like one big computing machine. Put a success story in one end; money and promotion come out the other.'

'OK,' Johnnie interrupted. He fixed me with that glare again. 'They want this man, Semitsa – then, by God, I'll get him.'

'That's the boy,' I said, but I don't know how I got any kind of enthusiasm into my voice.

28

Development for its own sake is insufficient. There
must be a keen purpose in every move.

London, Thursday, October 17th

'It's no good trying to blame Hallam,' Dawlish was saying.
'He's given you more co-operation and information than
you could reasonably ask for. Good Lord, you should have
worked with the Home Office people when I was seconded
to them.'

'Let's not talk about when coppers wore high hats,' I
said. 'I've got my problems *now* – I don't want to hear
your chilling experiences.'

'And bringing the San Sebastian people into this – it's
a grave error of judgement. Grenade's people will have
listened to the whole thing.'

'Don't worry about Grenade,' I said. 'I gave him that
girl and said she was working from Bonn. That was quite
enough to have them all busy for a couple of days.'

'You don't have to sit here and sort it all out,' said
Dawlish. 'You just make a lot of trouble right across Europe
and leave it for me to curtsy, kiss your hand, apologize,
explain that we all make mistakes sometimes and carry the
can for you.'

'You do it so well,' I said. I turned to go.

'Another thing,' said Dawlish, 'that young Chillcott-
Oakes came up here the other day babbling about books

and thistle stamens. Couldn't understand a word of it except that he'd got it from you.'

'I just said that you were interested in wild flowers,' I said. 'It's true, isn't it?'

Dawlish began to move items off the top of his desk like he was going to climb on it and do a Gopak. It was a sign of deep emotion.

'Do you know, even the wife likes it now? People have heard about it and they come to see it. They come to scoff. I know they do, but they stay to admire and one or two people have brought me plants. I have cornflowers – I don't know why I didn't think of those right from the start. I have some lovely scarlet pimpernel, corn camomile (you may know that better as mayweed) . . .'

'Yes,' I said.

Dawlish was looking into the far, far distance now as his crop paraded slowly before his eyes. 'Sweet alyssum, *galinsoga*, the yellow ox-eye daisy and some quite remarkable grasses, and wild birds and butterflies.'

'You aren't going to encourage pests then. You aren't going to have wire-worms and Colorado beetles,' I said.

'No,' said Dawlish.

'What about poisonous plants?' I said. 'What about foxglove and monk's-hood or deadly nightshade and wild arum or some of that great agaric fungus? Deadly as hell.'

Dawlish shook his head.

He switched his squawk box on and asked Alice for a dossier he needed, then switching the box off for a moment, he said: 'Whatever else you conclude, right or wrong, don't make any mistakes about Hallam. He's a damn good chap; whatever you may feel about him personally, the HO would hardly function without him. Leave him well alone or you will be tackling me – in person.'

I nodded. Dawlish passed me a flimsy message form. 'I would appreciate it if in future you didn't request even routine information from field units without permission. You don't understand . . .' He waved the flimsy sheet. 'These things cost us a fee.'

'OK,' I said. Dawlish had a happy knack of indicating when a meeting was at an end, even though he would often feign surprise when one made towards the door.

'I say,' he said. 'All that twaddle about my writing books and meadow flowers.'

'Yes,' I said.

Dawlish shrugged in embarrassment. 'Good of you,' he said and suddenly busied himself with work on his desk top.

29

Players who relish violence, aggression and movement
often depend upon the Spanish Game.

Thursday, October 17th

To	Unspec. field unit via London	
Immediate Destination:		W O O C (P)
Source:	Cato 16	

Further to your query. The number plate you mention
is that of Dr Ernst Mohr who is under a four-year surveillance. (Future queries should refer to him as Thrush.) Your
(London) records will show a detailed account. Briefly:
height 6' 1"/Weight: 12 stone 12 lbs/Eyes: brown/Hair:
almost bald. No scars or distinguishing marks. Born Leipzig
1921. Qualified as Dr (of medicine) Leipzig 1941. Entered
German Army 1941. Served in base hospitals in Germany
1941–4. Served in Eastern Front 1944–45. Captured Hamburg 1945. Witness at British Army War Crimes Inquiry
Hamburg 1946 (ref: 275/Crime/nn). Released to work
British military hospital 1946. Released to work in German
civilian hospital 1946. Under contract to Bonn Government
(Intelligence, not Gehlen) 1948. Began work as representative radium therapy machinery 1948. Assigned to Northern
Spain as radium therapy equipment salesman 1949. Began
buying land locally (N Coast Spain) 1951. Resigned radium

LEN DEIGHTON

equipment company 1953. Began forming Spanish companies 1953. Married Spanish citizen 1953. 2 children.

Dr Ernst Mohr is now a Spanish citizen. He continues to submit reports to Bonn but we think that this is known to Madrid with whom he has probably come to an agreement. Bonn has him marked as a very low credulity.

He spent five hours with JV on date you mention and French immigration have since refused him entry. We assume this is your contact point. We have nothing of JV on record here. Trust this is of some help.

CATO 16

30

Range in chess is measured not by distance but by the
number of squares to which a legal move can be made.

Thursday, October 17th

I took the message sheet down to my office and read it
again twice. I looked quickly through my 'In' tray, then
the phone rang. The operator said that Hallam had phoned
twice in the last half hour. Did I want to be connected?
Yes.

'Hello, Hallam here. Special Import Service.'

'They tell me that you are after me.'

'Go along with you,' said Hallam, 'I'm not after you.'
We both had a jolly good giggle about that. Then I said,
'Well, what is it?'

'Just to tell you that everything is ready.'

'Every what thing is ready?'

'Customs, immigration, car will be available for you at
Southampton or Dover. We have a guest house near Exeter.
He'll go there for a week or so.' Hallam's voice trailed off.

'Oh yes,' I said.

'That's why we'd prefer Southampton,' said Hallam.

'Well, isn't that cosy?' I said. 'Is he going to bring his
own hot-water bottle?'

'These things have to be attended to,' said Hallam in his
snotty voice. 'It's not a bit of use you being upstage about
the domestic arrangements. You'd look rather silly standing

on the deck of the cross-Channel packet holding the hand of a "refused entry".'

'Not half as silly as I'd look holding hands with . . .'

'Now now,' said Hallam sternly and rang off.

I spoke the remainder of the sentence into the dead phone as Jean came in. She said 'Hallam?' and put two cups of coffee on my desk.

'Right on the button,' I said.

'You mustn't let him get you down,' she said.

'He's so irritating,' I said.

'You think he doesn't know that?' said Jean. 'He's just like you; he takes a perverse delight in irritating people.'

'Do you really think so?'

'It's obvious,' said Jean.

'Do you know I never realized that? I'll have to revise my attitude to the chintzy old bastard.' I passed her the message from Cato 16 and began to drink my Nescafé-flavoured hot water. Jean read the message carefully.

'It's interesting,' she said.

'In what way?' I said.

'I don't know,' she said. 'But it must be interesting because you asked for it. It's meaningless to me.'

'I don't want to destroy your pathetic faith,' I said, 'but it's meaningless to me too.'

'What did you expect?' Jean said.

'I don't know quite. I suppose I hoped it would exactly fit the description that Gehlen gave me for the Broum documents, or that Vulkan would come into the résumé somewhere.'

'Perhaps he does,' said Jean, 'if you examine it closely enough. This Eastern front section. He and Vulkan were probably stationed in the same concentration camp unit, just as Vulkan says.'

'I suppose he might,' I said grudgingly. 'It's just that I was hoping for some big dramatic development.'

'But you are always telling me *not* to hope for some big dramatic development,' said Jean.

'You don't do as I do. Do as I tell you.'

Jean pulled a face at me and read the message through again. 'Do you want me to check his records through for any mention of Vulkan?' I hesitated. 'Things are very quiet just now,' Jean said. 'I'm having my hair done twice a week.'

'If you will find Mohr's file equally therapeutic, go ahead,' I said. 'I'll be happy to give an authorization for the records clerk.'

'See how your plant has grown,' said Jean. 'All that part there is new leaf.'

I took Jean to lunch at the Trattoria Terrazza where we had lunched the first day we met. We sat in the swish downstairs room and drank Campari sodas and I threw my waistline to the wind and had a vast portion of lasagne and followed it with chicken Kiev. Franco the proprietor brought us grappa with the coffee and we sat and talked about Soho and about Billy Big and Harry the Hanger Man and what the cross-eyed man from the fish shop shouted at the traffic warden. I leaned back and surveyed the empty wine bottles and the full ashtrays and wondered how I could get a job as a Michelin Guide inspector.

'You wouldn't like it,' Franco said.

'Wouldn't he?' said Jean. 'You don't know him.'

I just sat there smiling and fighting down the belches. There is not much point in going back to the office at 4.30 P.M. so I took Jean to see a film that the Sundays said was a poetical experience. All I got out of it was cramp.

Jean was being motherly. She had bought a bag of groceries in Soho and we went back to her flat in Gloucester Road after the pictures and cooked them.

Jean's flat is as draughty as a lettuce basket. We went into the kitchen and sat there with the oven full on and the oven door open, beating eggs and boiling artichokes while Jean read the directions from a cooking article in the *Observer*. I had just begun to warm up a little when the phone went. Jean answered but it was for me.

'Been trying to get you since four o'clock this afternoon,' the Charlotte Street switchboard said petulantly.

'I was in the toilet,' I said.

'It's the DST[1] Bordeaux office. You don't have a scrambler there, I suppose, sir?'

'No,' I said. 'This is Miss Tonnesson's private number.'

'Then when I reconnect with your Bordeaux party I shall have to scramble here and put it through to you in clear.'

'OK,' I said, but apparently I wasn't being appreciative enough.

'It's against orders really, sir. You should come to the nearest phone with a scrambler: that's the instructions. It's only because I've spoken with the Fremantle exchange supervisor and had him handle the call personally that I can risk it.'

'Well, it's certainly very kind of you to do that for me. I'll certainly be most discreet in my conversation.'

'There's no need to be sarcastic, sir. I'm only doing my job.'

I said nothing and there was a series of noises as Charlotte Street hooked itself into the official Government cross-Channel phone cable. Suddenly there was a din of unscrambled noise before Charlotte Street switched the scrambler into the circuit, then Grenade's voice said '. . . lucky to do it. However you'll just have to rely on Albert's memory. You hear me OK?'

'OK,' I said. 'Go ahead.'

'If he enters France again we will arrest him,' said Grenade.

---

[1] *See* Appendix 5.

'The hell you will,' I said. 'On what charge?'

'I'll tell you,' said Grenade. 'Until we spoke together, your friend was just a name buried deep in our files. Just someone we were interested in; but if he comes back again we will charge him with terrorism and murder and I daresay we will be able to find a few war crimes if we dig around carefully.'

'Can you be a little more explicit?' I asked.

'I'm sending you the usual written sheet,' said Grenade.

'But who did he murder?' I asked, 'and when?'

'End of 1942, he murdered a member of the Vichy Government,' said Grenade.

'Why?' I asked.

'Because he was in the FTP,[2] said Grenade. 'It was a political assassination.'

'Go on,' I said.

'Arrested by Vichy militia in Colmar in February 1943. We have the old war-time docket here, I'll send you a photostat of it. Claimed to be a German citizen and was sent for trial to Germany. We have no record of any of that, of course. Albert's got a hell of a memory, he says he got off with a prison term.'

'Albert would have to have a hell of a memory,' I said. 'It must have all happened when Albert was about five.'

'Albert used to be downstairs in the archives. He has a memory for documents. You know what I meant,' said Grenade and chuckled.

'I'm staggered,' I said. 'You mean to tell me that John Vulkan was a communist and killed a member of the Vichy Government. I just can't believe it.'

'I'm not talking about Vulkan,' said Grenade. 'We all

---

[2] Francs-Tireurs et Partisans: World War Two French resistance network organized by the Communist Party and kept entirely separate from all others.

know what Vulkan is. He is one of your riot squad, eh? I'm talking about Broum.'

'Broum?' I said in amazement.

'We were all surprised. I thought this man Broum was another figment of your over-active imagination. I told Albert so.'

'Oh no,' I said.

The operator cut in and said were we finished as the line was in great demand and I told her to wait. There was a buzz and Grenade was saying '. . . complaining that his girlfriend was missing. Ha. We knew that he was one of your boys but he kept his mouth shut, I can tell you.' There was a pause. Then Grenade said, 'We know perfectly well that Vulkan works for you.'

I grunted. Then Grenade said, 'Admit it, my friend. Tell the truth for once. You will find it an invigorating experience.'

'We pay his wages,' I said guardedly.

Grenade gave a triumphant little hoot of laughter. 'Very good, my friend. A subtle distinction and in the case of your friend Vulkan a necessary distinction.' He laughed again.

'Where is Broum now?' I asked.

'No trace,' said Grenade. 'Why don't you start doing a little work for yourself? Routine inquiries. Get your weight down a little.'

'Thank you, operator,' I said. 'You can disconnect us now.'

Grenade shouted, 'Albert drinks Dimple Haig.'

'Don't tell me your staff problems,' I said.

'You are a hard man,' said Grenade.

'Inside that layer of fatty tissue,' I said. Then the operator disconnected us.

Jean flung a clean tablecloth to me and brought supper. I told her the contents of Grenade's call.

'Why does it make any difference who this man Broum is or what he did in the war? Our task is just to move one man named Semitsa from East Berlin to London.'

'You oversimplify things as always,' I said. 'If it was as simple as that Carter Paterson would be doing it. The reason we are involved is because we want to learn as much about Karlshorst in general and Stok in particular as we can. Secondly, I have to know to what extent Vulkan is reliable, to what extent we can trust him if something really serious blows up. Thirdly, we don't know nearly enough about the Gehlen set-up; what's its allegiance to Bonn; to the State Department; to the US Army . . .'

'To us,' Jean said.

'Even to us,' I agreed. 'And then there's Semitsa, the crux of the whole problem. When he crosses Zimmerstrasse he will be Paul Louis Broum and armed with enough evidence to defy anyone to disprove it. That's why I want to know who Broum was and why Semitsa should be so desperately anxious to become him.'

'How are you going to start?' Jean asked.

'"Begin at the beginning," as the Queen said to Alice, "Go on to the end. Then stop."' Paul Louis Broum was born in Prague.

31

Czech Defence: a sequence in which pawn is matched
with pawn but the queen's bishop tips the balance.

Monday, October 21st

If anyone ever decided to illustrate Hans Andersen with
photographs he would start in Prague. The heights of the
city are a fairy tale of spiky spires; Hradcany castle and the
steeple of St Vitus stare down to where the fourteenth-
century Karluv bridge tucks the Three Ostriches tavern
under its arm before crossing the calm blue Vltava. The older
parts of the city are a maze of tiny twisting streets illuminated
by gas lights and so hilly that a careless driver can find himself
tobogganing down steep stone steps. It was twilight and the
city looked like a dusty Christmas tree. I parked my hired
Skoda car and walked back towards the Three Ostriches
tavern. The steps were worn to a glassy smoothness and the
inside was like something whittled three lessons before Pin-
occhio. The overhead beams were painted with red and green
vine leaves and varnished with about five hundred years of
tobacco smoke. A tiny radio balanced over the tiled stove
was beating out 'Walking my baby back home' with enough
violence to make the potted geraniums quiver. The tables
were as crowded as a Stakhanovite work schedule and merry
groups of men shouted for slivovice, borovicka or Pilsner
Urquell, and the waiters kept a tally of their progress by
marking each man's beer-mat with strange pencil marks.

Harvey was sitting in the corner drinking and talking. Harvey was a typical Foreign Service officer. He changed his shirt three times a day and used talc with a masculine perfume. He was a short, thickset, city-bred American, his arms a little too long and his hair cut short enough to disguise his receding hairline. His skin was nearer to olive than to any other colour. His face followed every syllable of the conversation and would grow serious or flash a sudden smile in response to the mood of the talking. It was this animation of his face muscles that made him good-looking – not handsome – but definitely good-looking.

'Less viable than the Munich project,' he was saying as I reached his table. He nodded to me to sit down. He didn't introduce me.

The man with him nodded and removed a signet ring from his finger and put it back again with considerable skill.

Harvey said, 'But I'd opt for it just the same.' He had that soft Boston accent that Americans acquire when they work for the State Department.

When the other man spoke it was in a light whisper. He said, 'Wages escalate, Harvey. You'd think that would make it better but it doesn't. It's counter-productive. I'll advertise again.' He turned to me. 'So long,' he said. Then he said, 'So long' to Harvey and drifted through the door like a smoke cloud.

'What was all that New Frontier jargon, Harvey?' I asked.

Harvey swept a small glassful of slivovice over his tonsils. 'We all talk like that now,' Harvey said. 'It's so the British won't understand.'

'We never understood before,' I said. When the waiter had brought two tall, ice-cold Pilsen lagers, Harvey said, 'You know, I thought I knew this town once. My old man was always telling me about the old country and even

LEN DEIGHTON

before I stepped on the boat to Europe I thought of Americans as aliens. But the longer I stay here, the less I understand.' Harvey laid his hand limply face up on the table in a supplicating gesture. 'I need a maid: check?'

'Check,' I said.

'For three weeks I'm trying to get a local girl to help with work around the apartment. It's not hard work but can I get one? No, sir. They tell me that no one does domestic work any more – "only in capitalist countries", they tell me. Today I said to one, "I thought the function of the communist state was to dignify labour, not to denigrate it."'

'Did you get the girl to work for you?'

'Negative,' Harvey said.

'You should take a lesson from European diplomacy,' I said. 'The purpose of political debate is to achieve results, not to win arguments.'

Harvey sank his lager in one long draught. Outside there was the constant noise of tram-bells and traffic-cop whistles. 'Slivovice,' said Harvey. 'How about a slivovice before I take you to see him?'

'None for me, Harvey, and none for you. Let's go. I'm starved.' Harvey wanted his slivovice but I knew the danger signs. Harvey was determined to get very drunk. We left Harvey's new Dodge where it was under the trees in Na Kampe, and took my Skoda which gave me a better excuse for insisting that I drive. We drove out through the dusty area of rebuilding with Harvey slouched well back in his seat saying 'Right' and 'Left' and 'Straight on' every now and again.

The roads out of Prague are lined with cherry trees; in the spring the blossom follows the road like smoky exhaust and in the summer it is not unusual to see a driver standing on top of his lorry munching at the fruit. Now it was autumn and the trees had just the last few tenacious leaves

154

hanging on like jilted lovers. Here and there young girls or tiny children dressed always in trousers attended to a cow or a goat or a few geese. High-wheeled bullock carts moved ponderously along the narrow roads and sometimes a big truck filled with mocking gesticulating girls being taken home from their work in the fields. Their clothes weren't peasant weaves and hand-printed headscarves but hard-wearing trousers, mass-produced blouses, and plastic scarves.

Ahead of us was an ancient car with a bulbous brass radiator and landau coachwork. I overtook it only to find ahead of me a red and white diagonally striped pole with a sign 'Objizd'ka' on it. Diversion.

'I thought our luck couldn't last,' said Harvey. 'Now we'll encounter something that will make the previous three miles look like the Washington Turnpike.'

I opened my mouth to speak just as we hit the first of the pot-holes. We battled against flint with rubber, and beat mud into cake-mix with our treads. We scraped a way between trees and bored a hole through a great rolling cloud of white dust. We climbed back on to the main road again like the sole survivors of a ship-wreck.

'Do you know where you are?' said Harvey.

'No idea.'

'Good,' he said and fell back in his seat. 'Don't want the whole British colony to find the place.' The road became paved. Ahead of us was a tiny group of houses.

'What are they going to come here in – half-tracks?' I asked.

'You'll love it,' said Harvey. 'Turn in here. Decelerate.'

I stopped the car and let one of those heavy trucks with two trailers that they call 'road trains' pass us, then pulled in to the side entrance. To the left a range of hills was summit-deep in mist and ahead the road curved to skirt a forest. On the corner house a vast oval-shaped traffic mirror with a red and gold frame pictured the intersection in distorted reflection. Above it, looking like something wrenched out of the HMV trademark, was a loudspeaker that spoke the words of government. Across the front of the brown stone building on the left the name of the pre-communist proprietor could still be read in the faded paint-work from which solid wooden letters had been taken down. From the first floor there hung a plastic sign. As we looked at it in the gathering dusk it was switched on. We read the words 'State Hotel'.

At the side entrance a small boy in a pink sweatshirt was pulling open the enormous wooden doors. I drove through into the cobbled courtyard and the noise of the engine sent a flock of white geese cackling and calling in flat-footed rage to the far side of the yard where chopped logs were stacked in neat wooden honeycombs. The boy pointed to the open-sided barn and I drove under it and shook Harvey fully awake. Suspended under the roof of the barn was a huge horse-sled, spun with cobwebs and dust. The courtyard was growing dark and through the back windows of the hotel I could see the kitchen and the dining-room lit by blue neon.

Clouds of steam rolled out of the kitchen door and tip-toed stealthily across the cobblestones, diminishing at every step like shy ghosts. The kitchen's stone floor was shiny with moisture and plump women with handkerchiefs drawn tight around their heads stepped in and out of the noise and steam like a team of formation dancers.

From the restaurant came a heavy sweet smell of beer. The plastic table-tops supported countless leather elbows and at the counter the standard meal of one hundred grammes of goulash was being carefully and lawfully measured by a cheerful woman in a stained apron. Except for the waitresses there were no women to be seen in the dining-room. Harvey led the way right through with scarcely a falter. Upstairs there was a powerful smell of antiseptic. Harvey knocked at a door on the first floor and waved me inside.

It was a tiny room. Lenin shared the floral wallpaper with the local football team. There was a glass-fronted dresser containing mass-produced local glassware, five uncomfortable wooden chairs that had been moved there from the dining-room after suffering minor damage, and a table. On the hand-embroidered cloth were three place-settings of plain white china with the government hotel symbol, three tumblers and two unlabelled bottles of local wine, which glowed like garnets in front of a large paraffin lamp.

At the far side of the table was the dark vole-like man Harvey had brought me here to see – Jan-im-Glück – Lucky Jan. The girl brought us the roast goose and heavy dry dumpling slices almost as soon as we sat down. Harvey poured two glasses and finished the bottle himself.

Harvey probably *knew* how to carve a goose but it was his co-ordination that proved such a handicap. We all got large torn pieces of hot, crisp, juicy, oily goose and we had a large plate of those breadrolls that come with great chunks of sea-salt and poppy seeds baked to the top of them. There was slivovice which Harvey liked and tiny pots of Turkish coffee of which he wasn't so fond. We ate in greedy silence. 'Why can't I have American coffee?' he asked me, and he took the oil lamp and left the room while the old man and I talked about the price of butter in England, the role of the trade unionist in US politics and what became of the Austro-Hungarian Empire. When Harvey came back he was shouting 'Obsazeno, obsazeno'.[1] He pointed a finger in no definite direction and said, 'Why is it that in this damned god-forsaken country, where everyone

---

[1] Obsazeno: occupied.

is filling out small rectangular forms in triplicate, there is never any god-damned paper in the WC?'

Without smiling the old man said, 'Because someone has filled it out in triplicate.'

'Affirmative,' said Harvey. He let the weight of his fist bring it down on the table with a thump that made the dishes jump. 'That's right.' And having solved the problem he put his head on his hands and went to sleep.

The old man looked at him and said, 'If God had made the world for humans we would have alcohol that made the head clearer instead of drowsy and the tongues of men more articulate instead of slurred. For it is when a man has consumed alcohol that he has the most important things to say.'

'What *did* God make the world for?' I asked, 'if not for humans?'

The old man spoke more sharply. 'For building speculators and generals, any fool knows that.'

I smiled but the old man's face was unchanging.

'Did,' I nodded my head towards Harvey, 'tell you what I wanted to talk to you about?'

Jan-im-Glück took a slim metal case from his pocket. It was worn smooth and burnished like a flat pebble from the seashore. He prised a thumbnail into its edge and it opened to reveal a silk interior of royal purple in which the serpentine coils of a pair of spectacles nestled. He put them on.

The old man took the oil lamp with two hands, turned up the wick just a fraction of an inch, and held it near my face. The lamp illuminated the old man's face too. The skin had the texture of a jute sack so that a small scar went almost undetected in the coarseness of the complexion. The few days' growth of white bristles across his lower face shone silver in the light. His eyes were bright and moved quickly behind the bent spectacles that were artfully placed upon his nose to allow him to look over them when he preferred to do so. As his head turned in the lamplight, the circular spectacle glasses took turns to become silver pennies and clear again to reveal the small black eyes behind them. He nodded his way out of the spectacles and put them back into the cloth lining of the metal case.

'It's my job to investigate war crimes,' I said.

Wizened was about the only word you could apply to him. He would have been tall if he ever stood upright, he would have been thin if he had ever removed the layers of black overcoat, and may have been bald under the wide-brimmed black hat of orthodox Judaism.

'War crimes?' he repeated. 'What war is it that you speak of?'

'The Second World War that finished in 1945,' I said.

'It finished then, did it?' he said. 'I wish someone had told me. I'm still fighting it.'

I nodded. He wrapped a layer of overcoat across his knees.

He said, 'We all have to, you see. Every Jew has won a desperate battle against the world the day he is born. For a Jew, you see, just *existing*' – he squeezed the word through his palate – 'just *existing* is a triumph; a victory against fascism.' His eyes moved slowly from my shoes to my head without any sort of rudeness. 'So they are still sending men to write legal papers so that lawyers can talk about war crimes. Every crime is a holiday if you are a lawyer, eh?' He laughed soundlessly, his small eyes shining and his crisp little hand patting his knee.

'I want to talk about Treblinka Camp,' I said.

He closed his eyes. 'Then either you have never been there,' he paused, 'or you are a German.' He added hurriedly, 'Not that I bear any ill will to Germans . . .'

'Nor me,' I said. 'In fact many of my best friends are anti-semites.'

LEN DEIGHTON

'Meschugge,' said the old man, 'ganz meschugge.'² He slapped his thigh and cackled. Harvey snored. The old man turned to examine Harvey. There was a huge tuft of cotton wool poking out of the old man's ear in a demoniacal fashion.

'Camp Treblinka,' I said, to prompt the old man.

'Yes,' he said. 'They were using monoxide gas there. It's not efficient.' He smiled like a crack in the lino. 'At Auschwitz they managed things better. They moved with the times. With Zyklon B they killed two and a half million at Auschwitz – they could never have done that with monoxide. Never.'

'It's about Paul Louis Broum,' I said. 'You knew him.'

The old man spoke with deliberation, choosing each word like a lawyer. His voice was shrill and yet dignified. 'I did. Yes. I knew Broum.'

'Well,' I said, 'did you know him well?'

'Well?' said Jan-im-Glück. He thought about it. 'I knew him *ill.* That's the only way you know anyone in a concentration camp. You watch the ones that are taken away to die and you are happy because you are left alive. That's our guilt, you see; all Europe suffers from a feeling of guilt. That is why the world is so spiteful. The ex-gaoler remembers someone he has beaten or selected for beating, the people who watched us move through the towns remember that they forgot five minutes afterwards, and we victims remember that we were happy to see our friends die because it meant that we lived. So you see we are all racked with guilt.'

'About Broum,' I said.

'Ah,' the old man cried. 'My conversation embarrasses you because you too feel it.'

'If the world is guilty,' I said, 'who remains to pass judgement?'

² ganz: completely; meschugge (Yiddish): batty, crazy, nuts.

160

The old man patted his knee and said, 'Ganz meschugge.'

'Can you tell me about Broum's life in prison?' I said.

'Better than that,' said Jan-im-Glück. 'I'll tell you of his death.'

'Tell me about that,' I said.

32

JAN-IM-GLUCK, 1945

It was moving-day at the camp. Everyone suspected that the Russians were getting closer but there was no way to find out. At the week-end the Germans detonated the crematoria in explosions that went on all night. Sunday was devoted to burning down half the huts, which meant that on Sunday night each remaining hut was twice as crowded as usual. Scarcely anyone slept that night; it was early summer and the windows were shuttered to make the sentries' job easier. Inside the huts the temperature was unbelievable. Most of the huts put two or three unconscious people out of the front door the next morning before the march had even begun.

One side of the camp was a railway siding. All the sick were taken there just after dawn. Someone asked a guard what was happening and he said that the sick were being taken to Siedlce by train, but that all the others must march. The sick left before the food was distributed; it was an ominous sign.

The next group to leave were the children. They were marched away before the shutters were taken down from the huts, but everyone was listening.

The remainder of the prisoners formed up in the main compound. There was an acrid smell of burnt wood and burnt bedding. Great pieces of soot floated on the air like dandelion seeds. The guards were all carrying new automatic rifles and outside the gates there was a large group of soldiers. They wore camouflage smocks and steel helmets and were dirty and unshaven. They were front-line troops, not Waffen SS. The guards had formed up nearby too, but the two sorts of soldiers didn't speak to each other. Each prisoner was given four raw potatoes and some hard dried meat. Some of the prisoners got extra potatoes but only those in the front rank. They began to eat the food as they walked out of the gate.

Everyone knew that they were walking westwards because the shadows stretched very long and very thin in front of them as they walked. They walked for two hours, then they rested, then they walked for another two hours. The second or third time they stopped, there was the distant sound of heavy artillery. It was very faint and, when the march recommenced, the sound of moving feet made it impossible to hear.

At noon the soldiers and guards lit fires and began to cook food that came out of the carts that were being hauled by manpower. They spoke and laughed together. The soldiers didn't speak to the prisoners at first. It was as though the very existence of the concentration-camp prisoners embarrassed them; that although they were guarding them they didn't want to admit that the prisoners existed. The first soldier to have a conversation with any prisoner was a middle-aged Latvian who heard two prisoners speak his language. They exchanged the names of their birthplaces, then marched in an awkward silence until one of the regular guards came near to them. Then the soldier moved farther down the marching column. Later he brought a small piece of tobacco for his countrymen; they chewed it but it made them feel sick, for their stomachs were not strong enough for such things.

In the fields there were only women. They attended to their work and seldom turned to watch the great shuffling army. In the villages there was no one to be seen at all, but if a prisoner watched carefully he saw a movement of lace curtain or a door opening an inch or two.

There were many crucifixes at the roadside and some of the prisoners would shake their fists as they passed. One man spat. Broum said, 'Do not blaspheme,' and the man replied, 'Our very existence is a blasphemy.' Then the man who had spat shouted a prayer as loud as he could shout and a guard came along and hit the prisoner. Broum called to the guard, 'Don't strike him, let him grow weary.' Strangely enough the guard moved away and the man who had spat became quiet.

Soon after that, other men began to tire and fall to the rear of the column. It was a long line, the tail of it seldom visible to the men at the front, so they didn't know what happened to those who lagged behind, but all day there had been the sound of rifle shots. Some said that the soldiers were shooting birds and hares for food.

Jan and Broum found themselves walking side by side. Broum began to talk. They talked about their days in the prison camp and the prisoners they both remembered. Later Broum began to talk of his life before he came to the camp. This was unusual; origin and family were topics prisoners preferred to leave undiscussed. At first Jan thought that he must be some sort of Kapo employed to ferret information, but he seemed more interested in speaking of himself than in discovering facts about Jan.

Broum's father was a Frenchman who came to Czechoslovakia to work in the wine business. His mother was a member of one of the best Jewish families in Prague. 'I'm a Jewish Roman Catholic,' Broum said to Jan. 'I was ten before I realized that not everyone in the world has a Jewish mother and a Catholic father.' At home they mostly spoke German although his mother also spoke fluent French.

Broum's mother was an accomplished amateur musician and sometimes would participate in the musical soirées they regularly held. His father used these occasions to get silently drunk, sitting glassy-eyed in the back of the room and none of the guests dared to turn round.

Broum was studying at the German University in Prague until 1940 when the Germans expelled him because he was half-Jewish. Even then he had no strong political ideas, not even feeling hatred for the Nazis after he was expelled. He described himself as a 'political virgin'.

He found it impossible to get a job – not because the Nazis were persecuting him but because the Czechs were anxious not to provoke them. Ironically the job he finally got was working for the Nazis direct. The fall of France brought an urgent need for French-speaking interpreters. Broum went to France as a civilian interpreter for the Wehrmacht.

Even as a civilian Broum found himself a member of the master race: a strange and frightening experience for a young man visiting his father's native land for the first time. Broum became an interpreter with the HQ group 312 Geheime Feldpolizei in Caen. The job of that unit was investigating crimes committed by local civilians against the German Army.

Many of the French prisoners reminded Broum of his father. In spite of himself, he became emotionally involved in their fate. Sometimes he was ordered to be present as a witness at executions, sometimes information was gained only by torture and as a translator he was required to be present.

Broum began to dread each day's work. Sometimes he would stay awake all night knowing that the moment he fell asleep morning would arrive next. Indigestion became stomach pains – the stomach being the focal point of fear – and these developed into severe abdominal cramps.

Sometimes he used his fast, fluent French to slip a word of sympathy or advice into the translations. The word spread that Broum was a sympathetic German. For some time Broum played a double game, revealing pieces of information that he would never have got had the prisoners not trusted him to a limited extent.

Finally Broum cracked. Perhaps the local French knew enough to blackmail him. Perhaps he started out as a betrayer but stayed as a believer. In any case he made contact with local resistance leaders. He reported to them regularly; train times, barge concentrations, movements of prisoners and rations. When his position became too precarious the French resistance gave him false papers and sheltered him in Douai with a Jewish family. Broum became a Jew in manners and thought. He passed himself off as a Frenchman but eventually he was caught – as they were all caught – by betrayal.

He was passed from civil prison in France to Wehrmacht prison in Holland to civil prison in Essen. No one knew quite what to do with a half-French, half-German civilian who had deserted from the Army, until he told them how proud he was to be a Jew. He was a figure that attracted legends as a magnet attracts iron filings. Stories were told of Broum's close friendship with Goering until Goering coveted Broum's wife – or in other stories his art collection – and had him imprisoned. There were stories that made Broum a relative of Pierre Laval, in jail as a hostage for the latter's collaboration. Some stories insisted that Broum was a member of the German General Staff who had been secretly working for the Russians. Whatever the truth was, it had brought Broum to Treblinka. It was an extermination camp but Broum found ways to stand aside from the stream of prisoners who entered and died within a week. Jan too earned his nickname. The art of survival – the old man said – was the only Jewish art form.

The great dirty column of ragged, smelly prisoners kept moving west. There were several times when the old man Jan would have slipped behind and solved the riddle of the rabbit guns but for the voice and the arm of Broum. The column halted before it was dark. Fires were built but there were no axes to chop wood and the food didn't last long.

The prisoners were counted endlessly, when all the totals tallied the food was distributed. Each prisoner got three raw beets and a slice of black bread which they were permitted to dip into a canister of hot soup. One man dropped his bread into the soup. He was a strong, intelligent man but he wept like a child. The guards laughed. The prisoners crowded together in vast groups – some of a hundred or more – and shared their body heat to stay alive.

All night the horizon flickered with gunfire. All night long men were getting to their feet and flailing their bodies to move their thin blood. As dawn broke the guards ordered everyone to their feet. Some didn't get to their feet; the cold had nibbled the last calories of life away from them. Counting began. The live moved hastily away from the dead. Broum was one of the dead. The cold hadn't killed him; he had, they said, been strangled. No prisoner was surprised, for Broum had many enemies, but the Germans were surprised and angry. Death was something which only they dispensed. They began to ask questions. They wanted to know who slept near Broum. Jan-im-Glück had slept beside him and had heard nothing and seen nothing. Jan-im-Glück said nothing to anyone. An SS medical officer examined the body and then questioned five suspects. Jan was one of the thousands of prisoners who looked on. The wind was screaming and tugging at the flaps of their clothes like an angry child. The officer questioned each suspect in turn. Sometimes the words were

LEN DEIGHTON

audible to the watchers but generally the wind tore the words away from the wide-moving jaws. The prisoners watched with unseeing eyes the moving mouths of the men; not hearing, understanding or caring that they were arguing, pleading, crying for their lives.

Some of the guards grew impatient at this lengthy attempt at justice. They pointed to the enormous column of men and to the horizon and they too wasted their pleas upon the deaf ear of the wind. The officer sent two of the suspects back into the ranks and motioned for the other three to kneel. They knelt. He drew his pistol without haste and shot the first man in the neck. He stepped forward and shot the next man in the neck, the third man got to his feet and began shouting – his hands cupped to carry his voice better. The officer shot him in the chest.

As the column began to move again Jan-im-Glück noticed that the man next to him was covered in blood and tiny splinters of bone. He had been standing in the front row. Three soldiers pulled the executed men to the side of the road and the SS officer looked pleased as he threw an army greatcoat over the body of Broum who had caused it all. The prisoners were pleased that something had been decided, for as they walked the circulation began again in their cramped frozen limbs.

33

Two hostile bishops can be used to block the advance
of passed pawns since between them they control
access to all squares of both colours.

Monday, October 21st

I shook Harvey and his head revolved on his folded arms
until his cherubic features smiled at me sideways.

'Let's go,' I said. Harvey reached for the bottle of slivovice.

'Come along, Harvey,' I said and unlocked his fingers
from around the neck of the bottle. The old man blew his
nose loudly into a handkerchief that was covered with the
cross-hatching of meticulous darns.

The night was as clear as a planetarium. Once outside Harvey did a little gavotte and sang a tuneless, improvised song.

> 'You've got to escalate or even quantify
> For pre-emptive counter-strateg-y-y-y-y.'

The cross-country detour was softened by the independent suspension of the slivovice. When we turned on to
the sealed surface of the main road to Prague we began to
pick up speed.

'Did you hear all that, Harvey?' I asked.

'What do you think I am?' said Harvey. 'A goddamned
snooper?'

169

'Yes,' I said and Harvey laughed and belched and went back to sleep until I woke him up.

'Something ahead,' I said.

'An accident,' said Harvey. He was sober. Harvey could get drunk like some people cat-nap. There was a vehicle with its lights on and a red and white illuminated bull's-eye device was swinging in blurred arcs across the road.

I stopped the car. The man holding the signalling light was wearing a white crash-helmet, leather riding-breeches and a brown leather jacket with huge stiff red epaulettes. He tucked the signalling-lamp into the top of his black jack-boots as I wound down the window. He looked at us both, then said in German, 'Who is the owner of this vehicle, please?'

He examined the insurance papers and the documents the hire company had given me and then he went over each page in our passports and tugged at the binding. Behind him was a motor-cycle and sidecar and on the far side of the road a jeep-like vehicle without lights. The man in the crash-helmet took our papers over to the jeep and I could hear the music of the voices; the questions were vibrato and flute-like Czech, but the decisions were played on a Russian bassoon. The two men in the jeep climbed out on to the road. One was dressed in the very English style of a Czech army officer, the other wore the uniform of a Russian corporal. They held the papers on the bonnet of the jeep and studied them with a flashlight before climbing back in. Then – still without switching on its lights – the jeep reversed at full speed a matter of twenty feet. Then the corporal gave it full lock and roared up the road, taking the pot-holes in easy style.

'Follow,' said the man in the white crash-helmet, pointing after the jeep.

'Better follow it, boy,' said Harvey. 'There go our passports and in this country an American passport is worth more than a sixteen-ounce can of instant coffee.'

The jeep turned down a wide fire lane. We turned off the road after it; the rough ground hammered the suspension. Above us the tips of the firs almost closed out the stars as we sped down the long claustrophobic track like bugs in a hair-brush. Through the fire gaps I caught glimpses of rolling countryside, dusty in the white moonlight. The jeep slowed and in a clearing ahead a soldier in a brown anorak was waving a torch. It was a large clearing and a small farm fitted snugly into the corner of it. Inside the hollow feudal plan of the farmhouse a cobbled courtyard held half a dozen soldiers, some motor-cycles and a close-harmony quartet of dogs. I parked behind the jeep and climbed out of the car. A soldier pointed from the back seat of the jeep, the curved magazine of a Model 58 Assault gun peeping from his cradled arms. We obeyed his signal and stepped through the small door.

The building into which we were ushered had one simple wooden table standing amid straw, three hens moving sleepily and a staircase leading up to a landing where the army officer was standing. As we entered the doorway he said 'Good evening' in English. Harvey turned to me and began to relight his cigarette. Americans don't often relight an inch of cigarette so I watched Harvey's lips. He mouthed, OBZ[1] under the cloak of his cupped hands. I didn't nod.

The Czech army officer pointed to two grey weather-beaten chairs and Harvey and I sat. Harvey had thrown his match down and the officer went across to where it lay and planted a carefully polished boot on it. He looked at Harvey in an admonishing way that could have meant anything from 'I wish this was your neck' to 'That's how

---

[1] OBZ: *Obranne Zpravodajstvi* – security police of the army.

fires start'. The Czech officer had a face like a half-erased pencil drawing. His skin and his eyes were grey. His forehead was tall and his ears, nose and chin a little too long, like a wax doll that has been out in the sun. Behind him on the stairs was the Russian corporal intent on opening a bottle. The corporal smiled widely at us. 'English,' he said. 'What a wonderful surprise, *poputchik*.'[2]

'You know this guy?' said Harvey.

'Colonel Stok,' I said. 'Red Army Security Berlin.' Stok pulled down the front of his brown soldiers' summer-issue blouse with its corporal's insignia.

One of the Czech soldiers brought in four thimblesize glasses and a plain tin the size of a floor polish tin.

'Only the best we have for you, English,' said Stok. The Czech smiled a tight smile, fixed like a piece of sadistically applied sticking-plaster; the slightest relaxation might rip his ears off. Stok prised the tin open. 'Beluga,' he said, holding it out to me. 'They sent me Ocietrova at first but I said, "This is for our special foreign guest. We must have Beluga".' Inside the tin were the light-grey veiny spheres of caviare, almost as big as a tiny pea. Stok opened a packet of small wafers and spooned a large portion on to each. He poured the vodka until the tiny glasses brimmed above the rim. Stok held up a glass. 'To travellers,' said Stok.

'Let's make it motorists,' I said.

The Czech ripped the sticking-plaster smile off with a sudden unexpected jerk. He would do himself an injury doing that one day.

'To motorists,' said Stok, 'all over the world.' We all drank and as Stok refilled the glasses he said, 'Here in Prague they say that although the traffic police are communists the drivers are fascists, which would be all right if it were not that the pedestrians are anarchists.'

---

[2] *poputchik* (Russian): fellow-traveller (lit. and fig.).

Stok was bubbling over with gaiety. He prodded Harvey and said, 'I tell you a joke. The factory workers say that it's impossible to do anything right. If you arrive five minutes early you are a saboteur; if you arrive five minutes late you are betraying socialism; if you arrive on time they say, "Where did you get that watch?"' Stok laughed and spilled his drink. The Czech officer looked at him in shy disbelief and offered round his packet of Memfis cigarettes.

'Another,' said Stok. 'Capitalism is the exploitation of man by man. Yes? Well socialism is exactly the reverse.'

Everyone laughed and swilled down another drink. Harvey was getting quite merry. He said to Stok, 'Where do you get all these gags – *Reader's Digest*?'

Stok grinned. 'No, no, no, no – from people. That one about capitalism and socialism – we arrested a man for telling that this morning.' Stok laughed his booming baritone laugh till the tears came into his eyes.

Harvey said to me softly, 'Is he kidding?'

'Who knows?' I said.

The Czech walked under the oil lamp. Beside the huge gasometer of Stok he looked like a walk-on for *La Bohème*. He had a pair of soft leather gloves. He dragged them on and smoothed the creases around the fingers and flapped the cuffs backwards and forwards as he walked.

'Eat, drink,' Stok roared. The Czech began to shovel the caviare down like an automaton. Stok's word was law.

We munched into the caviare, spooning it on to the wafer biscuits.

'To Henry Ford,' said Harvey holding up his glass.

Stok was doubtful. 'If Henry Ford had been born in the Soviet Union, he would be a name I could drink to.'

'If Henry Ford had been born in the Soviet Union,' said Harvey, 'he would still be making bicycles.' Stok laughed.

Harvey lifted his glass again. 'Henry Ford, philanthropist.' The Czech officer asked what the word meant and

Stok translated it. Harvey belched and smiled. It angered Stok.

Stok said, 'You Americans are generous and we Russians are not. This is what you wish to say. Well, it is true that we do not give other nations gifts and bribes. We do not give them nuclear weapons. We give them very little money and very few guns. What we give other nations is encouragement. Encouragement and ideas. No amount of guns can fight ideas. In China, Laos and Cuba you have discovered that.' Stok nodded to emphasize the point.

'In China,' said Harvey, 'you have discovered it too.'

There was a moment of tension. I proposed an old Russian toast, 'To my wife and my girl friend and to the woman I have yet to meet. I carry gifts for all three.'

Stok slapped his thigh in delight. We drank.

Then there was a toast to sputniks, the inventor of vodka, detour signs wherever they may be found, Shakespeare, Howard Johnson's ice cream (twenty-eight different flavours), and that 'famous English cathedral, St Pancras'. Then Stok held his glass up and proposed 'Czechoslovakia'.

'To Czechoslovakia,' I said. 'The best beer and animated films in the world. Where abortion is legal, homosexuality no offence and a divorce costs only ten pounds.'

'I never know when you joke,' said Stok.

'Nor do I,' I said. I downed the drink and so did the others. Stok refilled the glasses and said, 'Death to the fascists.'

Harvey said 'Fascists', quietly. He looked around. 'There is a deal of semantic confusion around that word. A sort of implied, inbuilt suggestion that there is a special counter-productive network of every bully, crook, swindler, rapist and short-order artist in the world confronting the gentle, honest, helpful, long-suffering, scholarly underpaid remainder.' Harvey swayed slightly and tapped his chest violently. 'Fascism is something in here. Right here in everyone in the world.' Stok and the Czech officer were looking at Harvey in surprise.

Harvey held his glass of vodka and, drawing himself up to a position of attention, said in a slow, dignified voice, 'We will drink to the death of fascism in Washington, in London . . .' He waved his head at each town. 'In Prague and in Moscow.' He tapped the chests of each of us as he repeated the towns again. By a small error of judgement I got Prague and the Czech officer got London and Harvey had trouble finding a Washington chest until he remembered his own.

'Yes,' said Stok dully. It was a situation that well fitted the native land of Kafka and the Good Soldier Schweik. There were more toasts after that but Stok had lost a lot of his bounce.

'Disadvantageous confrontation,' Harvey pronounced when we were back in the car.

Two huge trucks rattled past towards the state factory, the huge painted registration numbers on their side almost obscured by dirt. I waited until the dust and dense black exhaust fumes drifted out of my headlight beams, then began the return trip to Prague.

'Do you think he knew?' Harvey kept asking me. 'Is that what he meant by *poputchik*?'

'Don't worry about it,' I said. He was dying to talk.

'You are right,' Harvey said and dozed lightly as we drove back to Prague.

There were still plenty of people around when I parked outside the hotel. Here and there were groups of people in heavy overcoats sitting on wicker chairs in sidewalk cafés and making like it was Paris. The fat man in the kiosk was selling hot dogs to hungry pedestrians who all had transistor radios or battered brief-cases; some had both. Through the trees, big red and green neon signs were flashing and making strange abstract patterns in the shiny sides of passing trams.

'Coffee,' said Harvey and I nodded, because I knew that he would burst if he didn't say what I already knew but would pretend to be surprised about.

The hotel foyer was full of brown aspidistras and green silver, the floor was visible through the holes in the carpet, and a gnome-like clerk was turning the pages of a vast dusty ledger. In the centre of the foyer were twelve pieces of plaid-patterned matching luggage, two small children in bright yellow sweatshirts, a woman in a grey woollen dress with a large leather handbag and a frail-looking man in large spectacles and a golf jacket.

'Cold, cold, froid, say, Janie – what's the German for cold?' He turned to us as we entered. 'Hey, look, will you tell this guy that we got to bath the kids and we need hot water? The hot water tap in the bathroom just isn't working at all. Will you tell him . . .'

Harvey looked faintly annoyed that he'd been so easily tagged as an American. He said in German to the man behind the desk, 'He needs hot water.' The clerk said, 'By the time the idiot has his luggage upstairs the hot water will be running.'

The tourist said, 'You tell him that back home the health authorities would close a place like this down – the whole place is filthy.'

Harvey said to the clerk, 'The gentleman's mother was born in Prague – he says it's like coming home.' To the American he said, 'The management regret the counter-productive difficulty with the thermostat but if you return to your room the water will be running hot in a moment or so.'

'And tell him not to ask for someone to carry his baggage,' said the clerk. 'He's not in the land of slavery now.'

The tourist said, 'We have just the same trouble with our furnace at home.'

Harvey said, 'I'm afraid the baggage porter's mother is sick. If you could possibly manage a flexible response in order not to escalate the difficulties.'

'Sure,' said the tourist and he began to explain the whole thing to his wife while I grappled with the controls of the ancient lift. The tourist's wife said to Harvey, 'What time do the stores close downtown?'

Harvey said, 'I'm a stranger here.' The lift began to ascend.

'They are going to fire me,' Harvey said when we were finally in my room.

I opened the bottle of Black Label that I had bought on the plane. Harvey bounced full length on the hard bed with a great rumble of straining metal, and sang a snatch of his song, 'You've got to escalate or even quantify,' but he was no longer really drunk.

'Official?' I asked.

'More or less,' said Harvey. 'The last time I went to see the Embassy Security Officer, he gave me a printed form called "The Foreign Service Retirement and Disability System". What's more they've got me working in the visa section with an FSO 8[3] leaning over my shoulder all day.'

'And Jindriska?' I said.

Harvey got to his feet and walked across to the wash basin. He selected a cake of soap from my open case. He sniffed at the soap. 'Lemon,' he said.

'Yes,' I said. He sniffed the soap again and then began to wash his hands. 'She wants to stay here in some ways,' Harvey said. 'But she will do as I ask. There's no point in my persuading her to go Stateside when there's no slight chance of the State Department giving her a visa.'

'You work in the visa department,' I said.

---

[3] FSO 8: Foreign Service Officer, 8th Grade. Grades go from 1 to 8. 8 is lowest.

'That's just what they are waiting for,' said Harvey. He continued to wash his hands with Freudian preciseness. '. . . Hell, they're right. I'm not complaining. I'm in the Political section, I've got no business falling in love with a Czechoslovak girl, but . . .' He pulled a face at me in the mirror.

'Maybe *I* should marry her,' I said. 'That would make her a British subject. Then you'll have no trouble.' Harvey wasn't in a laughing mood. 'Yeah,' he said and continued to wash his hands until they had all but disappeared into great white boxing-gloves of sudsy lather. 'You see,' he said quietly, 'that's why those two comedians tonight gave me the jitters. I don't know what I'd do if I found that Jindriska was . . . working for . . .'

'Harvey,' I said sharply, 'don't get so maudlin. Just treat your work like a mistress: don't tell your wife about it *wherever* she was born.' Harvey grinned. I said, 'Stop trying to wash your troubles away and come and have a drink.' I was wondering where I would get another friendly contact in Prague half as good as Harvey.

He rinsed and dried his hands a little awkwardly, smiled and took his drink. Down the corridor I could hear the American tourist saying, 'Jiminy, Jane, there are no darned curtains at the window. I wonder which room those two guys are in.' We heard him walk down the corridor in our direction. He stopped, then he called, 'Is there a fellow American hereabouts?'

We listened to him calling all along the corridor. Then I said to Harvey, 'Where do I meet this second guy who was in Treblinka camp?'

'Jan-im-Glück's brother,' said Harvey, 'they hate each other.' He went and stared through the dingy lace into Wenceslas Square. 'But if you want to see the death of your guy in writing he'll be in the Pinkas synagogue at ten thirty in the morning. That's in the Staré Mesto near the Ghetto section. There are several synagogues there but Pinkas is where he'll be.'

'I'll be there,' I said. I poured Harvey another drink. 'I wish I knew what Stok was thinking,' said Harvey.

34

COLONEL ALEXEYEVITCH OLEG STOK

Monday, October 21st

'It's not my job to think,' said Stok. 'I employ youngsters to do that; their minds aren't so cluttered up with knowledge.' He eased his boots off and flexed his toes in front of the stove. Stok could pick things up with his toes when he was a kid. It was a long time since he had demonstrated that. They had a different set of values nowadays and not only about prehensile toes.

'Veal I'm having,' said the Czech officer whose name was Vaclav.

'Anything you have,' said Stok. He wasn't a fussy man. Something hot to eat, something cold to drink and a bed – with sheets if possible – and he wouldn't complain.

'Veal and strawberries,' said Vaclav. Stok nodded.

'They are tinned,' said Vaclav.

'Good God, man. I'm not Tsar Nicholas. Just heat it and bring it in.' Stok wished he hadn't said 'God'; he'd probably given the wrong impression the other way now. Vaclav went out to the kitchen. Stok lit up. He relished the taste of Makhora. He made a point of smoking fancy things when he was talking to Westerners but the coarsest Russian tobacco was what he enjoyed most.

Vaclav came back with two plates of meat. He had prepared them himself; he hoped Stok would understand.

There was no chance of getting servants, they were all working in the factories. The last one went back to the farm, could you imagine that?

'Easily,' said Stok. 'The only place anyone gets a square meal in this country.'

'I wouldn't say that,' said Vaclav but he relaxed into a smile.

'You can say anything you want when I have my boots off,' said Stok. 'That's what I tell all my people. Anything I hear while my boots are off is off the record, privileged you might say.'

Vaclav slipped his shoes off. He wasn't sure if Comrade Colonel Stok expected him to do that but they were damp anyway. He turned them soles upwards near the stove. He didn't want them to lose shape, for even in Czechoslovakia where shoes were a major industry – the Gottwaldov factory that used to be Bata turning out thousands of pairs – even here there was no excuse for waste. He stuffed the inside of the shoe with strips torn from *Lidova Demokracie*.

'Don't use that,' Stok bellowed.

Vaclav looked down at the torn paper. He had torn Walther Ulbricht into two irregular halves.

'*Pravda* is what I use,' Stok boomed. 'It's best for boots, seems to draw the moisture out somehow.' Vaclav smiled; he knew he was being teased.

Stok ate his veal and drank the whole of his lager in one go.

'You don't waste time,' said Vaclav.

'I had one knocked over once,' Stok said, and roared with laughter.

Vaclav arranged the complicated system of dampers on the large white porcelain stove and the fire began to whine and crackle.

'You should come up to Berlin,' said Stok. 'It's damned comfortable up there, I can tell you. They know how to look after themselves, Vaclav, these Germans. Sometimes I wonder how we managed to beat them.'

'The Nazis?' said Vaclav.

'Oh we still haven't beaten *them*,' said Stok. 'The Germans I meant.'

Germans. What went wrong with Lenin's dream of a marriage between the Russian and German proletariat? The same thing that went wrong with lesser marriages – the image of illusion is shattered by the hammer of reality. It was all very well extending the hand of friendship to the German proletariat until you found them in Wehrmacht uniform burning down your village. It went wrong then. Stok nodded to himself.

'I hate Germans,' said Vaclav, 'I was in the RG[1] at one time.'

Stok raised his eyebrows as though he hadn't known. 'We knew what to do with Germans,' Vaclav went on. 'The lucky ones took just their hand-luggage and went across the border in cattle trucks. Three million of them. They were glad to go. That's what to do with Germans.'

'That's what we did,' said Stok. That's what we did wrong, he thought to himself. Lenin would never have agreed to the forced shift of factories and populations. Stok looked at Vaclav's pale eyes. He's a Stalinist, Stok decided. They all are, the Czechs. Pushing the Germans across the border was a piece of pure Stalinism.

'The Germans are the wild animals of Europe, whatever sort of flag they carry.'

'Germans are more complex than that. I could give you a dozen examples.' Stok pulled his fleshy chin. 'I am faced

[1] RG: Revolucni Garda. This was a punitive group formed at the end of the war, to kill Germans for revenge. They operated mostly in the German-settled Sudeten parts of Czechoslovakia. Around the RG, the STB (Statni Bezpecpost) or Security Police was formed. Vaclav is a member of OBZ (Obranne Zpravodajestvi) – the military version of STB.

with a problem at this moment, which is a matter of under-standing the German character, and quite honestly, Vaclav, I don't know whether I'm a fit man to do it.'

'A man that stormed the Winter Palace?' said Vaclav.

'Ah,' said Stok smiling, 'the number of times I have stormed that Winter Palace. But it's no good, my boy. We can't go on storming our Winter Palaces for ever. We must storm new Palaces every day, for that's how we are judged, upon last week's desk work, not upon the night I had a little too much to drink and couldn't see the danger involved in charging riflemen with a rake. We don't want any more Winter Palaces, Vaclav, as I told that young fool tonight; ideas will infiltrate the most heavily fortified citadel.' Stok nodded to himself and fingered the flesh under his chin as though trying to tear it free.

'Ideas travel,' Stok said. Both ways, he added to himself. He thought of the young tough that poor Major Bykovsky had for a son. He wore leather jackets and pointed shoes and sat in his room getting ancient American jazz records word-perfect. Some say he wrote to film stars in Holly-wood. There should be a dossier on him, Stok thought, but he'd known Bykovsky since 1926; it would break his heart. When he got back to Berlin he would inquire into the whole business again. These sort of sloppy sentimental inefficiencies were a betrayal of all he believed in. But still . . .

'All societies contain within themselves the germ of their own destruction,' Vaclav said.

'That's about it,' said Stok. Not very bright, Vaclav, Stok thought. Even his quotes from Marx were wrong. There was a radio playing near by. 'The Motherland hears, the Motherland knows.' Stok softly sang a few bars.

'Have you been often to the West?' Vaclav asked.

'Often,' said Stok.

'I too have visited the West,' said Vaclav. Stok sipped

his lemon tea and nodded. 'You lived in Bayswater — a district of London — during the war,' said Stok. Then he laughed a deep-throated laugh. 'Don't blush, my son.'

Vaclav was angry at himself for being even slightly embarrassed. 'I went to join the Free Slovak forces on the orders of Moscow.'

'That's right,' said Stok, still grinning. He knew all about Vaclav.

'I enjoy a trip to the West,' said Vaclav. He was like a defiant child, thought Stok. 'Why not, lad?'

'But the fundamental inequality is what spoiled any pleasure there might be in material things. How can there ever be justice there?'

'We are policemen, Vaclav; and policemen can't get mixed up with justice. It's bad enough being mixed up with the law.' Vaclav nodded but did not smile.

Vaclav said, 'But as citizens we must consider such things. Inequality in the eyes of the state is the overwhelming sin of capitalism and will be responsible for its downfall.'

'Sin?' asked Stok. Vaclav had the pale features of a young priest, thought Stok. Although he wriggled with embarrassment, Vaclav continued, 'It's what makes our Socialist Republic strong: the guarantee of humanity, fraternity, justice and prosperity for all. In the West the one-sided invidious processes of commerce which dominate the system inevitably end in militarism, in which truth and justice are suppressed by corruption.'

He's like my own young men, thought Stok, well provided with answers. Stok pushed his feet against the hot porcelain of the stove and watched the steam rise from his damp socks.

'Not to believe in justice because of corruption is like not believing in marriage because of infidelity,' said Stok. 'A system works according to the kind of people running it. Even fascism would be acceptable if it was run by angels. Marxism assumes that countries are run by men – corruptible men.'

'Are you directed to ask me questions?' said Vaclav. 'To test me?'

'May my right hand lose its cunning,' roared Stok, 'if I abused my job and your hospitality.'

Vaclav nodded. Then, putting on his formal voice, he said, 'Comrade Colonel, what was the purpose of the meeting tonight?'

'There was no purpose,' said Stok without a pause. 'It's just a matter of letting them know we have our eyes upon them.'

'You never intended to arrest them.'

He was a mass round-up man, this Czech. He'd use an armoured division to shadow a suspect and wonder why he vanished. 'He's not a black marketeer,' Stok said. 'He is an employee of the British Government. This is all a matter of probing gently. Like a brain operation, Vaclav. A hammer and chisel is all right for getting through the skull, but after that you have to be delicate.' Stok pronounced it as though the word itself was fragile.

'Yes,' said Vaclav. Yes, thought Stok. He'd never understand in a million years. He wondered how the Englishman would ever manage, had he an assistant of this calibre.

There was a long silence. Stok helped himself to some slivovice.

'He seemed not very . . .' Vaclac groped for a word, '. . . professional.'

'In our business,' said Stok with a chuckle, 'that's the very height of professionalism. In fact it wouldn't surprise me if the Englishman came just to show us that they are probing.'

'Probing what?'

'Why must you be so unfeeling, my boy? Just probing:

the situation, the way we work, the way we think. Some of us,' he corrected himself.

'I understand,' said Vaclav.

'Get a drink,' said Stok. 'You're like an unemployed undertaker.'

Vaclav said, 'I have some Western gramophone records that we can play.'

'My oath,' thought Stok. He was going to be another jazz fan like Bykovsky's brat. 'The Aitchison, Topeka and the Santa Fé' and 'The Dark Town Poker Club' were two songs that Bykovsky's boy sang in word-perfect American. What an awful idea.

'Ideas travel,' said Stok, 'and there is nothing any of us can do about that except listen.'

'Yes,' said Vaclav. He didn't fetch the records, to Stok's relief.

Stok curled his toes around the warm metal of the poker. Vaclav watched him without seeing.

'This girl the American wants to marry. *Is* she working for you?'

'No,' said Vaclav.

'Now don't lie to me, you young blackguard,' Stok said loudly.

'No,' said Vaclav quietly. They smiled at each other.

'You can like people,' said Stok, 'without going into detail.' Stok's mind roamed off to the old General Borg. A desiccated old Prussian general, who would have thought that one could have made a friend of him? At first he'd only visited Borg because he was going to make a play for the elder daughter. Stok tugged at his chin again. And now here he was, the younger girl's *Pate* – A fine old fuss there would be if that leaked out. *Pate* – an old-fashioned godfather instead of having her attend the *Jugendweihe* ceremony that the Communist regime held instead.

Stok thought of all those books and papers, room after

room of documents that the poor girl collated and dusted. He knew that flat as well as any place in the world; it was perhaps the only place he could really call home. The greater part of his time he spent in his office, devoid of anything that could be construed as even the simplest bourgeois comfort. As for the great ocean liner of a place in Köpenick that one of his staff had furnished to impress visiting officials, well! It gave him the shudders just to go inside the door. No, Borg's place was the nearest thing to a home.

It had been difficult to keep up with the old man or his daughter at first. This division, that army corps 'wheeling southward on the Don', 'counter-offensive pinching out by concentric attack'. He had only been a captain during the war, and that only for the final seven weeks. Old Borg always spoke to him like he had the ear of Stalin. Stok remembered an American tourist that he had questioned a couple of months back. When Stok asked him where he had travelled on holiday, the tourist said, 'I don't know until I develop the film.'

Stok had laughed at the time. He knew how true that could be. He had never known what he had done in the war until old Borg had explained it to him. The old man wouldn't last long, Stok thought. He didn't know what Heidi would do when he died. Heidi, thought Stok, *I* don't know what *I* will do when the old man dies. Stok wondered what the old man would say to the idea of him marrying Heidi. It was a stupid idea and Stok rejected it from his mind. His toes gripped the warm metal of the poker but it slipped from the grasp of his damp sock.

'German man,' said Vaclav.

'What did you say?' said Stok.

'You started to tell me about a problem you have with a German man,' Vaclav said.

'Did I?' said Stok. He must try and cure himself of this tendency to daydream.

'Oh, yes,' said Stok. 'Well, the problem is this. If you have a German Jew, what is he?'

'I do not understand,' said Vaclav.

'It's quite simple,' said Stok loudly. 'Is he primarily a Jew, or is he primarily a German? Upon that depends what he will do in a certain situation. That's why we keep dossiers, my dear Vaclav, to provide matter for anticipatory calculations. My guess is that if a man behaves in a certain flashy, unscrupulous way for long enough he will develop behaviour patterns of that sort, no matter what fantasy life he may lead about retiring to a monastery or university or wherever errant capitalist intellectuals end up.'

'So you have decided what to do?' said Vaclav.

'In these tricky cases I always do the same thing,' said Stok. 'I make my plans upon the basis of everyone being untrustworthy.'

Vaclav admired that solution. It had a certain historic ring to it. 'What about the Englishman tonight?' said Vaclav. 'Is he another problem?'

'English?' said Stok. 'No, no, no.' He poured himself another drink. He'd had too many, he knew, but one more wouldn't make all that difference. '"English" is a professional just like you and me. Professionals never make problems.' Stok curled his toe round the warm poker and lifted it.

35

In medieval times it was the aim of players to annihilate every opponent instead of checkmating the king.

Tuesday, October 22nd

TEREZIN. BELZEC. OSVETIM. GLIWICE. MAJDANEK. SOBIBOR. BERGEN-BELSEN. IZBICA. FLOSSENBURG. GROSSROSEN. ORANIENBURG. TREBLINKA. LODZ. LUBLIN. DACHAU. BUCHENWALD. NEUENGAMME. RAVENSBRUECK. SACHSENHAUSEN. NORDHAUSEN. DORA. MAUTHAUSEN. STRASSHOF. LANDSBERG. PLASZOW. OHRDRUS. HERZOGENBUSCH. WESTERBORK.

The Pinkas Synagogue is a tiny grey stone fifteenth-century building, its Gothic Renaissance interior bare of all furnishings except the carefully painted lettering.

The walls of the little synagogue seem grey, grey with an intricate pattern of tiny writing. Jammed together like the victims themselves, and written with obsessional clarity, are the names of the camps and of the dead. The grey wall stretches away like infinity and the lines of names are as hushed as a Nuremberg rally.

The man I had come to see tapped the stone wall at shoulder height. Under the scarred finger tip I read the name Broum. As his finger moved in the cool light the name was revealed, hidden, revealed and then hidden again as his hand rested over it.

'The best book is the world,' said Josef-the-gun, 'that's

what the Talmud tells us; the best book *is* the world.' His
hand made a curious turning movement. He looked at it
like a stage conjurer, proud that by opening his fist he
could make fingers materialize. He looked at the wall as
though he had produced that too from his sleeve and he
tapped it to show what a solid manifestation it was.

'I know what you are going to say,' said Josef-the-gun.
His voice sounded indecently loud.

'What?' I asked.

'Now you understand for the first t-t-t-t-time.' I could
see the tip of his tongue vibrate as he stuttered. 'That's
what they all say and, believe me, it sounds silly.'

'Is that what they all say?'

'One man said "I went to St Peter's before I understood
Luther and I had to come here to understand Hitler".'

'Understand,' I said, 'that's a complicated word,
"understand".'

'That's right,' said Josef-the-gun. He moved suddenly
like a trout in a patch of sunlight.

'What is there to understand? You write a numeral six,
put six zeros behind it and you call it "Jewish Dead". You
write six zeros behind a numeral seven, and you call that
"Russian Civilian Dead". You change the first numeral to
three and you have a symbol for murdered Russian prisoners. Five: it's Polish corpses. Understand? Why, it's
simple mathematics. Just name it as the nearest round million.' I said nothing. 'So you are inquiring about Broum?'
he said finally. He removed his wide-brimmed black hat
and studied the band of it as though he had some secret
message inside.

'Broum,' I said. 'Yes. Paul Louis Broum.'

'Ah yes,' said the man; '*Paul Louis* Broum.' He emphasized the given names carefully. 'That's the voice of offi-
cialdom all right.' And he gave a secret little smile, then
ducked and bobbed away like he thought I was about to

strike him. 'Broum,' he said again; he rubbed his chin and moved his eyeballs up into his forehead in an attitude of deep thought. 'And you saw Jan-im-Glück yesterday.'

'Harvey took me there,' I said.

'Yes, yes, yes,' he said still rubbing his chin. 'Well, my brother is an old man . . .' He stopped rubbing his chin long enough to make a little circular motion with his index finger. '. . . it happens to us all as we get older.'

'He seemed lucid enough,' I said.

'I meant no d-d-d-disrespect,' said the man. He ducked away again. I realized that some of the physical movements were to cover his stuttering.

'You knew Broum?' I asked.

'Everyone knew him,' said the man. 'People like that, everyone knows them, no one likes them.'

'What do you mean?' I asked. 'People like what?'

'Very rich people,' said the man. 'Didn't you know he was v-v-v-very rich?'

'What's the difference,' I asked, 'rich or poor?'

The old man leaned towards me. 'The difference between the unhappy poor and the unhappy rich is that the unhappy rich can change.' He gave an abrupt cackle. He shuffled across the cold floor and when he spoke again his voice echoed around the vaulting. 'When the Gestapo needed a h-h-h-h-h-headquarters here in Prague they chose the Petschek House – that's a bank – they used the vaults and strongrooms as their torture chambers. A symbolic dwelling for the tortures of fascism, eh? The vaults of capitalist wealth.' He dodged away waving a finger.

I realized why he was called 'Josef-the-gun' – it was because of this stutter. 'But why was Broum unpopular in the camp?' I asked to try to get the conversation back on my lines.

'He wasn't unpopular with the G-G-G-G-G-G-Germans. Oh dear no. They liked him almost as much as his money.

Almost as much as his money,' he said again. 'They did favours for money, you see, the Germans.'

'What sort of favours?'

'Any sort,' said the gun. 'The medical officer for a start, he'd sell all manner of lovely things for money. For the right amount of money he could c-c-c-c-cure you.'

I nodded.

'Cure you,' said the old man. 'You understand what I mean?'

'Yes,' I said, 'they could make innocent prisoners suffer or let guilty ones go free.'

'Guilty ones,' said the man. 'What a strange vocabulary you have.'

'Who killed Broum?' I asked. I wanted to cut through the man's rhetoric.

'International disinterest,' said the man.

'Who personally killed him?' I said.

'Neville Chamberlain,' said the man.

'Look,' I said. 'Who actually strangled him?' I added 'Broum', in an effort to avoid another long flight of philosophy and paradox.

'Ah,' said the man, 'strangled?' He put on his hat like a judge about to pass the death sentence. 'The instrument of death?'

'Yes.'

'It was a guard,' said the man.

'An officer?' I asked.

Josef removed his hat and wiped the leather band with a handkerchief.

'Was it the medical officer?' I prompted.

'Didn't my brother tell you?' he said. 'He knew.'

'You tell me,' I said. The man put his hat back on. 'A Landser named Vulkan. Just a boy. Not good nor bad.'

He walked out of the door into the bright sunlight. Beyond him greenery sprouted between the white gravestones like they were gigantic mustard-and-cress sand-wiches. I followed him.

'Did you know this soldier Vulkan?'

He turned quickly. 'Just as well as I know you. What do you think Treblinka was – a Conservative club?' He stepped away. The bright sunlight made his skin waxy and yellow.

'Try to remember,' I said. 'This is important.'

'Oh, that's different,' said the man. He rubbed his chin. 'If it's important, I'll *have* to remember.' He chewed each syllable carefully and presented the finished word on the tip of his tongue, anxious not to mutilate a vowel or drop an aitch. 'I was getting it mixed up with the trivia of half a million people being fed into a gas chamber.' He looked up at me, frankly jeering, and began to walk towards the street.

'This prisoner Broum,' I said. 'What had he done?'

'Done?' said the man. 'What had *I* done? To be in a concentration camp you need only be a Jew.' He opened the cemetery door with a howl of rusty hinges.

'Had he been involved in a murder?' I asked.

'Have we not all been involved?' said the man.

'A communist,' I said. 'Was he a known communist?'

The man turned in the doorway. 'Communist,' he repeated. 'You may have heard someone in a concentration camp admit to being a murderer and many agreed that they had been spies. A prisoner would sometimes even confess to having at one time – for a short while – been a Jew. But a communist, no. No one would ever let that word pass their lips.' He stepped through the door into the street and walked slowly towards the old synagogue.

I walked alongside. 'You may be the last chance of bring-ing a guilty man to justice . . .' I pleaded. '. . . a traitor.'

The man seized on the word 'traitor'. He said, 'What's that mean? Is that another of your special words? What was a man who threw a piece of his bread ration into the children's compound when it was against his orders as a German soldier to do so?'

I didn't answer.

'What was a man who would only throw his bread for money?'

'What about a Jew who worked for the Germans?' I countered.

'No worse than a Frenchman who worked for the Americans,' said the old man cockily. 'L-l-l-l-look at the clock up there.'

I looked past the Staronova Synagogue to where an ancient clock with Hebrew numbers glinted golden in the sun.

'This was the Ghetto,' said Josef with a sudden sweep of his hand. 'Every day I looked at that clock when I was a young boy. I was eighteen before I discovered that it was different from every other clock in the world.'

Around the corner rolled a huge, glassy tourist bus sparkling like a paste brooch. A resonant, amplified voice inside the coach was saying, '. . . wealth of sculptural decoration presages the High Gothic. This is the oldest surviving Jewish prayer-house in Europe.'

'That clock goes backwards,' said Josef, 'anticlockwise.'

Solemn tourists cocooned with camera straps disembarked. 'It keeps the right time but every twenty-four hours it moves one whole day in the wrong direction.' He tapped my arm. 'That's what will happen to *us* if we spend our days remembering the Vulkans, Broums and Mohrs instead of moving forward into a world that can never give birth to such people.'

'Yes,' I said.

Josef-the-gun eyed me curiously, wondering if I would understand him. He said, 'We must live out our personal decisions and beliefs, for this is what I was taught. When one day I face my God, He will not say to me, "Why were you not Moses?" God will say, "Why were you not Josef-the-gun?"'

Josef-the-gun moved away past the disgorged tourists like a mechanical toy with a broken ratchet. The American from the hotel called to his wife, 'Quick, Janie, get some movie. That's so typical: the old guy under the clock.'

36

Switchback: to return to original position in any
given sequence.

Friday, October 25th

Someone from the Meteorological Office should discover
why it is that every time I fly into London Airport it is
raining. Perhaps I should ask Mrs Meynard. The great
silver wings shone with it and the motors made the puddles
sag and blew them into weird branch shapes as the plane
trundled towards the apron. There was the click of seat
belts being loosened and that sudden nervous chatter of
relief. Somewhere near the front, efficient men in camel-
hair waistcoats were on their feet probing for plastic raincoats and bottles and cameras amongst the salvage of their
holiday.

The stewardess shook off her lethargic disinterest in the
passengers and in a sudden surge of new-found energy
began to assemble her own belongings. The motors gave a
volley of pops before the blades came to a final sticky halt.
Outside on the wet tarmac shiny loaders clustered around
their siege ladders. The great door of the city swung open.
In the corridors there was a last-minute scuffle as the engines
of war moved closer – so must the greedy eyes have watched
Bokhara. From their positions of power men in uniforms of
blue and gold appeared, still strapping together their documents and treasures even as the sack began.

'Nice trip?' said Jean.

'All right,' I said. 'I read a history book for most of the way – and tried to forget the taste of the meal.'

'That can be quite difficult.' Jean had wangled a Jaguar from the car pool. I eased myself into the leather-work as the driver nosed his way into London Road traffic.

'Been working hard?'

'I've been getting my hair done almost every day.'

'It looks nice.'

'Does it?' Jean turned her head and prodded at the chignon. 'It's a new man who used to be an assistant . . .'

'Don't tell me the secrets,' I said. 'It spoils the magic for me.'

'There's a few things that you'll have to check. There are a couple of letters that I've written undated so that you can see if I've done the right thing. The only appointment you have is lunch with Grenade tomorrow but I haven't promised.'

'What's he want?'

'It's some conference that O'Brien at the Foreign Office has arranged. I said you probably wouldn't be back in time. I've told Chico that he must go.'

'Good girl,' I said. 'Why does Grenade bother with those things? They only have them so that O'Brien can write those long reports and have his neighbours in East Anglia along as guest speakers at twenty-five guineas a time.'

'Grenade goes to them because it's an expense-paid trip to London where, as you well know, he spends all his time on draughty railway stations watching trains.'

'Well, that's harmless enough.'

'It's not harmless when you make me entertain him. Last November I had ten days ill in bed with influenza through standing around on the sloping ends of railway stations. All I got out of it was where to find an ashpan drop-bottom, steam accumulators and why they are still used, and the ability to recognize a three-cylinder locomotive by sound alone.'

'I think you are secretly rather proud of yourself.'

'If he wasn't such a nice old character I'd flatly refuse to go again.'

'Then you are offering to go again?'

'You dare.'

'It's all guilt, you know,' I said.

'What, the trains?'

'Yes,' I said. 'He was in Resistance during the war. He destroyed any number of locomotives. Now that they are being exterminated by progress he feels he has a task to protect and preserve them.'

'Are you giving him lunch?'

'Yes. You can come too. He likes you.'

'I'll book a table then – Chez Solange?'

'No, make it King's Cross Station Restaurant – he'll like that better.'

'Over my dead body,' said Jean.

I scarcely recognized the office. It had been repapered; it was lighter than I ever remembered it before. I was deprived of those hollow areas of paper which made a drumming sound when you tapped them, but Jean thought that was a good thing.

The gramophone music from the dispatch department hadn't changed, though, and the sound of Munn and Felton's (Footwear) Band sailing through the 'Thunder and Lightning Polka' was clearly audible from the second floor. I flipped the switch on my intercom. The duty dispatch clerk answered, 'Sir.'

'Angels Guard Thee,' I said and flipped the switch off.

'And the new window,' said Jean. 'You haven't mentioned that.'

'I noticed,' I said. 'And the Mother-in-law's Tongue is coming on a treat.'

'I've been oiling the leaves,' said Jean. 'It's a lot of trouble but the man in the shop said it was well worth while.'

'He was right,' I said. 'It looks great.' I turned over the stuff on my desk.

The trombone solo of 'Angels Guard Thee' filtered up from dispatch. 'Everything is great,' I said.

'I had a reply from Berlin Documents Centre[1] – nothing known there.' I grunted. 'I have one or two things though,' said Jean, 'if you'd like to see.'

'OK,' I said. 'In a minute or so.'

Jean walked across to her desk and the wet sort of light that envelops London on rainy days made a halo around her face as she stood near the window. I watched the movements of her hands as she picked up the large heaps of uncompleted work. Her hands moved without haste or irritation: like a skilled nurse or a croupier. She wore one of those shirt-style dresses with buttons and pockets and too many seams. Her hair was drawn back tightly from her face and her skin was taut and wrinkle-free like the very finest aero-dynamic design. She felt me looking at her and looked at me. I smiled but she did not smile back. She opened a small compartment of her desk. The dispassionate impersonal attitude made her very desirable. 'You are looking pretty damn sexy today, Jean,' I said.

'Thanks,' she said. She continued to process a heap of file cards and I read a memo from the Defence Ministry. Jean had that diligence upon which all intelligence work and all police work and for that matter all research of any kind must be based. Jean could sift through a haystack,

---

[1] BDC: an archive of Nazi Party Membership records saved from a paper mill at the end of the war.

find a pin and then look at it close enough to see the Lord's Prayer written on the head of it. It's that extra piece of effort at the end which makes the difference.

'Come on,' I said. 'You've signed the Official Secrets Act. You know that withholding information from me is a felony. Let's see what it is.'

'Now then,' said Jean, 'don't be all pompous.'

'There are days when I could cheerfully consign you to a job at the FO,' I said. 'You'd find out what pomposity really means there. They all talk like officers in English war films.'

Jean riffed through her desk. It was a large Knoll International desk that I had had to really fight the appropriations people about. There were so many drawers and sub-compartments that only Jean knew her way around it. She produced a limp paper file. She'd written 'Broum' in pencil on the front.

'There's no code name for him,' she said.

I lifted the key on the desk communication box. Alice answered, 'Yep.'

'Alice,' I said, 'can you let me have one of those code names we reserved for the Cuban Embassy people last year?'

'What for?' said Alice, adding a 'sir' as an afterthought.

'It's for those papers in the name of Broum that Hallam is supplying for us.'

'You want a depersonified one then?'

'No,' I said. 'We think there may be a real live Broum hanging around somewhere. If we have to make a claim to FO or HO for any documents on him it would make our position stronger to have an open file ready.'

'Death's-head hawk moth,' said Alice. 'I'll back-date the opening of the file a year ago today.'

'Thanks, Alice,' I said.

You couldn't fail by talking to Alice in terms of interdepartmental conspiracy. I told Jean the code name and the file date.

'Death's-head hawk moth,' said Jean. 'That's a terrible long code name. Do I have to type that out all through the file?'

'Yes you do,' I said. 'I have enough trouble with Alice as it is without asking her to change a code name after I've wangled one out of her.'

Jean raised one eyebrow. 'You're frightened of Alice.'

'I'm not frightened of Alice,' I said. 'I just want to work without unnecessary friction.'

Jean opened the brown folder. Inside there were some flimsy typewritten documents. Printed at the top it said 'Sûreté Nationale'. Under that, the typing was single-spaced and the open part of many of the round characters was clogged with dirt. I read it through slowly and painfully. It was a transcript of a judge's preliminary hearing of a murder case.[2] It was datelined Colmar, February 1943.

'Just an ordinary murder,' I said to Jean. 'This fellow Broum was a murderer?'

I read the transcript through again. 'The way this reads, he was about to get the chop,' I said. Jean passed me a photostat of a German Army document. The photostat was brown and spotted. It was a receipt for a prisoner taken from the civil prison in Colmar by a German Army major whose signature was like a piece of rusty barbed wire. 'Photo of Broum?' I asked.

'If you read it carefully you'll find you're holding a

---

[2] In continental trials the first stage consists of the judge examining the accused about his work, his health, his general ambition and demeanour in order to build a picture of the accused before hearing about the crime. In England the exact contrary happens. Any evidence about previous crimes or anything which might influence the jury against the accused is expressly forbidden. While the English system is clung to on the grounds of 'fair play', the continental system can in its way be more humane.

receipt for a prisoner *and* a dossier. Also notice,' said Jean, 'that the French documents have him as Monsieur Broum but the German one says *Obergefreiter* Broum. The Archives must have checked back to his desertion from Caen, and he probably had an equivalent army rank.'

'I noticed,' I said. 'Check Caen area court-martial records. The normal procedure is to return a man to his unit . . .'

'We know all that, darling, but his unit was no longer there and I can't find where they were. The group 312 Geheime Feldpolizei had vanished, as far as I can find, and Ross at the War Office says that the Germans didn't send their people back to the original unit.'

'He's an old know-all, Ross,' I said.

'He's been very sweet and helpful.'

'I hope you haven't been giving him access to our records,' I said. I shuffled all the stuff on the desk. 'Good, good,' I said. 'Send a thank you to Grenade through the usual channels, even though I will tell him tomorrow myself.'

'Grenade has got nothing to do with it,' said Jean.

'Didn't this come from Grenade?' I said.

'No,' said Jean. 'I got it.'

'What do you mean you *got* it?' I said. 'You climbed through the window of the Sûreté Nationale at dead of night, do you mean?'

'Silly,' said Jean. 'All I did was put a Green through to Interpol.'

'What?'

'Now don't blow your top, darling. I mixed it up with a lot of ancient old tat and even then I had Special Branch origin it.'

'Grenade will know,' I said. 'All Interpol requests go straight to DST.'

Jean said, 'If you sat over there for a couple of days –' she pointed to her desk: it was stacked with documents, dossiers, newspaper clippings, unsorted file cards, unanswered correspondence and IBM cards – 'you'd know how unlikely it is that Grenade or anyone else at DST is going to attach any significance to an Interpol Green. Even if they do, it won't have origined us. It origined Special Branch. Even if they dust it for fingerprints and find where it came from, so what? Is that what we're supposed to be doing here in Charlotte Street, working against Grenade?'

'Simmer down,' I said. 'It's not the role of this department to make political decisions. That's what we have Houses of Parliament for.'

'Which, coming from you,' said Jean, 'is very funny.'

'Why coming from me?'

'Because when Parliament wake up in the small hours of the morning bathed in sweat and screaming, you are what they are dreaming of.'

'Look, Jean,' I said.

'I'm joking,' said Jean. 'Don't give me the Dutch Uncle just because I made a joke.'

I took no notice. 'You only have the same sort of fear that everyone here has. That's why you are employed here. The moment we notice someone who isn't frightened that this set-up and all the other set-ups like it are a threat to democratic parliamentary systems – we fire him. The only way a department that pries can run is to admit of no elite which is immune from prying.

'On the other hand this is a Government department like all other Government departments; without money it could not exist. There is the danger that the people who allocate the money are going to feel that they should be immune from prying. That is why, every time someone is after my blood, Dawlish protects me. Dawlish and I have a perfect system. It is a well-known fact that I am an insolent intractable hooligan over whom Dawlish has only a modicum of control. Dawlish encourages this illusion. One day it will fail. Dawlish will throw me to the wolves. Until he does, Dawlish and I have a closeness in inverse proportion to our differences because that's his protection, my protection and, believe it or not, Parliament's protection.'

Jean said, 'And next week, schools, your lesson will be "Statesmanship for the under fives". And now back to Victor Sylvester.'

'Victor Sylvester,' I said. 'My God, did you fix with the BBC for him to play "Someday I'll find you"?'

Jean said, 'Good job I don't rely on your memory. You create an international incident by proxy. The tune was "There's a small Hotel" and it went out on the BBC Overseas request programme yesterday morning.'

'Good,' I said.

'Speaking of music, I've bought you a little gift.' She opened the vast filing drawer of her teak desk and produced a brown paper envelope. Inside was a twelve-inch gramophone record of Schönberg's 'Variations for wind band'.

I looked at it and wondered why Jean had bought it for me. I'd only heard it the previous week when I went to the concert with . . . Oh.

Jean was looking down at me like a protégée of Count Dracula. 'I was at the Royal Festival Hall that night when you had business with the celebrated Miss Steel.'

'So what,' I said. 'So were a couple of thousand other music lovers.'

'The operative word is lovers,' said Jean.

'Go down to dispatch,' I said, 'and borrow their gramophone.'

'I hope you feel guilty every time you hear it,' Jean said.

'I will if we break the gramophone,' I said.

The dispatch department had all put five shillings a week towards buying it. It was a good machine. Not like my hi-fi, mind you, but really good for a small mass-production job. The bass instruments came through with a fine clarity and the volume was such that when I started to play the record a second time Dawlish began to thump on the floor in complaint.

'Schönberg's "Variations for wind band",' I said.

Dawlish said, 'I don't care if it's the Treasury Choral Society. I won't have it in my office.'

'It's not in your office,' I said, 'it's in *my* office.'

'It might just as well be in my office,' Dawlish said. 'I can't hear myself speak.'

'You're not missing a thing,' I said.

Dawlish waved his pipe stem at me and at an armchair. 'It doesn't even make an irregular pattern,' said Alice to Dawlish. I sat down in one of the black leather armchairs. There was a great stack of newspapers on the table. I sorted through them carefully – finally selecting the *Herald Tribune*.

Dawlish said, 'The Liberal Party' to Alice.

Alice shrugged and put the finder card into the IBM 88 stacking a huge pile of cards into the sloping rack on the right. She switched the Collator on and there was a whirring noise like a piece of paper stuck into a cycle wheel. The cards piled up in the reject racks except for four cards which were flicked along the machine.

'Four,' Alice called like a croupier.

'Key-punch a finder card for the Tory Party,' said Dawlish.

'No,' said Alice. 'It will be far too many, it's not worth trying it.'

Dawlish laid a clean piece of paper on his desk, studied it, then produced a device from his pocket that looked like something on which the Spanish Inquisition would have taken out a provisional patent. He reamed the bowl of his pipe with it, shedding crispy, well-done pieces of

tobacco in a nasty little heap. 'Another way then.' He
prodded the detritus with his finger. 'Sort out the aircraft
companies who have given any sort of hospitality or
entertainment . . .'

'Not *aircraft* firms,' said Alice. 'This is missiles – we
need to have the engineering firms.'

'Where the Inland Revenue interim analysis shows over
£10,000 in the last fiscal year. We'll process any new firms
afterwards. It has to show up there somewhere, it's just a
matter of keeping at it. Put them on the machine later,
Alice, it makes such a terrible noise.'

Alice walked across to Dawlish's desk and carefully
folded up the tobacco ash into a neat envelope and put it
into the waste basket. Then she straightened the pen set
and went out. Dawlish said, '"Variations for wind band",
eh? Very nice. Very nice.'

I said, 'You know Harvey Newbegin – State Department.
Been in Prague for a few years now?'

Dawlish said 'Newbegin' softly to himself over and over
again putting the emphasis on every syllable I could have
thought of and a couple of syllables that didn't exist. Dawlish produced a shiny plastic pouch and began to pound
fresh golden tobacco into the bowl of his pipe. 'Trouble,'
said Dawlish quietly like that was another name that someone had asked him if he remembered. 'Trouble with a girl
in . . .' He looked up and, raising his voice and the stem
of his pipe in unison, he said 'Prague' quite loudly.

'That's what I said,' I said. 'Prague. I've just told you
that.'

'Told me what?' said Dawlish vaguely.

'Newbegin – State Department in Prague.'

'It's not worth arguing about,' said Dawlish. 'Why, we
could have got it from the records in a minute or two.
There's no need to take such a childish delight in remembering trivia.'

'I think we should employ him,' I said.

'No,' said Dawlish, 'I can't agree.'

'Why?'

'Four years with the US Defence Department before going to State Department. They will be as paranoiac as anything if we give him a contract.' I realized that Dawlish knew about Harvey being fired and had been giving our dossier on Newbegin a careful going over in spite of all that vagueness about his name. 'I think it's worth chancing it,' I said. 'He's a first-rate man.'

'What sort of money would he want?' said Dawlish cautiously.

'He's an FSO 3. I'd say he's making fourteen thousand dollars a year. On top of that he'll be getting Post differential, quarters, and whisky allowance . . .'

'Good grief, man,' said Dawlish. 'I know all that. That sort of money is out of the question.'

'But there is one thing that we can offer him that won't cost a bean,' I said, 'a British passport for his future wife – this Czech girl.'

'You mean naturalize Newbegin so that his wife will become British by marriage.'

'No, I don't mean that,' I said. 'Let Newbegin keep his US passport and give the girl a British one. It gives us slightly more control.'

'You've got it all worked out, haven't you?' said Dawlish.

'Yes,' I said.

'Do you think Czech intelligence have got a hold on the girl?' asked Dawlish.

'We would have to assume that,' I said. Dawlish pursed his lips and nodded. 'The State Department,' I said sardonically. 'They make me . . .'

'They have their own way of working,' said Dawlish.

'Finding out about things by not going near them?' I said.

207

Dawlish smiled.

'It's such a waste when they have such good people,' I said. 'Harvey Newbegin speaks Russian like a native.'

'Not surprising. His mother and father were Russian,' said Dawlish.

'You'd think the State Department would pay him a bonus for marrying a Czech girl. All they ever seem to do is order everyone to stand up and chant loyalty oaths.'

'It's a young country,' said Dawlish. 'Don't go on about it – what are you doing with that *New York Herald Tribune*?'

'It's a ladder,' I said.

'Good gracious, man, they have to go downstairs to be filed, don't tear them up – are you completely irresponsible? Suppose we wanted to refer to a new item for that date – by George, it's very long, isn't it?'

'It will go right from here to the window.'

'No,' said Dawlish.

'If you hold it there and pull the paper gently.'

'Remarkable,' said Dawlish. 'You must show me how to do it. My children would find that awfully good fun.'

'You need – keep going, there's lots more – you need one of these American newspapers really.'

'Look at that, it's remarkable,' said Dawlish. 'Open the office door and we'll see how far it will go down the corridor. Get Sunday's *New York Times* from my desk. That's even thicker.'

I opened the door only to find Alice standing in the corridor with an arm full of engineering companies' file cards.

'Don't drop your end,' Dawlish shouted. Then he looked up and saw Alice too.

37

A committed piece is one given a specific duty. It
often becomes the focal point of an opponent's attack.

Saturday, October 26th

It was a good thing that Jean had booked a table at Chez
Solange because it was packed tight. The tables were gar-
nished with tomato salads, slices of pâté and bowls of
fruit. Grenade made his way through the wild French menu
handwriting and kept patting his face with his table
napkin.

'. . . tool box in the Stroudly position,' he was saying.
'There probably aren't more than half a dozen of them on
the whole of British Railways, but we are boring Miss Jean.'

'No,' said Jean, equally gallantly. 'It's interesting when
you talk about it.'

Grenade dabbed his lips again before finishing the sole.
'That girl claimed to be an American citizen,' he said. Jean
pretended not to hear.

'I told you she might,' I said.

'Said you had stolen her passport and wanted to phone
the American consul.'

'Made a fuss, eh?' I said. I dipped a piece of bread into
the sauce — it's something I feel free to do in bourgeois
French restaurants.

'She wanted me to have a road patrol stop you and
search you.'

'Waste of time,' I said.

'That's exactly what I told her,' said Grenade cheerfully. 'I said if it's not true he has stolen your passport, then we will find nothing. If, on the other hand, it *is* true, he won't be walking around with it in his pocket.'

'She was happy about that?' I said. I poured the last of the wine. 'A lot of people like a fragrant hock with fish,' I said to Grenade, 'but I prefer something really dry.'

'This Pouilly-Fuissé is perfect with sole,' said Grenade. 'Happy? No, she was demented with rage. She broke a heel kicking Albert's shin.'

'You should have let her have a go at your central heating,' I said. 'Where is she now?'

'She told us that she wanted to go to New York, so we gave Pan-American airways a letter to say that if she was refused entry at Idlewild we would take her back. We never heard of her again.

'By the way,' said Grenade. He searched in every pocket of his serge suit. It had many pockets. He finally found a wallet crammed with tickets, cuttings, money and letters; from it he drew a photograph. 'Look at that,' he said, 'took it out of your friend Vulkan's pocket. Forgot to give it back to him.'

It was a photograph of eight men. One man wore the uniform of an SS major. He wore metal-rimmed spectacles and stood with arms akimbo, thumbs tucked into a shiny leather belt. He was smiling. The other seven men wore the wide-striped pyjama-like uniform of concentration-camp inmates. They were not smiling. Behind the group there were two cattle trucks and a lot of railway lines.

'Mohr,' said Grenade, tapping the SS officer, 'owns a lot of villas near San Sebastian. Terribly nice fellow, they say.'

'Really,' I said.

'One of those others looks a lot like your friend Vulkan, don't you think?' Grenade asked.

'These sort of old smudgy photos look like everyone,' I said. 'The man on the end looks a bit like you.' Grenade smiled and I smiled but we both knew that neither of us was being fooled.

'Well I'm glad it all worked out OK,' I said. 'I've just remembered something I must do this afternoon. Why don't you two go off and look at trains and I'll meet you for tea?'

'Miss Jean doesn't want to look at a lot of trains,' said Grenade with irrefutable truth.

'Nonsense,' said Jean. 'I'd love to come but I must get a warm coat from the office.' I smiled at her and, because Grenade was looking at her, all she could do was smile back.

Straight from lunch I went down into Leicester Square Underground station. There was a group of children sitting on the stairs with painted faces and rattling tin cans. 'Penny for the guy, mister,' they repeated dully to each passer-by. I bought a threepenny piece from them and phoned the office. The Charlotte Street number gave the usual out-of-order sound before clearing automatically and ringing GHOST exchange. I gave the operator the week's code: 'I want the latest cricket scores.' The operator said, 'Are you a subscriber to the service?' and I said, 'I have country membership of two years' standing – Mr Dawlish please.'

The operator was careless with the key and I heard him say to Dawlish, 'He's on an open line, sir, please remember.' I made a note of the time in order to report the operator. Then Dawlish said, 'Hello, you've finished lunch early, it's only a quarter to three.'

'They have phones on each table at the Caprice now,' I said, and there was a silence while Dawlish tried to decide whether I was really at the Caprice or sending him up. 'What is it?' he said finally.

'Gas and electricity at Samantha Steel's old flat.'

'Why?'

'Just a hunch,' I said.

'Well, since the Home Office are in on this there can't be any repercussions, so go ahead. I'll tell Hallam.'

'Good,' I said. 'Thanks.'

'We'll see,' said Dawlish. He was never enthusiastic.

Sam's white Alpine car was parked outside. I turned in at the gate and crunched my way up the path through damp brown leaves. There was a small panel just inside the Gothic porch – it said 'Flats 1–5'. Against the bell-push of number four it said 'Steel' in typewritten characters. At the foot of the metal plate it said 'Caretaker – side entrance'. I pushed flat four's bell and waited, watching the curtains. There was no movement. I went down the side of the house to where a cat was asleep on a crate of dirty milk bottles. I rang the caretaker's bell. A man in a Fair-Isle pullover came to the door. In his bright red face was a small cheap cheroot.

'I've gone out,' he said. He sucked in his cheeks theatrically a couple of times. I got my matches. Stepping forward into the protection of the door I lit one and held it up. The red-faced man reached out and held my wrist steady using a little more pressure than was needed as he pushed his big red face forward towards the match. He sucked the flame into the open end of the cheroot and without removing it from his mouth exhaled.

'Can I do for you?'

'Flat four,' I said. 'I want the key.'

'Do yer?' he said. He grinned. He put one hand on the frame of the door and crossed one foot over the other resting it toe down on the floor. 'And who are you – exactly?' He was still looking at his toe.

'Electricity Emergency Service.' I produced a small red

printed notice which said, 'Under the Gas and Electricity Boards Act 1954, the undersigned officer is legally entitled to enter any premises to which gas and/or electricity is or has been supplied to operate, service or disconnect equipment.' From somewhere inside I could hear the gentle lowing of cattle.

The Fair-Isle pullover read this through. 'You are holding it upside down,' I said.

'Regular joker, ain't yer.' He folded the card with his long dirty fingernails and handed it back. 'Got no keys,' he said.

'Well that's OK,' I said. I flicked the hollow door with my finger. 'It shouldn't be difficult to bore a hole through this jerry-built jungle. It'll just be another repair for you to add to the list. I'll get you to sign here to say you know the entry has been forced.'

'I'll sign nothin',' he said. He uncrossed his feet and moved his shoulder up behind the door. The door moved slowly.

'How would you like me to come in and disconnect *your* telly-palace?' I said moving in through his doorway, taking the initial weight of the door on my arm. 'I'll . . .'

'Nar then,' said Fair-Isle pullover. 'Don't throw your weight about. I'll get the keys to number four.' He went off mumbling into the deep, dark Augean confines of his flat. The speculator's face-lift had been more perfunctory here in the basement. Cobwebbed into a dark corner was an ancient house phone, a dusty pantry shelf and a shallow mahogany box with striped indicator flags marked, '1st bedroom, 2nd bedroom, dining-room, study and front door'. On the right was a room lit by the glow of a cocktail cabinet, the floor was bare boards and the only other furniture was a plastic covered armchair with a box of Black Magic chocolates on the arm and a twenty-one-inch TV that was saying, 'Making it one of the beauty spots of

Shropshire,' to the accompaniment of English documentary-film music and a picture of a flying buttress.

Fair-Isle pullover came jingling his way up the passage. 'Don't snoop in there,' he said, ''sall paid for.' He prodded me in the back and I walked along the side path and up the carpeted stairs to flat four. He pushed the chiming door-bell and twisted the key twice in the lock. I walked straight to the kitchen; but not so straight to it that it looked like I'd been there before. I looked at the big modern stove and sighed a long deep sigh. 'We might have guessed it,' I said. 'We've had a lot of trouble with these.' I turned to Fair-Isle pullover. 'You'd better get a big spanner, or I can let you have one, I suppose, and you'd better have overalls on or you'll get properly messed up. They look spotless these things –' I leaned close to him '– underneath they are crawling.' It had a good effect so I said it again – 'crawling'. That put him off his Black Magic chocolates for the afternoon. I told him that it was the caretaker's job to help, but he wouldn't stay. He had to go downstairs to do something that couldn't wait.

I started again. I went through each room very carefully. I didn't take the furnishings to pieces but I lifted everything up and put everything down. The scientific equipment was missing. A woman had been in the flat fairly recently – there was still perfume on the sheets and towels. There was a tin in the kitchen that wasn't quite rusty enough. In the front room there were some flowers that just weren't old enough and the water tank just wasn't cold enough. I looked in the mail-box behind the door. There was a small yellow telegram envelope that was unopened; inside the telegram said, 'Confirming Monday. Have enough money with you. John.' It was all so circumstantial even if Monday next *was* the day we were expecting to get Semitsa. This telegram could refer to any Monday and there were hundreds of Johns in Berlin.

I went to the back window and looked down. It was a fine example of a London garden: luxuriant concrete lawn. A gay section of trellis hid the dustbins. It was being tied into position with a length of string by Fair-Isle pullover who stood on a heap of sand and spent more time watching the back window than putting his finger on knots. I moved back from the window and jarred against the phone; when I looked into the garden again he had gone. I sat down in the only comfortable armchair. Outside, an ice-cream van chimed a twentieth-century carillon. Just suppose that no one had used the flat since the last time I had seen Samantha Steel? What else? A red-faced man in a Fair-Isle pullover doesn't like me coming up into this flat. When I am here he doesn't watch the front of the house – he watches the back of it. In any case he drags himself away from an afternoon of telly. Suddenly he goes back into the house.

Fool. Of course. I went back across to the telephone and followed the wire back to the junction box. I found a small freshly bored hole in the skirting board and as I stood up I took a Morley stretch Bri-nylon (11/12 fitting) full of wet sand across the side of the head. I knew what it was because the torn stocking and the sand were underneath me when I recovered consciousness.

It was a very well polished toecap that I saw first. It was prodding me not very gently in the chest. In an out-of-focus zone beyond I put together an image of a helmeted policeman and two men in belted raincoats. The shiny toecap said, 'He's coming round now – who did they say he was?'

I couldn't make out what the other voice said but Toecap said, 'Oh is he – I'll electricity him,' so I closed my eyes again. It was Keightley, the military liaison officer at Scotland Yard, who had them 'yessiring' and 'threebagsfulling' around. Jean had phoned Dawlish when I didn't turn up for tea. Dawlish had told the Yard to come and sort me out.

Two of the Special Branch people broke in the door of the caretaker's flat while I rubbed my sore head. On the TV, the quizmaster was saying, 'And now, for a stream-lined washing machine that will make every washday a pleasure. What is a secretaire?'

There was enough blue light for me to find a hard centre in the box of Black Magic. The two back rooms were papered with wallpaper that had a motif of motor cars and crash-helmets and contained some dark-stained furniture with coloured plastic handles, dirty underwear, three packets of cheap cheroots, two bottles of Dimple Haig, one sticky glass, an opened packet of Kraft cheese slices, half a pound of margarine and a packet of soft white bread slices with Wonderloaf printed on the wax paper. The tiny kitchen was almost empty, except for an enamel bowl full of dirty underwear and two large family-size packets of Tide. Three quart bottles of brown ale were standing in the sink among the tea-leaves. On the draining-board was a stack of books, some of them about enzymes.

On a slatted shelf in the airing cupboard there was a clean enamel bucket. The older Special Branch man with the shiny toecaps got it down gently. 'Smell that,' he said. 'Strewth.' I sniffed at the warm frothy contents. There was a strong yeasty sweet smell.

'A drop of good home brew,' said the younger man. 'Used to be able to pinch them for that – brewing beer without a licence.'

Toecap said, 'All beer and dirty underwear, this bloke.' and the young one made a joke based upon the alimentary canal.

I pushed past the two of them to get to the bathroom. The white tiles shone brightly in the pink neon light. Across the bath there was a door placed to make a table top; drawn up to it was an old kitchen chair.

'Naughty,' said Toecap behind my shoulder, 'very

naughty.' I looked at the layout; it seemed complete. There was a dark brown US Army surplus telephone handset, a small condenser and a wire leading to a pair of crocodile clips. Two GPO phone wires had been brought in from the back garden and could be attached to the handset or to a small Grundig tape recorder for amplification of the speech or recording the message. Also on the makeshift table there was a small Woolworth's reading light, a large scribbling-pad and four ballpoint pens stuck in an empty cream bottle. A do-it-yourself telephone-tapping kit.

'Makes me curious about the locked room,' said the young SB man. He took off his roll-brim hat and put it on a chair. I said, 'I'll want a copy of the phone bill and the phone agreement and anything else you can think of – this flat and number four.'

'We usually do the whole block in these sort of cases,' said the cop.

'Fine,' I said.

'We've got some Elastoplast in the squad car,' he said. 'You'd better get something on that cut.'

'What, Dave?' said the young SB man.

'I said I don't like the look of his head,' said Dave.

'No, nor do I,' said the young SB man. Then they both looked at me quizzically for a couple of minutes. Finally the young man went and gazed at the steel padlock with the same forensic dispassion. There was a little glass pea set in the fresh black paintwork at eye level. When Dave had decided that he was trying to see through it the wrong way he said, 'Well this won't do,' to the young man, who produced a large screwdriver from his raincoat pocket.

It took him only two minutes to rip the hasp out of the shoddy cardboard panels of the door. 'Landlords who rent places like this,' said the young SB man rapping the door, 'that's who we should be locking up.' He raised his foot and gave the door a great superfluous smash of his boot that caved in one panel. The older SB man stepped inside and switched on the lights. He whistled very softly to himself.

It was a semi-basement room. It got any daylight that could be spared by the architect and God between them through four small slots set high along one wall. There was some cheap lino of large black and white squares carefully cut to shape but not nailed down. Across the long side of the room was a low bench with two Anglepoise lamps and a gramophone. Draped over the bench was a huge red flag with a white circle and a black swastika in it. Upon the very centre of the swastika was a plaster cast of a rather idealized head of Hitler; around it were a few books, including a signed copy of *Mein Kampf*, some ceremonial daggers and a box of medals and badges. There were a few travel brochures and a notice that said: 'Hameln in Lower Saxony. Waffen SS Rally. Organized by the Welfare Association of former Waffen SS members. Members wishing to attend give in their names by next week. Friday 6.30 P.M to 7.30 A.M. Monday. Comfortable hotel, all meals, a visit to a nightclub and attendance at the rally: by air both ways £30 inclusive.'

Behind the gramophone there were some records put out by an American company which gave the connoisseur a chance to hear Hitler speeches and Nazi bands in hi-fi, even if they couldn't afford the thirty quid for the SS week-end. There were well-framed official portraits of the Nazi leaders on the wall, including one of the American Führer in his home-made uniform. There was army surplus seating stacked around the walls and a large very well-cleaned blackboard on an easel. Propped on the mantelpiece there was a piece of wrapping-paper with a message pencilled on it: 'Tell Mrs Wilkinson there will be a big turn-out Thursday. Please order extra pint milk.'

'Very nice,' said the Special Branch man. 'Did you expect that something like this was going on?'

From the next room I heard the telly shout gaily, 'No, I'm afraid that it's a writing-desk with pigeon-holes for keeping papers, but thank you, Mrs Dugdale of Wolverhampton, for coming along and being such a good sport . . .'

I said, 'I heard him say, "Take that, Yid," when he hit me.' The Special Branch man nodded. The telly gave a great fanfare of trumpets and a descending series of chords on an electric organ.

38

A player who uses two moves to do something possible
in one is said to have 'lost tempo'.

'Very pretty that plaster looks,' said Jean.

'You have the flat well covered?' I asked.

'Policemen are standing on top of policemen,' said Jean.

'And the white Alpine?'

'Give them a chance,' said Jean. 'The police have got plenty of things to attend to without interfering with the march of Crime.'

'Didn't you tell them it was urgent?'

'So is the Armistice Sunday rehearsal.'

'But if they do stumble over anything, put it on the teleprinter,' I said. 'It could be important.'

Jean smiled.

'I'm serious,' I said.

'I know you are,' said Jean and she smiled again. It was so difficult getting even the simplest things done.

'Keightley says you don't want any D notices[1] sent out,' said Jean.

'Keightley,' I said. 'He loves them, doesn't he? Sometimes they do more harm than good – they can attract attention when no one would have bothered.'

---

[1] D notice: instruction from Government to newspapers, etc.

'It's probably getting quite a splash – Nazis and all that – it's good circulation-building stuff,' said Jean.

'Sometimes you talk like a Press Officer,' I said. 'Just as long as I'm left out of it, they can have their swastikas across the front page. It could even help in the long run.'

'You mean catching the man who socked you on the head.'

'Socked is a good word,' I said.

'Special Branch are throwing a Section 6[2] at him.'

'Good,' I said. 'That'll learn him to sub-let.'

'Who is he?' asked Jean.

'No idea,' I said, 'but he's certainly not fussy who he rents his rooms to.'

'What do you know about him?' she coaxed.

'An agent for the United Arab Republic who carries a flick-knife.'

'How do you know that?'

'He had to use something to spread the marge on his processed cheese sandwiches,' I said.

'I mean the UAR,' said Jean.

'I'm guessing,' I admitted, 'but Samantha Steel is undoubtedly on the payroll of Israeli Intelligence, whatever private shenanigan she may be up to with Vulkan. This character downstairs had done a neat job of tapping her phone right where it did the most good, so I'm guessing that he's a conscientious anti-Semite and maybe Egyptian Intelligence.'

'It's a terrible over-simplification,' Jean said.

'You're right,' I agreed, 'but it's all I've got.'

'What about the neo-Nazis?'

'I'm no expert,' I said, 'but I don't see those boys running away without their baubles.'

'That's ingenious,' she said. 'You are probably right,' and gave me one of her rare admiring looks.

---

[2] Section 6: *see* Appendix 6.

39

In Burma and Japan a general is the piece we call a
queen, but in China and Korea a general is the piece
we call a king.

Saturday, November 2nd

Pankow is a sort of Hampstead of East Berlin, comfortable
and bourgeois; the dogs wear little overcoats and the kids
play without shouting. Fist-sized shrapnel holes pock-
marked the grey face of number 238 and as I mounted the
wide stone staircase, the smell of *Eisbein* and fried onion
walked alongside me.

Apartment number 20 was on the top floor. The small
brass plate said 'Borg' in the Gothic script. Ex-Wehrmacht
General Borg lived here.

A young girl answered the door. She wore one of those
short frilly-edged aprons that maids wore in the 'thirties.
The room she showed me into was over-decorated but
under-furnished. A fierce-looking woman with her hair
drawn tightly back into a bun glared out of a plain oval
frame like a tiger leaping through a hoop. Under the large
photo sat Colonel-General Erich Borg, Commander Panzer
Group 'Borg'.

General Borg was a tall thin man. Sitting low in the
ancient armchair, all knees and elbows, he looked as delicate as a stick insect. His face was very white and very
wrinkled like a big ball of string, loose to form eyes and

mouth. Under his right hand was a pad of paper and an ancient fountain pen. With his left hand, he raised a tall glass of lemon tea to his face and sipped secretively at the almost transparent liquid.

At Borg's feet there was a large tray of sand in which the contours of central Belgium had been carefully moulded. Tiny strips of coloured wood and bright drawing pins were meticulously arranged in neat rows. I walked across to the sand tray and studied it. 'Four-fifteen P.M.,' I said.

'Good,' said Borg. The girl was watching us both.

'Just before the British artillery start to fire double-shotted charges.'

'You hear that, Heidi,' said Borg. He prodded the sand around the rectangle of Hougoumont with a thin length of cane. 'Ney's cavalry are cantering up there towards the British guns, five thousand horsemen and not a grain of intelligence between them. Just shouting "Vive l'Empereur!" and hoping for the best. When they reach the guns, they don't know what to do, do they?'

The General stared up at me. I said, 'You can't spike guns without spikes or drag them away without horses and harness.'

'They were stupid,' said Borg. 'Hammers and nails would have done it.'

I shrugged. 'They could have smashed the sponge staves,' I said.

Borg beamed. 'You hear that, Heidi?' He nodded. 'The sponge staves, yes, that would have been something.'

'I learned about the battle from an artilleryman,' I explained.

'No better way,' said Borg. 'Artillery was the key to the battle. Read *War and Peace*. Tolstoy knew it.'

'Napoleon should have known it too. He was an artilleryman.'

'Napoleon,' said Borg. He prodded deep into Rossome Farm until the cane bent and flipped a small red cube across the room in a spray of sand. 'Vollidiot,' snarled Borg as the Emperor disappeared under the sideboard.

'I'm glad he was,' I said, 'or Waterloo Station would be in Paris.'

'What would you care?' said Borg.

'I live behind Waterloo Station,' I said.

Borg rapped me across the ankle with his cane. I cowered back to avoid the next blow. Borg smiled icily. It was a Prussian gesture of friendship. The girl made a seat for me by moving a map of central Poland, a book of medieval armour and *Der Deutsche Soldatenkalender* for 1956. I sat down.

'Droll men, you French,' said Borg.

'Yes,' I said. The walls of the garret room sloped like a tent and the big windows fitted into it like an awning. Along the window stood a line of potted plants, which shone in the artificial heat. Condensation dribbled down the glass, making an impressionist painting of the view across the dusty roofs.

'Heidi,' the general's voice was high and clear.

His daughter brought me a small cup of strong coffee. She watched me as I tasted it and asked if I was too hot.

'No,' I said. I felt a trickle of sweat move down my forehead and sweep across my cheek like an errant tear.

She laughed. 'Papa feels the cold so,' she said.

'I understand,' I said. I polished the condensation from my spectacles again.

'What's that?' said the general in a loud voice.

'You feel the cold,' I said.

'I *am*,' said the general.

'What?' I said.

'I am old,' he said patiently. The girl patted his shoulder and said, 'Of course he doesn't think you look old.' She spoke to me. 'Papa lip-reads; you must face him when you speak.'

'Then he must be a fool,' said the general.

I looked out through the dribbly glass; there was a banner on the building opposite. 'Peace must be armed', it said.

General Borg said, 'The passing of time is like the passing of two trains; when you are young the other train is travelling at almost the same speed. Time hangs upon your hands. You grow older, the train gains speed slightly. Then it's rushing by faster, faster and faster until it's gone and you see the green countryside again.'

'Yes,' I said. The general gazed at me intently. 'I'm trying,' he said very slowly. 'I'm trying to remember you. Were you in the war with me?'

'Yes,' I said. 'I was on the other side.'

'That was wise,' he said and nodded in admiration.

'It's about your collection of regimental diaries,' I said.

The general's face brightened. 'You are a military historian. I knew it. We have a large collection of records – are you interested in cavalry uniform – that's my principal interest at present – I am writing an article.'

'It's a simple enquiry,' I said. 'It's a Wehrmacht unit that was evacuating people from a concentration camp. I'd like some details of the personnel.'

'Heidi will look it up for you,' said the general. 'That's a very straightforward matter. We have a roomful of unit records. Eh, Heidi?'

'Yes, Papa,' she said. 'I can hardly get in it to clean,' she said to me. I gave her the details written on a slip of paper.

'I'm sure you manage,' I said. She pattered off to get the files.

The general sipped his tea and talked about nineteenth-century cavalry uniform.

'You came on the advice of Colonel Stok?' the general said.

'That's right. He said that you have one of the best collections of military records in the whole of Germany.'

The general nodded. 'Fascinating man, Stok,' said the general. 'He has let me have some most interesting Red Army historical material, most interesting. Very kind. It's rare, you know.' I wondered whether he meant Red Army history or kindness.

'Have you lived here very long?' I said finally, to break the silence.

'Born in this very building,' said the general. 'And I'll die in it. Used to have the whole thing when my father was alive. Now we are just a small apartment in the roof, eh? All under Government control, the rest of the building – still people are homeless, can't have everything, mustn't complain.'

'Have you ever thought of living in the West?' I asked.

'Yes,' he said. 'My mother was very keen to move to Köln. That would be about 1931, but we never went.'

'I mean since the war. Why do you live here in East Berlin since the war?'

'My old friends cannot visit me,' he said.

I pursed my lips to reform the question, until the general's quiet simper told me he had answered it.

'Do you do any work for Bonn?' I asked.

'For those ruffians – certainly not.' He tapped the arm of his chair as though his fist was a gavel. 'For a decade after the war, I was too much of a Nazi for any decent German to take coffee with me.' He put the words 'decent German' into roughly tongued inverted commas. 'My only conversations were with two colonels from the American Army Historical Department. We fought all the way from the Bug to the Volga together. Do you know . . .' He leaned forward confidentially. '. . . every time we did it, I made less mistakes. I tell you, a couple more visits from those Historical Department colonels and I think I might have *taken* Stalingrad.' He laughed a humourless treble laugh. 'For a whole decade I was too much of a Nazi for the German politicians.' He sipped his tea. 'Now I'm not enough of a Nazi for them.' He laughed again, without humour, as though he had made that joke and laughed at it many times before. Heidi came back with a bundle of large brown envelopes.

'Do you know Colonel Stok?' she asked me.

'My girl's rather taken with him,' said the general and laughed as heartily as he could laugh without shattering into a million fragments.

'She could do worse,' I said, wondering if I had been guilty of impropriety.

'Exactly,' said the general.

'Are you a colleague of Alexeyevitch?' the girl asked.

'I'm a business rival,' I said.

She laughed and set before me the big envelopes that contained more details of the life of Broum.

40

A king cannot be captured nor need it be removed
from the board. It is enough that the king is put into a
position from which it cannot escape.

Sunday, November 3rd

I had begun to look upon Berlin as my home. The room
at the Frühling was warm and comfortable. I went to bed
early, got up late and let the morning trickle through my
fingers like silver sand. The sky was heavy and the air
unnaturally warm. I bought a copy of *Time* and a *Daily
Express* at the U-bahn station across the road and sat down
in Kranzlers at a table from which I could see the whole
width of the Kurfürstendamm as far as the Gedächtniskirche. The waitress brought me a *Kännchen Mokka*, soft-
boiled eggs, marmalade, bread and butter and I even
remembered that Karlsbader Hörnchen were croissants.

There was plenty of traffic on the Ku-damm. Taxis full
of sightseers were cruising, huge furniture vans with trailers were leaving for long trips and double-decker buses
were making short ones.

Oddly enough, Berlin is one of the most relaxed big
cities of the world and people were smiling and making
ponderous Teutonic jokes about soldiers and weather and
bowels and soldiers; for Berlin is the only city still officially
living under the martial command of foreign armies and if
they can't make jokes about foreign soldiers no one can.

Just ahead of me four English girls were adding up their holiday expenses, and deciding whether the budget would let them have lunch in a restaurant or if it was to be Bockwurst sausage from a kiosk on the Ku-damm and eat it in the park. Beyond them were two nurses, dressed in a grey conventual uniform which made them look like extras from *All Quiet on the Western Front*. And all around me people were munching and drinking. A white-faced man on my left was working out all the permutations on coffee, doughnuts and tiny glasses of Steinhäger, and drinking in the scene around him like any moment he might wake up in Siberia.

I had the table all to myself until the Science section of *Time* and my fourth pot of coffee. The man asking if he might sit there wore a very clean white shirt and a suit made from wool and mohair cut with that sort of high roll lapel that Continental tailors think is English. He cleared his throat and adjusted the set of his necktie.

'If I sit at one of the outer tables I shall get wet when the rain begins,' he apologized. I nodded but he was anxious to talk.

'The crops need it,' he said. 'If you live in a town, it's difficult to understand how welcome it is in the country.' He smiled and drank his coffee.

'If you live in *this* town it's difficult to *get* into the country,' I said.

He smiled. 'It's a little . . .' He paused. 'Claustrophobic. Is that right?'

'In every possible way,' I said. There was a distant roll of thunder, very faint, like a mouse walking across a drum. One of the English girls said, 'We won't be able to picnic if it rains.' The man with the white face was trying to get doughnut sugar off his tie and the German nurses were surreptitiously easing their shoes off.

'They come from the Baltic Sea at this time of year,' said

my companion. One of the English girls said, 'We'll just sit in the Mini and eat it.'

'You get a cold front,' said my companion. 'Low pressure zone – moves quickly, brings the rain. See that cu-nimbus; when that's gone, it'll be fine again.' The thunder sounded again. He nodded his head knowingly; he was the only mortal in on the secret. He raised his long, carefully mani- cured hand without looking to see where the waitress was. She initialled his bill with a hasty flick of the pencil, pre- sented it to him on a saucer while confiscating the sugar with the other hand.

'Thunder,' he said. 'Sinister sound, eh?' I nodded. He said smiling, 'My mother used to tell me that was God having his coal delivered.' The slow drum-roll of thunder sounded again. I sipped my coffee and watched him as he finished writing something on the back of the bill. He placed the bill face-down on my saucer. The pencilled message was light grey on the poor-quality paper. It said, 'I will attend to ALL. Go to zoo NOW. See KING.' The final word in each sentence was underlined three times. The message existed for only a few seconds because I lowered my cup quickly on to it. The dark coffee spilt in my saucer, defiling the coarse fibres into a soggy brown pulp. I twisted my cup and shredded it.

'It sounds just like coal; you must admit it,' said the man.

'Just like it,' I said. The thunder sounded again, a little closer this time, and he raised his hand as though he had demonstrated the sound to jog my memory. As I got up to leave, he gave a stiff little bow of the forehead and backed into the table behind him. If he hadn't tried to save things it would have been all right, but his hands hit the tall pot of coffee. There was a howl of pain as the scalding coffee swept across the table. I could hear the weather man's voice apologizing in the verbose formalities of German middle-class conversation and the doughnut man's staccato Berlin accent with its consonant-heavy exactness. A number 19 stopped at the lights and, as I got aboard, I glanced back to see them still at it. The weather man was talking and bowing like a well-made puppet and the doughnut fancier was standing awkwardly holding his steaming trousers away from his tender thighs. The English girls were giggling and one of the nurses was groping under the table for her shoe.

Ahead of me was Monte Klamott,[1] a hill of the Tier-garten made from old flak towers and concrete shelters that were too solid to eradicate; across the top of them the storm clouds were clamped like a stainless steel saucepan-lid. I got off the bus almost immediately and clapped down two marks at the zoo's main gate. The damp air held musky scents and there was a restless movement of animals. I could see the bison kicking at the ground and somewhere over on the right an elephant was trumpeting. There were a few moments of intense sunshine that photographed the shape of the trees on to the light-brown earth. Some visitors were moving towards the enclosures to avoid the rain. It was hard to believe that this was the heart of the city, except when modern concrete buildings leaned over the trees to reflect themselves in the bright blue ponds. Now that the rain was no longer in doubt, the wind had climbed down from the trees and chased the last crisp, brown leaves around in circles across the gravel paths. A bison rumbled its low threat from somewhere near at hand.

I saw Vulkan, dressed in a heavy green trenchcoat. He leaned against the waist-high railing in a tense posture. There was no one else in sight. 'All right?' Vulkan said and looked behind me in case any one was lurking in the bushes.

---

[1] Klamott: ancient rubbish.

'Relax,' I said. 'It's all right.' A large leaf, as crisp and brown as a piece of breakfast cereal, spun in the wind and settled in Vulkan's hair. He brushed it aside angrily as though it was a prank that I had played on him.

'You got rid of your tail?' I felt the impact of a warm raindrop.

'He got a lapful of *Pfannkuchen* and scalding coffee,' I said.

Vulkan nodded. He ran a finger around his lips as though deciding whether to grow a beard. We walked towards the pool marked 'Flusspferdhaus'. The moisture drew a fresh astringent smell from the grass, which was still dry enough to cling on to the tiny tear-drops of rain.

'There has been such a lot of trouble,' said Vulkan. We stopped in front of the still blue water. 'They have taken four of Gehlen's people in the last week.'

'Who have?' I asked. A large raindrop hit the water and expanded until it disappeared.

Vulkan shrugged. 'I don't know. STASI or Stok's people, someone in the East has taken them. They say it's all your fault.'

'That's what they say, is it?' The surface of the water heaved and exploded into a vast shiny grey-mottled mound.

'They say you talk too much with Stok,' said Vulkan. The hump split into two as a vast hippopotamus throat opened.

'Those bright boys,' I said. 'They are so keen for applause they disembowel themselves as an encore, then they want to sue the audience for damages.' There was a noise like a U-bahn train and the hippo sank under the water.

'Two of the people they have lost have been tailing you,' said Vulkan.

'What am I supposed to do?' I said. 'I didn't ask them to tail me.'

I noticed how spruce Johnnie's clothes were, from the crisp white collar to the highly polished Oxfords that had picked up a layer of grey dust from the path. Even as I watched, a perfect circle of black shiny leather appeared on the toecap of one shoe. A bright geometrical shape that sagged gently and warped into an oval until the blob of rain drew a black line down to the welt of the dusty shoe and fell into the ground, a grey sphere of water.

Vulkan leaned forward with his eyes wide open. I realized for the first time that he might be frightened of me. 'You didn't give them to Stok?' he said. 'You wouldn't do that, would you?'

'Wouldn't I?' I said. 'I only wish I had thought of it.'

Vulkan smiled nervously and twisted a cigarette in his dry lips to prevent it from sticking. He produced a gold lighter and put his head down inside his trenchcoat like a canary going to sleep. He lit the cigarette and tossed his head well back and sucked air in like an addict. 'I suppose you think that Gehlen's people are expendable,' he said.

'You are damn right they are,' I said. 'That's what they get paid for: knowing this town well enough to take risks and get away with it.' He nodded agreement. I went on, 'My boys have an entirely different job which is to sink into their environment like butter into hot toast and then not move whatever happens – especially for juvenile little pranks like this one. Gehlen's mob can't think of any greater ambition than kidnapping the premier of the USSR. Our aim is to have him working for us.'

Vulkan laughed nervously but I think he got the idea. He said, 'You knew that someone was tailing you then?' There was the screech of an animal somewhere nearby. I buttoned up my raincoat collar and a large raindrop hit Vulkan's cigarette with a loud hissing noise.

'Listen, Johnnie,' I said. 'One of my great advantages in this business is that I look a little simple-minded; but I don't stop there; I *act* a little simple-minded; I'm crafty, nasty, suspicious and irritable. I look under beds and I rap lamp-posts for hollow compartments. The moment that you think that you know who your friends are is the moment to get another job.' The rain began a slow disconsolate tattoo and far in the distance the thunder was soft and muffled.

'They were sold,' said Johnnie, 'those men.' The circles from the raindrops were describing more and more complex designs on the water.

'Sold or bought,' I said, 'what's the difference?' The hippo yawned out of the pool again, snorting and blinking and rolling buoyantly so that little waves splashed near our toes.

'They were men,' said Johnnie. 'That's the difference. They weren't packets of detergent. They were men; with wives, sisters, kids, debts, worries. And they suddenly aren't going to see them any more. That's the difference.' Small areas of earth under the trees were still dusty and grey, while elsewhere the ground became a rich dark brown as the rain beat it gently all over like a goldsmith's hammer on foil. The animal screeched again and from the same building there came a hard, almost human cry that could have been joy or pain or just something that wanted to have its voice heard.

'It's no good letting personal feelings wreck you up, Johnnie,' I said gently. 'I know how you feel . . .'

'He was such a good man,' said Johnnie. The rain was falling hard enough to make tiny rivers in the gravel, and the rough bark of the trees was wet and shiny and so was Johnnie's face.

'Keep a foot in each camp, Johnnie,' I said, 'and they'll build the barbed wire through you,' and Johnnie nodded and the rain dripped from his face.

41

Strong square: one placed well forward, secure from attack and firmly under control.

Monday, November 4th

German merchant banks are more conservative in their methods than their London counterparts but they still return a generous measure of profit. One small bank near the Ku-damm can hardly fail; it is backed by the Bank of England and is used by three British Intelligence groups as a clearing house for information. For obvious reasons each unit keeps to its own codes. My message only said, 'HOLD FIXED INTEREST ANNUITIES'; but to Dawlish it meant:

Further to your instructions, the Gehlen Bureau has been thoroughly penetrated by Soviet Intelligence Groups in East Berlin. The agents now in Soviet hands will have had the list of 'tactical objectives' with which we provided them last month. There is good reason to hope that the Russians will not realize that this information has been deliberately planted upon them by us.

I had also arranged a call from the bank to Hallam's office. Hallam was waiting at the Home Office for the phone to ring.

'You've made me late for lunch,' said Hallam.

'Well, that's too bad,' I said. His voice was crystal clear. The arrangement was that I merely had to say the code

236

words 'Action imminent' to tell the Home Office that I was expecting the exchange to take place within four hours. His reply to indicate all standing by was 'Unanimous agreement': but he said, 'Bogey, old chap, bogey.'

'What do you mean "bogey"?' I said. 'Bogey' was the alternative code word that meant the whole operation was cancelled.

'Semitsa's been made persona non grata,' said Hallam. 'I'm not permitted to discuss it.'

'You bloody well are permitted to discuss it,' I said. 'The whole thing is arranged.'

'What's happened to the papers?' Hallam said.

'I've given them to Vulkan,' I said. This wasn't strictly true as I had them in my pocket.

'Oh well, that can't be helped. Leave the documents in his possession. Let him handle everything as he wants. We officially withdraw all sanction and agreement. I'm putting that in writing immediately after lunch and pushing it round to your people early this afternoon. This operation is off as far as my people are concerned. We find that the other Government' [he meant the Soviet Government, of course] 'are not aware of the transaction. It is unofficial and we want to have nothing to do with it. My personal advice, for what it's worth, is to withdraw without notice.'

'And leave Vulkan in the lurch,' I said.

'You are an employee. Vulkan is an indirect employee. Your employers are responsible to Vulkan, not you.' Hallam made it sound like an edict from the Institute of Directors.

There was a lengthy silence. Then Hallam said, 'Hello, Berlin. Are we still connected?'

'Yes,' I said.

'Is that understood, Berlin?'

'It's all understood, Hallam.'

'It's no good taking that tone. It's official. It's a top-level decision, nothing to do with me.'

'No, it wouldn't be.'

'We are closing points of entry as far as those documents are concerned, so it's no good Vulkan or you trying to use them. It's the Home Secretary's decision.'

'—— off, Hallam,' I said.

'Don't talk out of turn.'

'It's my native language.'

'Sorry you're taking it all personally. Don't forget. Bogey, bogey. I have my recorder going.'

'Bogey —— bogey to you, Hallam,' I said. 'Play that back to yourself this afternoon when you've finished lunch.'

42

The Exchange: when a player sacrifices something for
an opponent's piece of lesser value he is said to be 'the
exchange down'.

Monday, November 4th

The first thing you see is the 'No Entry' sign. It's on the
corner of Friedrichstrasse and beyond that the whole thing
is laid out. There is the little white hut sitting in the middle
of the road with 'US ARMY CHECKPOINT' written in huge
letters on the roof. Then above there is a flagpole flying
the Stars and Stripes and there are always a few olive-and-
white Taunus cars and jeeps about. There are some West
German policemen standing around in long grey overcoats
and Afrika Korps caps and inside the hut a couple of young
pink-faced GI's in starched khaki shirts write in a vast
ledger and sometimes talk on the phone. There are lots
of notices but the biggest one says, 'You are leaving the
American Sector' and then says the same thing over again
in French and Russian. Filing past that, prim old lady
journalists go crowding up the short flight of steps that
lead nowhere, like it's the royal box for the last public
hanging.

The wall itself is a shoddy breeze-block affair that looks
as though one of the old ladies falling off the steps could
tumble the whole thing from here to Potsdamerplatz. The
West German policeman stands very near the wall on the

West side and he lifts the long-hinged barrier for the traffic. On the Eastern side there are three solid concrete barriers that block three-quarters of the road's width. Since the gaps they leave are staggered, a vehicle driven through has to zig-zag at full lock slowly past the barriers. That's what the big hearse had to do after they had removed the coffin.

Six uniformed men were hastily pressed into service as coffin-bearers. There were Vopos, Grepos, policemen and soldiers stumbling along under the heavy weight and swinging their caps in their hands at arm's length to help them keep their balance. A policeman at the front missed his footing at one moment and almost fell, but an elderly NCO began to sing out the time in the idiom of the old Army. They rested the coffin down on to the stretcher-like grid of the bier at the second barrier. The policeman who had nearly fallen wiped the inside of his shako and then held it up to adjust the cockade so that he didn't have to look at the others.

It looked as though the DDR had chosen a representative of each of its services as they stood there dusting off their blue, green and grey shoulders where the coffin had left an epaulette of dirt. Beneath me on the American side of the barrier were thirty men, all dressed in khaki light-weight raincoats. Each of them had a strange-shaped leather box at his feet. There were boxes for bassoons and boxes for bass clarinets, boxes for French horns, trombones, violins and cornets. The kettledrums were wrapped in soft black velvet bags. Two girls stood among the men dressed in the same raincoats but wearing long white woollen stockings. From where they were standing below me they couldn't see as well as I could. 'Some kinda procession, ain't it?' one said.

'Bringing a funeral through by the look.'

'Say, ain't that sump'n?'

Two of the musicians unlocked the leather cases and looked inside before locking them again. One of the men tapped the belly of a double bass and said, 'Gee, I sure didn't think I'd be toting a bull-fiddle when I moved in among the commies.'

The flautist got his instrument out of the case. 'It's as lethal in your hands as an M-60,' he laughed and played a little riff. In the silence caused by the attention to the coffin, the passage he played was the only sane thing for a hundred yards in every direction and, even before the overtones of that had faded, an American MP shouted, 'You want a goddam water-cannon to wash you across the sidewalk, fella? Put it away before they get the idea it's a telescope.'

'I told you not to point it at anyone,' said the string player to ease the tension. The flautist said, 'But I had the safety on.'

'Here she blows,' someone said.

They had the coffin back inside the long black unstreamlined hearse that looked very Al Capone-like especially with Stok standing on the running boards. Stok was dressed in his corporal's uniform in order not to alert the newsmen who constantly gaze across the border from Checkpoint Charlie to the Friedrichstrasse Kontrollpunkt.

There were two wreaths with the coffin; they were great lifebelts of fir-tree leaves with intertwined flowers and huge decorative ribbons of silk with 'Last greetings from old friends' and the date printed across them. The driver drove very slowly, nodding feverishly at Stok every now and again. The hearse stopped again and the driver produced a map, unfolding it across the steering wheel. In the no-man's-land of the world, two men in a hearse were looking at a map and discussing where to make for.

Stok was talking energetically to the driver, who was

probably a Red Army transport soldier, and the driver was nodding like mad. The glass panels at the sides were decorated with a complex engraved palm-leaf pattern, and the big coffin, chosen to give Semitsa room to stretch an elbow, could just be seen inside.

The hearse moved slowly again and one Grenzpolizist was walking ahead of it, brandishing the documents like a royal flush. Two East German soldiers, leaning against the flower boxes and talking, made a joke about the hearse and then straightened their jackets and walked away in case they should be reprimanded. Overhead a US Army helicopter clattered along the line of the wall, saw the hearse and circled, watching the activity around it. It crossed. One of the two GIs stepped out from the glass-sided box to salute a captain who had just arrived in a white Taunus with a spotlight and the words 'Military Police' on its side.

The GI waved the hearse forward and, as the Western barrier was flipped open, the captain leaned into the shop downstairs and shouted 'Let's go, feller' to me. I turned away from the window, but not before taking one last look at Stok. He grinned and held his clenched fist in the air – a salute from worker to worker across the last frontier of the world. I grinned back and gave him the same salute in return. 'Let's go,' I heard the captain say again. I rattled down the ancient creaking staircase and jumped into the Taunus. By now the hearse was way down near the canal. The captain pumped the accelerator and jammed the siren on. 'Hoo-haw, hoo-haw,' the doleful bray had the traffic pulling aside and halting at the roadside.

'This isn't the St Patrick's Day Parade,' I said irritably. 'Switch the bloody thing off, can't you? Didn't anybody tell you that this mission is secret?'

'Yes,' he said.

'Then why collect me in this carnival wagon?'

He flipped the siren off and it died with a whimper. 'That's better,' I said.

'It's your funeral, bud,' said the officer. He drove in silence, overtaking the hearse at the Tiergarten, at which stage of its journey it was attracting no attention at all.

At the address in Wittenau Johnnie was awaiting me. 'Wittenau,' I thought; to a Berliner the word is invariably linked with the lunatic asylum here. The car stopped in a sordid street.

It had perhaps been a shop at one time or maybe a tiny warehouse, but now it was a garage. There was a large wooden double door big enough to back in a lorry – or a hearse. At the rear there was a heavy bench with a metal-working vice and a few simple rusty tools and junk that the previous tenant had abandoned. As I opened one half of the door a thin shaft of daylight connected me with Johnnie Vulkan – like a carpet unrolling across the stone floor to where he was leaning against the bench. The single unshaded light bulb that looked so infirm in the daylight became newly significant in the darkness. I shot the large rectangular bolts and noticed how smoothly they moved into their oiled slots. There was grease underfoot too, and that smell of carbonized oil and spilt petrol that hangs around motor-car repair places.

The light was directly above Vulkan's head and his eye-sockets were great piratical patches of darkness and under his nose was a moustache of shadow. He put a cigarette into his mouth and it gleamed under the light.

Johnnie was watching me intently. He removed the unlit cigarette.

'Get through to London?' he asked.

'Just fine – clear as a bell.'

'What did they say?'

'They said "Unanimous agreement", the code word. What did you expect them to say?'

'Just checking,' said Johnnie.

I squinted at him in an obvious sort of way. 'Do you know something that I don't know, Johnnie?'

'No. Honest. Just checking. You got the documents in the name of Broum?'

'Yes.'

'Spelt correctly?'

'Knock it off will you,' I said. 'I've got them.'

Johnnie nodded and ran his fingers through his hair and carefully lit his cigarette with an expensive lighter.

He began to recount the plan to himself to be sure he remembered it.

'They'll go to the mortuary first. They will put him into a station wagon there. It should take at least another forty minutes.' We had both discussed the plan a dozen times. I nodded. We smoked in silence until Johnnie threw his cigarette butt on to the floor and stepped on it carefully. In the area around his feet the white rectangles of flattened cigarette ends were strewn like confetti. Overhead I heard the rattle of the low-flying helicopter which was watching the movement of the hearse between Checkpoint Charlie and the West Berlin mortuary.

As my eyes grew more accustomed to the darkness I could see the junk that had accumulated in the building. There was a disembowelled motor-car engine with old torn gaskets hanging off it. The cylinder head had been hastily slid back on to its bolts without being seated and it rested drunkenly upon the engine. Beyond it was a heap of bald tyres and some dented oil drums. Vulkan had looked at his watch so often that he finally tucked his shirt cuff under the gold rim to make it easier to glimpse the time. He heaved deep sighs and every now and again he would go up to the engine and kick some part of it gently with the very tip of his hand-lasted Oxfords.

'There's a funeral,' he said.

I looked at him quizzically. 'That's what's delaying the transfer at the mortuary, a *real* funeral.' I looked at my watch. 'There's no delay,' I said, 'and if it doesn't arrive for another five minutes they will still be on time according to the schedule.'

We both stood there in the dismal light of the bare bulb when suddenly Johnnie said, 'I was in prison once in the next street to this one.'

I offered him a Gauloise and lit one myself and, when we had finished lighting them and having that first inhalation that makes you dive for a cigarette, I said, 'When was that?'

'Spring of 1943,' said Vulkan.

'What charge?'

Johnnie grinned and stabbed the shadows with his cigarette. 'I was a communist, Roman Catholic Jew, who had deserted from the Army.'

'Is that all?' I said.

Vulkan gave a sour smile. 'I can tell you,' he said, 'it was grim. There wasn't much to eat for heroes in 1943 – for prisoners . . .' He drew on his cigarette and the garage was full of the pungent aroma of French tobacco, and he drew on his cigarette again like this was all some complex dream he was dreaming while really he was in prison just a few year-yards away.

He rubbed two fingers of his left hand and then put them under his armpit as you do when you've hit them with a hammer – put them into some dark, warm place where they can stay for ever and never come out into the daylight.

'Defined areas,' said Vulkan suddenly. 'Defined areas of hatred.' His voice was firm and yet seemed to originate from another time and another place, almost like a voice speaking through a medium, a voice that was just using the larynx and sound apparatus of Vulkan's body. 'It's easy then. When I was first arrested I was badly knocked about.' He made that motion of the hand that in some Latin parts of the world is a sign of pure joy: he flung his hand around on the end of his wrist like he wanted it to spin away into a corner. He held it up to me and I saw the skin grafts along the last two fingers. 'It wasn't so bad for me, those beatings. The French had arrested me; they were so anxious to demonstrate to their German masters how well they had learned from them. Those Frenchmen were the most evil men I had ever seen – they were sadists, I mean really, in the medical sense of the word. When they beat me they beat me for their own special sexual delight and just by being beaten I was participating in a sexual relationship with them – you understand me?'

'I understand,' I said.

'It was filthy,' he said. He clawed at his lip to find a shred of tobacco and finally spat heartily. I waited to see if he was going to continue; for a minute or so I thought he would say no more. Then he said, 'But it was uncomplicated for me. I could understand that a Frenchman felt hate for a German.' He stopped speaking again and I guessed that the conversation was proceeding in his head. 'The French prisoners were worse off because they . . .' He stopped talking again and his eyes were fixed on something from another time and place. 'But the first time I was ill-treated by a German – I don't mean pushed to one side or knocked off a chair, deliberately and systematically tortured, beaten – it was . . . I don't know, it threw me out of equilibrium. That's why the communists were almost the last to crack, they were able to cling to their "in" group, they had sharply defined areas to hate.'

I said, 'Most prejudice tends to operate against groups that it's easy to recognize. It's no accident that minorities only suffer where the prejudice has had time to develop its power of detection. Mexicans don't have trouble in

New York City; it's down on the Mexican border they run into it. Pakistanis are honoured guests in Birmingham, Alabama. It's in Birmingham, England, that they run into prejudice.'

'That's it,' said Johnnie. 'Well, after the war, communists had the best chances of rehabilitation. They'd always known that the forces of reaction (that's to say non-communists) were swine, so nothing had surprised them. The Jews had known about anti-Semitism for a few centuries. It was the ones who had suffered at the hands of their own people who were faced with an insoluble enigma. The Frenchman who had been tortured by other Frenchmen, the Italian partisan captured by the Italian fascists. We have this terrible thing to live with.

'I have more in common with the Germans than with any other nation on the earth. I've lived among them, I understand them in ways I could never get to understand you, no matter if I was chained to you from now until the day I die. But I never go into a roomful of Germans without thinking to myself: is there a man here who tortured me? Is there a man here who killed my friends? Is there a man who just stood beyond the door while I screamed and believed that nothing outside of my torn body was real? Is there a woman here who was the daughter of such a one, a sister or mother of such a man? And such is the power of mathematical reasoning that I am sure that often the answer has been "Yes" if only I had known.' He spat again in some sort of cathartic endeavour.

Johnnie spoke suddenly. 'They might pull some sort of trick,' he said.

'Could be,' I agreed.

'Do you have a pistol or a knife?'

'I don't think they are likely to try *that* sort of trick,' I said.

'Do you have a pistol or a knife or a persuader?'

'I have a persuader,' I said. 'Two hundred dollars in singles.'

'The Americans,' said Johnnie. He walked over to the old engine. 'You shouldn't have told the Americans,' he said.

'How would we have got it past Checkpoint Charlie?' I asked.

'I don't know,' he said petulantly and kicked his collection of cigarette ends to the far corners of the building.

He turned his back to me and began to toy with the junk on the bench, setting up some monstrous chess game. He tapped the rusty sparking plugs and squeezed valve springs in the palm of his hand. At the side of the bench was a thick polished oval of wood. There were twelve different sizes of drill stuck into it like matches in a peg board. Johnnie amused himself throwing the springs over the shiny drills. 'Schmidt's of Solingen,' it said on a scroll around the wooden base. 'Best drills in the world.'

He arrived right on time, the same Red Army driver in a black station wagon. He rapped at the ancient wooden doors, but the joins in the woodwork were so warped that we had both already seen the car arrive and back up to the doors. Johnnie moved quickly. The doors swung back smoothly, the car chugged back in as far as the bench. Then the gigantic coffin slid out of the back of the car with just the three of us pulling. Johnnie and I one on each side and the Russian at the front of the car, bracing himself on the dashboard and pushing the end of the coffin with the soles of his boots. It wasn't very dignified but it was smooth and fast. As soon as the coffin was on to the bench the Russian stepped round to the driver's seat and came back bearing the two gigantic wreaths that I had seen on top of the hearse. There were great sprays of lilies and chrysanthemums and a bright red ribbon with 'Letzter Gruss' printed on it in Gothic script. 'Take those back,' said Johnnie to the young Russian. The Russian said he couldn't and there was a small argument.

The Russian said he had tried to leave them at the mortuary but they didn't want them and he couldn't take them back through Checkpoint Charlie or it would seem highly suspicious. Johnnie argued in fluent Russian but it didn't do him any good: the boy wouldn't take the wreaths away with him. The more Johnnie swore, the more the Russian shrugged. Finally Johnnie turned away and the Russian jumped into the driver's seat and slammed the door. I opened the doors and the boy gunned the motor and gave the car full lock as he sped out into the street and away towards the border.

Johnnie had climbed on the bench by the time I had turned round. He was using one of the big rusty screwdrivers to scratch the wood-filler from the sockets above the countersunk screws. He was so frantic in his haste that he had been working feverishly for five minutes or more before he noticed that I wasn't helping.

'Get the items out of my case,' he said.

There were two small suitcases. One was a midwife's set adapted to take an oxygen bottle. In the other case Johnnie had put a bottle of Glenlivet malt whisky, one of those sand hot-water bottles that keep hot for hours, a heavy sweater, sal volatile, smelling salts, a box containing a hypodermic needle and four small ampoules of megimide, four vials of aminophylline and a dark bottle that I guessed was nikethamide – a circulatory stimulant – a mirror to detect breathing, a short Piorry's wooden stethoscope, a thermometer, a pen torch suitable for examining pupils, and a marking pencil.

'It's really complete,' I said. 'You take this pretty seriously, don't you?'

'Yes,' said Vulkan. He hadn't removed his coat and he was sweating profusely. Sometimes in the exertion of the work his head would set the bare bulb swinging and all the shadows would dance crazily and his face glistened with sweat as I remembered it glistening with rain.

'That's the last one,' he said.

'Just like the last scene of *Romeo and Juliet*,' I said and Vulkan said 'Yes' over his shoulder and started to chip at the seam where the lid and bottom joined, but I doubt if he even heard what I said.

'Help me,' he said. He began to strain at the heavy lid. It must have been inlaid with lead for it was so heavy to move that at first I felt sure that there were still some screws holding it – then it began to move.

'Look out,' shouted Vulkan and the bottom end of the lid fell on to the bench, missing our toes by only inches. The crash was ear-splitting and the vibration rocked the bench. At first the shadow of the coffin lid obscured the view, but, when it slid away, even Vulkan could cling to his hopes no more.

'Six reasons why the Deutsche Demokratische Republik should be represented in the West.' There were hundreds of them, stacks and stacks of leaflets stuffed into the huge coffin – Stok's last joke. I climbed down to the floor.

'It doesn't look like you'll need your hot-water bottle,' I said to Vulkan, and for just one split second reflexes pulled his face into a smile, but only for a second. 'They can't,' he said. 'They dare not, they promised – your Government must take action.' I suppose I laughed again, for Vulkan became past all rational argument.

He held his splayed fingers before his face like he was studying an invisible hand of cards. 'You and Stok,' he said, over-salivating slightly. 'You planned this.'

'He doesn't consult me,' I said. Vulkan was still standing on the bench three feet higher than I was.

'But you are not surprised,' Vulkan shouted.

'I'm not in even the slightest way surprised,' I said.

'That Red Army boy didn't even hang around to get a signature. Let alone for forty thousand pounds. I'd never believed any part of the whole deal, but that really convinced me. It's about time you came to grips with reality, Johnnie; there is no Santa Claus. People just don't give away anything for nothing. What could Stok gain?'

'Then why did he go to all this trouble?' said Johnnie. He leaned down and moved some of the leaflets around in the coffin as though he thought he might find Semitsa in there if he dug deep enough.

'He arrested four boys from the Gehlen set-up, didn't he?'

'Five,' said Johnnie. 'Another failed to report in this morning.'

'Exactly,' I said, 'and you got a little extra pay and some expenses and London will read your report and say what a good boy you have been.'

'And you, you slimy bastard. What's *your* angle?'

'I have my methods, Watson,' I said. 'I've been arranging the Berlin hit parade and you've slipped five notches to nowhere. You and that girl thought you had a nice deal, didn't you? Well, your big mistake was trying to exploit me as a part of it. Papers,' I said. I picked up a couple of the pamphlets from inside the coffin and let them flutter to the floor. 'There are the only papers you're getting, they aren't made out in the name of Broum but on the other hand there are probably no spelling errors.'

'You ——' said Vulkan and from his superior position on the bench-top tried to kick my head in. I backed off.

'I'll tell you your trouble, Johnnie,' I said from a safe distance. 'You've become a professional phoney. You've become so good at pretending to be different that you have lost contact with your identity. You've learnt so much jargon that you don't know which side you are on. Every time you move through the frontier of space you slip through the frontier of time. Perhaps you like that. OK. Be a Waldgänger,[1] but don't expect me to pay your expenses. Be a freelance, but don't expect a salary. You would be playing along with me now if you were smart. Stok's boys won't have anything more to do with you, you are poison to Gehlen . . .'

'Through you,' Vulkan shouted. '*You* messed up Gehlen.'

'You are poison to Gehlen,' I continued. 'And if you foul up with me there isn't a place left in the whole world where they would let you get a sniff of a job. You are dead, Johnnie. Dead and you don't know it. Dead and you can't afford the funeral expenses. Get clever!'

There was a long silence broken only by Johnnie's feet knocking against a valve.

'I always return the things I am given,' said Johnnie menacingly, 'and that especially includes good advice.' He reached into his jacket and I saw his fingers flicker as he eased them around his ugly little Mauser H SC. 'I've planned this operation for fifteen years and I've worked out every conceivable contingency, including Semitsa's non-arrival. That's unfortunate but it won't impede the remainder of the programme, whether you choose to stand in the way or not, because this time they are going to be building the barbed wire through *you*.' He clicked the gun casing to show he meant business. Now we both knew the gun was ready loaded and cocked.

'The girl and I did a deal,' Vulkan went on. 'Her interests and my interests complement each other: there is no conflict. Her side of the deal has gone on the rocks but that's too bad. I'm going to cut my losses. I need four days without you sounding off your big mouth. It's going to cost me eighty pounds per day to keep you on ice so you can see that I'm prepared to be out of pocket – because I

---

[1] Waldgänger: one who walks alone (in the woods).

could have you knocked off for one hundred pounds.'

'Listen, Johnnie,' I said in an all-good-pals-together sort of voice, 'cut me in. I can get back that photo of you in prison clothes with Mohr.'

'You lying bastard,' said Johnnie.

I said, 'It's the papers you want?'

Johnnie said softly, 'If you don't have them I'll kill you. You know that, don't you?'

What could he do in four days? Knowing Vulkan, I could risk a guess. 'Can you get the money and be clear in four days?' I asked.

'I told you I've been planning this for fifteen years. I laid the claim ages ago. I have three lawyers and a witness standing by – I . . .' he smiled '. . . talk too much,' he finished. I began to see the pattern but I didn't want that to be the last thing I ever saw.

'Mohr is the witness,' I said. 'You met him in Hendaye and told him that Samantha was a Shinbet[2] agent after him for war crimes. You told him that you could call her off if he did as you told him over the next day or so. Mohr saw Broum die. He's important to . . .'

'Shut your crummy mouth,' said Vulkan. 'I'm a Waldgänger, just like you said.' He walked along the bench, the light glistening on his face. He walked slowly, picking his way among the set of drills, the mallets and rusty sparking plugs and little tin boxes of nuts and bolts, his shiny shoes moving, hesitating and placing themselves down like little flying saucers playing tag on a desolate landscape.

Every now and again he flexed his fingers before easing them back around the handle of the pistol. I had seen Vulkan use that gun on the range; I knew he could put the whole eight-shot magazine into a six-inch group before

[2] Shinbet: Sheruter Betahan, Israeli Intelligence Service.

I could swing open even one door-bolt. It seemed as though an hour went by as he moved along the bench but it probably wasn't more than forty-five seconds. That's the theory of relativity, I thought.

'Get them,' said Vulkan.

I had the big manilla envelope in my raincoat pocket. It had the royal coat of arms on the outside and 'Home Office' printed in prim roman letters across the corner. On the front was a white label that said that to help the war effort one should use envelopes as many times as possible. I moved towards the bench and handed the envelope to Vulkan who reached down with his left hand to take the corner.

'Careful,' he said, in a genuinely solicitous voice. 'I want no complications at all. Let alone shooting you.' I nodded. 'I *like* you,' he added.

'That puts a new complexion on the whole thing,' I said.

The envelope had one of those little card circles that you wind string round. If you don't know what I mean, believe me you need two hands to open it, because that's the important point. Vulkan kept his finger on the trigger but held the corner of the envelope with his gun hand, using his left hand to unravel the string. It's the timing that was so important, because as soon as the string is unravelled you need two hands for only as long as it takes to get your hand inside and around the papers. Added to this factor was the risk that the longer I stayed there the more chance there was of Vulkan moving me back to a safe distance.

Vulkan's knee was level with the top of my head. I judged my distance with care. There is a groove in the fibula just below the knee where the lateral popliteal nerve passes close against the bone. A sharp blow here paralyses the lower leg – 'dead man's leg' we called it in the school playground.

'They are all falling out,' I shouted suddenly in panic. 'The papers.' Johnny clutched the bottom of the envelope as I pushed it – and the gun – upwards away from my cranium. I jabbed at his knee. I hit but not accurately enough. My head sang like a massed-voice choir as the nasty sharp front edge of the magazine hit the side of my head. I had already begun to fall back. Again I punched out, scarcely able to see Vulkan's leg for the bright crimson pain that sang its song in the empty echo chamber of my head.

I felt him go. He toppled like a felled redwood, the spilled papers spinning and drifting all around him. The crash of his body collapsing full-length across the bench was followed by the clatter of dislodged junk. An insurance renewal slip fell like a sycamore seed into the open tin of grease. 'I've hurt my back,' he said urgently; but training won out and the Mauser stayed firmly in his fist. Its chamfered snout made a little circling motion like a clerk's pencil just about to write. I waited for the bang.

'I've hurt my back,' he said again. I moved towards him but the foresight made that tiny movement again and I froze. His leg was crossed under him like a stone figure on a knight's tomb. I saw the real, ageing man behind the careless young mask. He twisted his shaken body and, more slowly than I had ever seen him move before, he eased his feet over the edge of the bench towards the greasy floor. His voice was a soft growl, 'Es irrt der Mensch, so lang er strebt.'[3]

I watched him with that sort of hypnotic horror that venomous insects evoke, but between me and Johnnie Vulkan there was no glass. His feet took the weight of his body and his face took its pain. He groped along the bench towards me. I moved back. He stepped awkwardly as

[3] Man errs till his strife is ended *(Faust)*.

though his foot had gone to sleep, his muscles unco-ordinated, his face twitching, but the Mauser always steady. His foot descended gently into the big tin of grease. Vulkan looked down at it. Now was the time to jump him. 'I've ruined my suit,' he said. The grease spattered around his leg and the Oxford made loud squelching noises inside the tin. He stood with one hand on the bench, one foot in the tin of grease and the Mauser H SC pointed at my middle. 'My suit,' he said and he laughed gently, keeping his mouth wide open, like imbeciles and drunks do, until the laugh became a gurgle, like soap suds going down a kitchen sink.

The bare bulb was in my eyes, so it took me a few seconds to see the blood that was flowing out of his mouth. It was light pink and very frothy. He swayed, then crashed to the stone floor and the grease keg unstuck from his foot with a 'chug' and rolled across the garage, rattling as it struck the old debris, and bounced into the greasing pit. Johnnie was face-flat on the petrol-shiny floor. His whole body contracted and arched like someone was pouring salt on to him, and then the flat of his hand slapped the con-crete, making three loud cracks like pistol shots. Suddenly he was relaxed and still. Stuck fairly high on to Vulkan's back was the thick oval of polished wood with the words 'Schmidt's of Solingen', and under that, 'The best drills in the world.' Vulkan now had their complete range driven deep into his dead body.

It was all so in character. This little Faust, seeker of salvation by striving. This Sturm-und-Drang artist, with his two demanding masters, who tried to die with Goethe on his lips but was carried away by concern for his suit. I wondered whether Samantha was Gretchen or Helena. There was no doubt about my role.

I stacked Stok's pamphlets in a pile near the door and, buttoning my trenchcoat tight around me, I lifted Johnnie's bloody carcass into the satin-upholstered coffin. Death had cut him down to size and I could hardly recognize the man whose ankle showed a four-inch scar. I took a grease pencil from the medical kit and, after wiping the blood from his face, I wrote '1 G. Na Am' on Vulkan's forehead. I looked at my watch and wrote '18.15' under it on the tanned skin. Anything that would increase the confusion when that box was opened was working in my favour.

I had only four of the screws in when I heard the lorry outside. The place seemed to smell of blood, which perhaps was my imagination, but I tipped a little petrol on the floor just to be on the safe side, and hid my bloodstained coat.

I swung the doors open. It was dark now and it had begun to snow. They drove in. I helped the driver unlock the rear doors of the truck. A figure stood inside the van holding an old Mark II Sten gun: a figure in a battered leather coat that bulged agreeably in just the right places.

'Act your age, Sam,' I said. 'If there's only three of us it's going to be enough trouble lugging this thing into the truck. Lower that gun.'

She didn't lower the gun. 'Where's Johnnie?' she said.

'Lower that gun, Samantha. If you'd seen as many accidents as I've seen with those shoddy Sten guns you wouldn't behave that way. Don't they teach you anything in Haifa?'

She smiled, pulled the cocking handle back, pushed it up into the lock slot and lowered the gun. 'Johnnie knows you're here?'

'Of course he does,' I said. 'This is Johnnie's show, but you will never get away with your end of the deal.'

'Maybe I won't,' she said, and leaned her face very close to mine, 'but my pop became a piece of soap in this goddamned country so I'm going to try.' She paused. 'We found out what happens if you don't – six million of you amble forward gently to die without too much mess or inconvenience – so from now on we Jews are going to try. Maybe I won't get away very far, but this boy . . .' she stabbed a bright red fingernail towards the driver, '. . . is right behind, and behind him there are plenty more.'

'OK,' I said. She was right. Sometimes it doesn't matter what the chances are. 'Plenty more,' she said. I nodded.

The military-style leather coat suited her. It suited the aggressive boyish stance that she had picked up along with the machine-gun. She leaned an elbow against the van and fanned her fingertips across her cheek as though the coat was the latest fashion and the machine-gun a photographer's prop.

'You should have told me that you were in on it.'

'Over that telephone of yours?' I said.

'I saw the newspapers,' she said. 'We were careless.'

'Is that what you call it?' I said.

'I suppose the man downstairs burgled my flat too.'

'There's no doubt,' I said.

'Haifa thought your people had done it.'

I shrugged and made the international sign for money with the index finger and thumb. 'How much of it's in German money?' I asked.

'It all is,' she said. 'All Deutsche marks.'

'That's all right,' I said. 'We have to pay the people at the mortuary for the turn-round there.' She was still a little suspicious.

'He's had one gramme of sodium amytal.' I waved towards Vulkan's medical supplies and the coffin. 'He's sleeping quietly, we didn't use the oxygen, but Johnnie said to take the unit and antidote with you. I've marked the dose and time on his forehead so even if you forget to warn the people you pass him to, you'll be OK.'

She nodded and put down the gun and tried to push the coffin. I said, 'He'll be out for eight hours solid.'

'It's heavy,' she said.

'There's just one little thing,' I said, 'before we put him into your van. I would like the money here.' I held out my hand as Stok had done to me. She went to the cab and from a large leather handbag produced a bundle of new 100 DM notes. She said, 'You realize there is nothing to stop me blasting you and taking Semitsa.' The driver came around the back of the lorry. He was carrying the gun, not aiming it, just carrying it.

'Now you know why Johnnie isn't here,' I said.

Her face showed great relief. 'Of course,' she said. 'I might have known he'd think of that. He's "Mr Angle": Johnnie Vulkan.' She gave me the money like she was sorry to see it go.

'It's extortion, ghoul,' she said. 'He's not worth this much.'

'That's what the Roman soldiers said to Judas,' I said. I put the money into my raincoat pocket and we all began to heave at the coffin.

There was a time when I thought we weren't going to get it in, but slowly it inched into the truck. When it was far enough in for the rear doors to close (and we tried three times before it was) we stood there drinking in the smell of petrol by the deep lungful without enough energy to speak. I poured a big shot of Johnnie's Glenlivet whisky into the small plastic cups that he had been thoughtful enough to provide in his kit. My whole body suddenly began to shake. The neck of the whisky bottle chattered against the cup in a tiny shudder of sound. I saw Sam and the driver watching me. 'Bottoms up,' I said and poured the smoky malt fluid into my bloodstream.

Sam said, 'You told those French cops that I was working for the Krauts.'

'Yes,' I said. 'I have an unpleasant sense of humour.'

'You knew I was working for the Israeli Intelligence.'

'Is that who you work for?' I said in mock innocence.

'Um,' she said and sipped her whisky. The driver was watching us both.

'It's all a game for you,' she said, 'but it's life and death for us. Those Egyptians have so many Kraut scientists working for them that their laboratory instruction manuals are printed in German as well as Arabic. With this guy we can really even things up.'

'Enzymes,' I said.

'Let's not kid each other any longer,' she said. 'Sure in Israel we can use Semitsa's knowledge of insecticides, but that's not half the story and you know it.'

I didn't say anything. She buttoned her leather coat tighter around her chin. 'These insecticides Semitsa is working on are nerve gases! They've had lots of horticultural workers go crazy already. They attack the nervous system, they say they're the most deadly substances known to man. It's true, isn't it?'

She needed to know. 'It's true enough,' I said.

She spoke more quickly, relieved to know that her assignment was as important and factual as she wanted to believe. 'One day those Egyptians are going to come back,' she said. 'One day soon. When they come they are going to have weapons that those Kraut scientists have built for them. Our people in the *nahals*[4] have got to pack a punch.' There was a sharp click of plastic as she put down the empty whisky cup. 'That's why nothing that you or I could think or do stood a chance. This is something that could be the finale of the Jewish nation; no one is more important than that.'

'If I'd known you were that keen I would have let you collect him from the Adlon.'

She gave me a playful punch on the arm. 'You think we couldn't have done it? If there's one thing we know

[4] *Nahal:* a military kibbutz.

260

something about, it's cities divided by a wall. We've had a wall across Jerusalem ever since I was a kid. We've mastered every technique there is for getting over, round, through and under it.'

I opened the rear doors of the truck and heaved the two dark shiny wreaths in. 'From old friends,' one of them said. It had hooked itself over a coffin handle. 'We don't want those,' said Sam.

'You take them,' I said. 'You don't know when you are likely to need a wreath from old friends. None of us does.'

Sam smiled and I slammed the truck doors. I opened the garage doors with their carefully oiled bolts and I waved good-bye solemnly as the truck moved slowly forward. Sam was smiling out of her leather coat. Behind her head I could see the big polished box that contained the mortal remains of John Vulkan and just for a moment I felt like calling this over-confident child back. It's OK to have soft feelings knowing that years of training preclude me from obeying them.

'Bis hundertundzwanzig,'[5] I said gently. The car lurched forward and Sam had to twist her head to keep me in sight. 'Mazel Tov,' she called back. 'My darling ghoul.' Florins of snow hit the ebony windscreen and slid gently down the warm glass. The driver flipped his lights on to reveal long yellow cones of fast-moving snow. I closed out the sound of the engine and promised myself another Glenlivet whisky; it wasn't cold but I had the shivers again.

[5] Jewish toast for a long life. (Moses lived 120 years.)

43

HANNA STAHL alias SAMANTHA STEEL

Monday, November 4th

Snow already, Samantha Steel thought. What kind of winter was it likely to be? Whatever kind of winter, it would be good to be back in her flat in Haifa, where from the bedroom window umbrella pines framed the intense blue water of the bay, and the whitewashed walls reflected back a glare too bright to look at, even in December.

She watched the big snowflakes hitting the grimy streets as they passed through the Reinickendorf district of Berlin. The whisky had warmed her and she was quite capable of dropping off to sleep. She pressed her face about with her hands, stretching the cheeks and pummelling her eyes. What a relief that it was all over, there had been so many traps and pitfalls. Now she felt torn, shredded, used — sexually used almost. She combed her hair through her fingers. It was soft and young; fine silky hair. She let it fall against her neck like murmurs of love. She dragged it up again, her eyes closed; it was like taking a warm shower, combing her hair through her fingers. It would be nice to have it blonde again. She felt her whole body drift into relaxation.

She would like to see Johnnie Vulkan again before she got on the plane; not for any romantic reason, he was just the sort of tough self-sufficient character that had no attraction for her at all. Vulkan was a big phoney. He wasn't even German, in spite of the way he always called Berlin his home town. He was a Sudeten German – you could hear it in his voice when he was angry. She didn't like him but she had to admire him. He was a professional; by any standards he was a professional. Just to see him work was a pleasure.

The Englishman was the exact opposite. There were times when she could have 'gone for' the Englishman, nearly did in fact. Given other circumstances, where there was no element of business involved, it all might have been different. She wished she had known him many years ago when he was at his red-brick university, this provincial boy wandering through the big city of life. She envied him his simplicity and briefly wished she had been the girl next door in Burnley, Lancs – wherever *that* was! He was cuddly, kind and malleable, he would make the sort of husband who wouldn't fight about her dress allowance all the time.

Why the English used men like that in Intelligence work was something she would never understand. Amateur. That basically was why the English would never be good at doing anything: they were amateurs. Such amateurs that finally someone standing by couldn't watch their bungling any longer, and took over. That's what America had done in two World Wars. Perhaps it was all part of a vast British conspiracy. She giggled. She didn't think so.

The driver offered his cigarettes. She looked round and tapped the coffin to make sure it was still there. She never trusted things she couldn't see and touch. Thank goodness Johnnie had supervised the morphia dosage and the details, the Englishman would forget or get it wrong. He had to be led, that Englishman. She had found exactly the same thing in her relationship with him. He has to have someone around like Johnnie Vulkan; or Samantha Steel, she added to herself. He would make a good father. Vulkan could perhaps be moulded into a good escort but the English guy would have been a good father to their children. She compared her memories of the two of them as though they were fighting some sort of tournament for her favours. She snuggled deeper in the seat and pulled her coat collar up to her eyebrows to think about that – to keep it more secret.

Vulkan was the worst sort of womanizer and had some idea that women were an inferior race; he had used that word – *Männerbund* – too; the bond that unites men, comradeship – her mother had told her that that was a dangerous sign. Men can get away with that sort of attitude in this country where there had been nearly two million surplus women in 1945. He would have got the shock of his life in Israel, where women were really gaining a place for themselves.

She lit the cigarette. Her hands shook. It was natural, it was the after-effect of all the work and worry, but there was still the airport to deal with. If she was still in this sort of condition when they got there she would let the driver handle it; he was unimaginative enough to be calm, thank goodness. 'Where are we?' she asked.

'There's the Siegessäule,' said the driver and pointed to the tall monument to ancient victories that stabbed into the Tiergarten like a pin through a green butterfly. He detoured to avoid the police cars that always sat around at the base of it. 'Not far now.'

'Thank goodness,' she shivered. 'It's damn cold in here,' she said.

The driver said nothing but they both knew it wasn't cold in there.

She went back to thinking about the Englishman; it was a nice warm pretence to indulge in and quite academic, now that she would never see him again. He smelled good;

she thought smell was important. You could tell a lot about a man by his smell and the taste of his mouth. His smell wasn't particularly masculine. Not like Vulkan – all tobacco and untanned-leather smells, which she knew came from a bottle, ever since she had looked for aspirins that night and found his hair-net. She laughed. The Englishman smelled of something softer; more like warm yeasty bread, and sometimes he tasted of cocoa.

She remembered that night. It was the night she decided she would never understand men. Vulkan had made love to her in his usual fashion, which was like a specialist performing major surgery. She had promised to buy him some rubber gloves and he had made some wisecrack about her acting like she was anaesthetized. It was about three o'clock in the morning when she had found not only the hair-net but the parts for the half-finished string quartet. Vulkan. King Vulkan. The way he delighted in his big, secret-agent, undercover life. She ought to have told him that the secretive attitude he had about his intellectual life was a guilt syndrome centred upon his parents. Vulkan preferred to think it was 'the mental casualties of war'. Phoney.

Why was the car stopping? She looked out at the densely packed traffic jam. It was a miserable town full of men in ankle-length overcoats and big hats. As for the clothes the women wore, they were unbelievable, she had hardly seen a well dressed woman all the time she had been here.

She wasn't worried about the traffic jam, there was ample time, she had worked out the schedule to allow for such things. The van crept forward a little then stopped again. It was as bad as New York. She wondered whether to visit her mother at Christmas. It was a lot of expense and she had only recently been there. Mothers, however, had some special metaphysical regard for Christmas. Perhaps she should ask her mother to come to Haifa. The traffic had begun to move again, there was a cream double-decker bus slewed across the road. An accident. The road was probably slippery with the snow. At first the big flakes had melted as they hit the ground but now they were beginning to build up a white pattern. People too were wearing lace shawls of snowflakes. The driver switched the windscreen wipers on. The motor whined in a monotonous rhythm.

There was a fire engine and a lot of people in the centre of the road. It could take ages at this rate. She leaned back to relax. The taste of the whisky recurred in her throat. She recounted the programme in her mind from the moment they had backed the truck through the doors of the Wittenau garage. Haifa had told her to let the money go only if she had to. It would make them suspicious, they had said. She wished she had bargained with the Englishman now: what had he said about 'That's what the Roman soldiers said to Judas'? It was a typical sour English remark. She should have just taken the coffin at gunpoint. It had been in her mind to do so at one time. It was Johnnie Vulkan who had forced her hand, by not being there. He was probably watching from a window across the road. You had to admire Vulkan. He was a real professional.

It was quite dark now, dark with the claustrophobic weight of the cloud from which dirty flakes of snow fell relentlessly. That's better; they were edging forward again now. Great lights illuminated the firemen operating the jacks under the bus. One fireman was kneeling in a great pool of oil, so was a policeman. Now she could see what had happened. The fireman was talking to an old man whose legs were under the wheels of the bus. They were trying to take the banner he was holding away from him but the old man was gripping it tightly. The policeman waved them past. The old man wouldn't let go. The snow covered his face. The banner said, 'No man can serve two masters. Matthew vi. 24.'

'This is Schöneberg,' said the driver. Tempelhof must be just ahead.

44

In China, Hungary, India, Korea and Poland pawns are called 'foot soldiers', but in Tibet they are called 'children'.

Tuesday, November 5th

The green-shaded lamp in Dawlish's office is rigged up with a complex series of cords and counterweights. From its present position its light cut the figures round his desk in half and illumined them only from the waist down. Dawlish's disembodied hands reached into the circle of yellow light. The fingers shuffled and riffed through the thin new unwrinkled paper money like serpents' tongues.

'You are probably right,' he said to me. 'It's counterfeit.'

'I'm only guessing,' I said. 'But she gave it to me like she was playing Monopoly.'

Dawlish flipped through it and read that little paragraph that they have on German money that says how they don't want anybody to feel free to print their own. Dawlish handed the money to Alice.

'They're being very cagey about Newbegin filling the Berlin vacancy,' said Dawlish. 'They say you are Americanizing the department in dress, syntax and operation.'

I said: 'That's their way of compensating for the orders I get from Washington.'

Dawlish nodded. He said, 'The Yard have had a cable from the Munich police.' He watched my face in the darkness. I said nothing. On the other side of the desk Alice was plucking an elastic band that held the money that Sam had given me. The elastic made a loud crack in the still room.

'A girl was transhipping a coffin at Munich – travelling with it between Berlin and Haifa. There was a dead body in the coffin.'

Dawlish looked at me again, wanting me to speak. I said, 'Coffins often contain corpses, don't they?'

Dawlish walked across to the tiny coal fire. He prodded it with a bent bayonet, there was a sudden flicker of flame and a tiny army of red sparks marched across the side of the grate.

'What do you think we should say?' he said to the fireplace.

'We?' I said. 'I thought the Munich police were asking the Yard. If you want to get yourself involved with girls going to Haifa with coffins, it's up to you, but I don't know what you're talking about.'

Dawlish gave the largest piece of coal an in-out and on-guard and it split into five small blazing pieces. 'Just as long as I know,' he said, putting down the poker and walking back to the desk. 'It's no use my saying one thing if your written report says something completely different.' He nodded like he was trying to convince himself. He didn't have to convince me.

'Yes,' I said. Outside there was a steady noise of starlings fidgeting about on the guttering. Through the window, dawn was revealing crippled roofs, and painting bloody reflections in the dirty glass of the window panes. The senile light above Dawlish's desk was losing its battle against the daylight with bad grace. Dawlish walked across to a leather chair and sank into it with a sigh. He took off his glasses and produced a crisp handkerchief which he carefully patted over his face. 'Could you find us a little

cup of real coffee?' he asked in a gentle voice – but Alice
had already left to make some.

Dawlish read the newspaper clipping I gave him.

FASCIST VICTIMS' ASSETS WILL BE RELEASED BY SWISS
BANKS

BERNE, OCT 21ST (R)

THE SWISS PARLIAMENT ON THURSDAY APPROVED A
GOVERNMENT BILL DESIGNED TO RELEASE UNCLAIMED
ASSETS OF LONG-DEAD VICTIMS OF FASCISM DEPOSITED IN
THE COUNTRY'S BANKS.

THE NEW LAW SUPPORTED BY 130 DEPUTIES WITH NO
OPPOSITION LIFTS A CORNER OF THE CURTAIN OF SECRECY
WHICH ENSHROUDS MANY A FOREIGN FORTUNE DEPOSITED
IN SWITZERLAND'S CONFIDENTIAL ACCOUNTS.

THE BANK SECRECY ACT WILL NOW BE SET ASIDE
FOR A TEMPORARY PERIOD OF TEN YEARS SO THAT
THE GOVERNMENT CAN TAKE OVER THE UNCLAIMED
FUNDS.

UNDER THE NEW LAW, BANKS, INSURANCE COMPANIES
OR ANYBODY ELSE ARE OBLIGED TO DECLARE UNTOUCHED
ASSETS BELONGING TO PEOPLE UNTRACED SINCE THE WAR
AND WHO ARE RACIALLY, POLITICALLY OR RELIGIOUSLY
PERSECUTED FOREIGNERS OR STATELESS PERSONS.

THE GOVERNMENT'S MOTIVES IN PUSHING THE BILL
THROUGH ARE TO REMOVE ANY SUSPICION THAT SWITZER-
LAND WOULD BE PREPARED TO PROFIT FROM THE CASE
OF EUROPEAN JEWRY IN HITLER'S EXTERMINATION
CAMPS.

DISPOSAL OF THE ASSETS IS TO BE DECIDED BY FEDERAL
DECREE, WITH THE STIPULATION THAT THE ORIGIN OF THE
DEAD OWNER WILL BE CONSIDERED.

JEWISH CHARITIES, OR PERHAPS THE STATE OF ISRAEL,
ARE EXPECTED TO BENEFIT.

THE HEIRS TO THOSE DECLARED MISSING, BELIEVED
DEAD, WILL HAVE FIVE YEARS TO CLAIM THE DEPOSITS,

BUT SWISS AUTHORITIES BELIEVE THAT MOST OF THEM
ARE PROBABLY DEAD TOO, AND THERE WILL BE FEW APPLI-
CATIONS.

NOBODY KNOWS HOW MUCH IS INVOLVED, ALTHOUGH
THE SWISS BANKING ASSOCIATION HAS STATED THAT IT
MAY AMOUNT TO LESS THAN ONE MILLION FRANCS.

Dawlish read the newspaper cutting for the fourth
time.

'Money,' he said, 'Vulkan was just after money.'

'It's highly thought of,' I said.

'Money isn't everything,' said Dawlish seriously.

'No,' I said, 'but it buys everything.'

Dawlish said, 'I don't really understand,'

'There's nothing to understand,' I said. 'It's perfectly
simple. In a concentration camp there is a very wealthy
man named Broum. Broum's family left him about a quarter
of a million pounds in securities in a Swiss bank. Anyone
who can prove he is Broum can collect a quarter of a million
pounds. It's not hard to understand; Vulkan wanted those
papers to prove that he was Broum. All the other things
were incidental. Vulkan made Gehlen's people ask us for
the papers to make it appear more genuine.'

'What did the girl want?' said Dawlish.

'Semitsa,' I said, 'for the Israeli scientific programme.
She was an Israeli agent.'

'Um,' said Dawlish. 'Vulkan wanted to give Semitsa to
the Israeli Government. In exchange for this they would
endorse his claim to the Broum fortune. The Swiss banks
are very sensitive to the Israeli Government. It was a brilliant touch, that.'

'Nearly,' I said to Dawlish, 'very nearly.'

The system upon which we ran the department was that
I took responsibilty for all financial problems, although

what might be called 'accounts' were seen by Alice and I merely initialled them. It was my special knowledge of finance which had brought me into WOOC(P) and compelled them to put up with me. Dawlish ran through a foolscap sheet of notes that he had prepared. It was comfortable sitting back in Dawlish's battered armchair in front of the fire, which every now and then exploded a little firework of sparks.

Dawlish's voice summed up the circumstances of each problem neatly and cogently. There was little for me to say except yes or no, unless Dawlish required an explanation or amplification of my decision. He seldom did.

Suddenly he said, 'Are you asleep, old boy?'

'Just closed my eyes,' I explained. 'I concentrate better.'

Dawlish said, 'You look about all in, now one comes to look at you.'

'Yes,' I said. 'I feel like hell.'

'It's the business with Vulkan, isn't it, old lad?'

I didn't answer and Dawlish said, 'Of course it is – you've been fighting his battles here and down the road for the last eighteen months. It's a nasty business.' Dawlish stared into the fire for some time. 'Are you worried,' he finally asked, 'about the written report?'

'Well,' I said, 'it's tricky.'

'Um,' said Dawlish, 'it's tricky all right.' He closed the file on his knee. 'Well, leave this for now – go home and get some sleep.'

'I think I will,' I said. I suddenly felt absolutely done in.

Dawlish said, 'I think I might be able to get you that interest-free loan if you still want it. Was it eight hundred pounds?'

I said, 'Can we make it a thousand?'

'I daresay we might,' said Dawlish, 'and if you leave that gun here I'll get one of the messengers to return it to the War Office.' I gave him the Browning FN pistol and three 13-round magazines. Dawlish put them into a large manilla envelope and wrote 'gun' on the flap.

45

The End-game: this often centres around the queening of a
pawn. Here a sudden threat can arrive on home ground.

Tuesday, November 5th

I got to my flat at 10 A.M. The milkman was just delivering
next door and I bought two pints of Jersey and a half-
pound of butter from him.

'You've got the same trouble I've got,' the milkman said.

'What's that?' I said.

He slapped his belly with a noise that made his horse
flinch. 'You like the cream and butter.' Then he gave a
loud hoot. The horse walked slowly towards the next
house. 'Don't wear your old clothes tonight,' he said.

'Why?' I asked.

'They'll have you on top of the fire.' Then he laughed
again.

I had trouble opening the door, so much mail had
jammed there. Copies of *Time* and *Newsweek*, bills from
the electric company, adverts, fly to Paris for £9 17s, the
RSPCA needs old clothes, and a sale of fire-damaged car-
pets gave me a chance to buy them for only ten times what
they were worth. Inside the flat was a musty smell of stale
air and two pints of penicillin under the sink. I made coffee
and took that strange pleasure in handling well-known
implements in a well-known place. I lit the gas poker with
a comforting plop, placed a log on the fire and drew a

chair up to it. Outside, the dawn sunlight had given way to low dark cloud that was sitting there thinking of some way to unload snow over the city.

The whistling kettle interrupted me. I opened a tin of Blue Mountain coffee and poured a lot of it into the French drip-pot. The heavy aroma scented the air and from the living-room there was a crackle of sound as the log began to catch. I switched on the electric blanket and stood for a moment staring out of the bedroom window. Men were smashing dustbins on to huge council lorries and the publican was having his windows cleaned by Mr Boatwright. Down the road, the milkman was slapping his belly and laughing with the postman. I pulled the curtains close and as suddenly it was all gone. I went back to the kitchen and poured my coffee.

The sun was trying to penetrate the cloud layer and the man five leafless gardens along was setting fire to old garden rubbish and tidying his hideous little yard for winter's onslaught. The smoke from the bonfire rose straight up on the windless air. Several of the gardens had huge heaps of inflammable material and the summit of one of them was crowned with a crippled human shape wearing a top hat. November the fifth, I thought. I suppose that's what the milkman was laughing about. Even as I watched a little boy came out of the house next door and threw an armful of firewood on the heap.

I returned to my bonfire, prodded it with the toe of my boot and sipped at the strong black coffee. There was the third volume of Fuller's *Decisive Battles of the Western World* on the table. I opened it and removed the marker. For thirty minutes or so I read. A light sleet had begun to fall outside and the streets were deserted. There were a number of bottles on the coffee table. I poured myself a large measure of malt whisky and stared into the fire.

As I caught the rich aroma of the malt it all suddenly

came back to me. I was transferred to the dirty little dark garage with its spilt petrol and its dismantled engines. The smell of the whisky clawed at my nostrils and ripped open my memory. Johnnie was lying in a mixture of spilt petrol and pink frothy blood, and as I moved him I was covered in a Faustian nightmare. I sank into a vortex of imaginings in which Walpurgis Night and Vulkan and the smell of petrol and whisky were indissolubly linked. Four hours later I woke up sweating in front of a cold fireplace. I had just enough strength left to get undressed and go to bed.

Unless one is a master player the Queen's Gambit –
when a pawn is offered for sacrifice – is best declined.

Tuesday, November 5th

'Papers,' said Hallam. 'P-A-P-E-R-S.'

'Wait a moment,' I said. 'I've only just this moment
woken up. I've been working all night, hang on.' I put
down the phone and on the way to the bathroom downed
half a cup of cold coffee. I splashed lots of cold water on
to my face and looked at the time. It was 5.30 P.M. Already
it was dusk. The back-gardens all along the block were a
chessboard of lighted windows. The light inside the houses
was very yellow in the blue evening of a London winter.
I went back to the phone, 'That's better,' I said.

'There's been a frenzy here, I'll have you know,' said
Hallam. 'It's about the Broum documents. Where are they?'
Without waiting for a reply, he went on, 'We give you
full co-operation. Then you don't . . .'

''Arf a mo, Hallam,' I said. 'You told me to clear out of
Berlin and leave the documents with Vulkan.'

'That's all very well, old boy. Where is he and where
are they?'

'How the hell do I know?'

'You sure you haven't got them?'

'No,' I lied. I didn't want the documents but I was
fascinated to hear why just about everyone else did.

'Would you care to come across here for a drink?' said Hallam, changing his manner abruptly. 'Fireworks night tonight, you know. Come and have a drink. There are a couple of things I want to ask you.'

'OK,' I said. 'What time?'

'About an hour,' said Hallam. 'Do you think you could bring a bottle? You know how these firework parties are. In the dark people sneak off with the booze.'

'OK.'

'Jolly good,' said Hallam. 'Sorry if I was a little shirty just now. The PUS have been giving me a frightful telling-off about those papers.'

'Don't mention it.'

'That's jolly decent,' said Hallam.

'Yes,' I said before I rang off.

47

> The power of a queen often encourages its use single-handed. But an unsupported queen is in a dangerous position against skilfully used pawns.

Tuesday, November 5th

The fog had descended on the town. Not fog to stop the buses running or make the policemen use fog masks, but drifting areas of fog that would suddenly throw the headlight beam back through the windscreen. It had pedestrians wrapping their scarves a little higher than usual and coughing and spitting the sooty layer that formed on the mucous membrane like scale in a kitchen kettle.

At Parliament Square they had a couple of acetylene lamps roaring and flaring their distinctive green light. Two policemen in white raincoats stood in the centre of the road amid the swirling mist like spectral puppets, raising their white arms as the visibility lengthened and scampering aside when it closed in. Here and there around the entrances to the Tube stations, kids were begging for money for the guys, most of which were little more than shapeless sacks with a mask and a hat stuck on them. Near South Kensington Tube there was a wonderful one, though. It was as big as a scarecrow and was dressed in an old dinner-suit complete with white shirt and bow-tie, while on its head was a dented bowler. There were four children around it and they were doing great from what I saw of passers-by throwing them money. I found a place to park just across the road from Hallam's flat. There seemed to be far more parked cars than usual because Gloucester Road was the kind of district where drinking cocktails and setting off rockets would be the right thing to do for young executives who like to play with fire.

'Capital,' said Hallam. His eyes were a little shiny. I guessed he had been at the decanter himself before I arrived. He ushered me into the echoing hallway. From upstairs I could hear an old Frank Sinatra record. 'It's the animals I sympathize with,' said Hallam, walking down the corridor that was so dark I could hardly see him. As he opened the door to his room there was a halo of light around his silhouette. 'They get frightened,' he said.

Hallam's room looked different from the way it was, the last visit I paid there. There was a Braun stereo-radiogram across one wall and a superb carpet on the floor. Hallam stood by the door, smiling.

'Do you like it?' he asked. 'Sets the room off, I think.'

'It must have given your bank account a blood-letting, though.'

'Go on,' Hallam said. 'You're always thinking of money.'

I took off my coat. Hallam wanted to explain. 'My aunt died,' he said.

'No kidding,' I said. 'With something contagious?'

'Good heavens no,' said Hallam quickly, then he gave a hurried laugh. 'She died with too much money.'

'That's the most contagious thing of all,' I said, 'and what's more it can prove fatal.'

'You are a terrible tease,' said Hallam. 'I never know when you're serious.'

I threw my coat across the sofa without solving the enigma for him. I unwrapped the tissue paper from a bottle of rum and set it on the chest of drawers between the half-eaten pot of Tiptree marmalade and the Worcester sauce.

The pile of travel booklets had grown. The top one had a half-tone shot of a liner at dusk. Golden lights were twinkling through the portholes with a promise of cultured gaiety. In the foreground a woman with a small poodle in the bosom of her mink stole was emerging from the discreet legend, 'Luxury Cruises for the people who know.'

'Rum,' said Hallam, 'that's very nice. I'm just taking a bottle of Algerian wine.' He moved the wrapped bottle of Algerian close to the Lemon Hart Rum; then we stood looking at them for a moment. 'What do you say to a little drink now?' said Hallam.

'I'd say hello,' I said.

Hallam beamed. 'What about a little rum?'

'What sort?' I said.

'That sort,' said Hallam. 'The bottle you've brought with you.'

'OK,' I said.

Hallam bustled about squeezing some lemons and boiling water on the tiny gas ring in the fireplace.

'How's Grannie Dawlish?' he asked as he crouched over the kettle.

'Getting older,' I said.

'Ah, aren't we all?' said Hallam. 'Good chap Dawlish, in his way.'

I said nothing. Hallam added, 'Tends to play the heavy father a little. You know – Whitehall Top Level stuff, but a decent cove in his way.'

'Didn't know you knew each other,' I said.

'Yes, Dawlish was at Home Office for a little while. He had that office next to the lift on the same floor as I'm on. He said the noise of the lift got him down; otherwise I was going to move into there when he went.'

Hallam stood up with two steaming glasses of drink. 'Here we are,' said Hallam. 'Taste that.'

I tasted it. It was sweet combination of lemon juice,

cloves, sugar and hot water, with a trace of butter on the top. 'Not exactly alcoholic,' I said.

'Of course not, silly. I haven't put the rum in yet.' He uncorked the rum bottle and poured a slug into both glasses. Outside there was a sudden spatter of small explosions as a jumping cracker exploded.

'I personally have always been against it,' said Hallam.

'Alcohol?' I said.

'Fireworks night,' said Hallam.

I went across to the sofa, sat down and began to search through Hallam's gramophone-record collection. He had a lot of modern music. I picked out Berg's Violin Concerto. 'Can we hear this?' I said.

'Play this one. It's wonderful.' He shuffled through his collection and found Sam's favourite: Schönberg's Variations for wind band.

'It retains a strong melody even when the tonality is abandoned,' Hallam explained. 'A remarkable work. Remarkable.'

He played the haunting discordant work from which it seemed I could never escape. It could be just a coincidence, of course, but I didn't think it was. While the music played I could hear the odd bang and shout outside and sometimes the whizz and spatter of a rocket ascending. When the music stopped Hallam fixed us another drink. As he said, in the dark people at the party wouldn't notice whether it was full or not. Whenever there was a very loud bang Hallam went across to comfort one of the cats.

'Confucius,' he called. He had a special high-pitched voice that he only used for talking to the cats. 'Fang.' Fang was something like a large bath-loofah with a leg at each corner. It moved lazily from under the sofa, about four paces to the centre of the carpet, deflated itself gently and went to sleep.

'They don't seem very frightened.'

'They are all right now,' said Hallam. 'It's later when the big ones go off. I shall give them a sleeping draught before we go out.'

'If you give that one a sleeping draught it will fall into its saucer of milk.'

Hallam chuckled discreetly. 'Where's my Confucius?'

Confucius was the active one of the household. It came from its curled-up pose on the bed in that cross-eyed, bandy-legged way that Siamese cats do and clambered with unfaltering ease on to Hallam's shoulder. It gave a short regal purr and then Hallam stroked its head. 'Wonderful creatures,' he said, 'so dignified.'

'Yes,' I said.

'We shall need your help,' Hallam said.

'I'm no good with cats,' I said.

'No,' said Hallam abruptly. He picked Confucius gently off his shoulder and put him on to the carpet. 'Your help with the Broum papers, I mean.'

'Is that so?' I said. I took out my Gauloises.

'Could I?' said Hallam; I gave him one. He placed it precisely in relation to a gold cigarette lighter and lit it. 'One way or another, you are the only one who can help. The department is extraordinary about documents like that. I know I said give them to Vulkan, but I didn't know the department would create such a fuss.' There was an explosion and then another from the street outside. Hallam stooped down to pat the cats. 'There there, my lovely. It's all right.'

'It will cost money,' I said.

'How much?' said Hallam. He didn't say, 'Very well' or 'Out of the question' or 'I'll refer it to higher authority'. I couldn't see the Home Office paying to retrieve things that they owned. It wasn't like them somehow. I said, 'How much? That's difficult. What do you think the traffic will bear?'

'It's the time factor,' said Hallam. 'Are they in London?'

'I'm not sure,' I said.

'For goodness' sake be reasonable,' said Hallam. 'I'm supposed to phone the PUS tonight at his private number and tell him that the documents are safely in our possession.'

There was a meek tapping at the door. 'Wait a moment,' Hallam said to me. He opened the door about six inches. 'Yes?'

A voice from outside the door said, 'She won't let me do it in the passage, Mr Hallam.'

'She's an old busybody,' said Hallam. 'Do it outside.'

'On the pavement?' said the voice.

'Yes, under a street lamp,' said Hallam.

'They are throwing a lot of fireworks about tonight, the young boys.'

'Well,' said Hallam in a bracing tone, 'it won't take you more than ten minutes, will it?'

'No, that's right,' said the voice and Hallam closed the door and turned back to me.

'Foggy tonight,' said Hallam to me.

'Yes, in patches,' I said.

Hallam pursed his mouth like he was sucking a lemon. 'Taste it. I can taste the fog in the air.' He went across to the little writing-desk and lifted the lid to reveal the wash-basin. He rinsed his hands under the hot-water tap and there was a little boom and a flash as the gas heater began to operate. He dried his hands meticulously, opened a cupboard above the sink and took out a throat spray.

'I suffer on the foggy nights,' Hallam said. He said this while spraying the back of his throat. He stopped spraying, turned to me and said the same thing again so that I could understand him.

Outside the man had almost finished repairing Hallam's puncture. We drove in my car with Hallam shouting directions. The fog was worse around here. It was a great green swirling bank, punctuated by dusty yellow orbs of street lamps. It tasted sour and caked the nostrils. The fog was a wall that echoed back the sound of footsteps before swallowing the sound. A heavy lorry ground past in bottom gear, following the pavement edge anxiously. A man walked slowly, guiding a car with a flashlight, and behind that a little convoy came like a line of coal barges towed by an adventurous tug. I let in the clutch and followed them. 'It's always bad around here,' Hallam said.

48

Pawns can only move forward. They can never retreat.

Tuesday, November 5th

It was there in the sky: red. Red flickering brown, red
flashing pink, but always like some sinister dusk or neo-
lithic dawn. Chimneys were drawn up tightly in soldierly
rows across the skyline and as we turned the corner a long
low street of artisans' houses was bright with the firelight,
like some Kensington speculator had given them the pink-
distemper-and-brass-lion's-head-knocker treatment.

The crash of fireworks went on all the time and the
tear-away sound of rockets wooshed and pattered way
overhead. The lines of windows were twisting with
reflected flame and suddenly the bonfire appeared from
round the corner. It was a huge flaming altar of fruit boxes,
heaped together and twisted with flames into a fiery cubist
nightmare. The apex of the flame was about thirty feet
high and from the very tip a whirling vortex of sparks
moved violently upwards on currents of heat, and then
slid sideways towards the cold ground like a swarm of
wounded fireflies.

The bonfire was in the centre of a large open site that
had probably been flat since the bomb-damage squads of
the war had checked the number of corpses against the
list of residents, sprayed the site with chemicals and framed
it with the fencing that now was bent and trampled. The

site was covered with irregular clumps of waist-high weeds and nettles. I wondered if there was anything here that Dawlish would like for his garden.

From the far side of the site there was a sudden patch-work of flame. Tangled skeins of yellow, unravelled spools of green and neat scarlet patches tumbled across the ground like an upset sewing box.

'Toes,' said a laconic voice behind me. I turned to see two men pushing a huge Victorian pram full of old card-board cartons and pieces of wood. Behind them there was a hoarding full of wrestling advertisements. 'Doctor Death,' said one of them, 'versus the South London Vampire – Camberwell Baths.'

There were lots of people scattered across the site in large groups and small groups, not mixing but holding their own little parties. We walked across the uneven ground, avoiding the large pieces of junk that had been dumped there over the past twelve months. Only non-inflammable items had survived the survey of the bonfire tenders. As we skirted a deep hole a group of men were sharply silhouetted on to the white-hot centre of the bon-fire. I watched the two men who had passed us throw chunks of wood from the pram high on to the pyre. On the other side of the fire the spectators were drawn as if with yellow chalk on a blackboard, but each figure had only one side depicted, their backs melting into the dark-ness and the haze of the remaining wisps of fog.

Behind the fire, four men were standing round one of the few trees that remained on the site. I saw the sulphur-ous yellow glare of a firework. Then the group and the tree disappeared into the darkness again. There was a tiny flicker of yellow flame as one of the men thumbed his cigarette lighter. One said, 'It's gone out' and someone else said, 'Go and blow on it, Charlie,' and they all laughed. All around us there was the flare and bang of fireworks and a pitter-patter overhead where rockets were spitting at the stars. There was a soft buzz as something landed at my feet. 'Oops a daisy,' said a fat woman walking towards me and we both leapt aside as there was a great smash of sound.

Hallam had dropped behind to have a cigarette without offering them to me. I could see the outline of figures against the light reflected in the house-fronts, but it was hard to know which one was Hallam until there was the loud cloth-tearing sound of a rocket, then the intense white light of the parachute flare which it had contained. Suddenly the whole site was as light as midday. I looked back in the direction we had come. I saw Hallam. He was dressed in his black melton overcoat and bowler hat with a bright yellow silk scarf. The thing I noticed about him was that he was carrying a .45 pistol and it was pointing directly at me. The flare surprised him as much as it did me. I saw him push the huge pistol into the front of his coat. The flare was beginning to die now. I looked around and saw the small crater I had almost fallen into. I dropped into it as the flare went out. It was very dark, the fire was behind me and Hallam in front; I peeped over the edge of the hole to see if I could see him.

He was standing in the same place. He had wrapped his scarf around the gun. Two old women were picking their way carefully past the crater. 'Look out, Mabel,' said one of them and the other one caught sight of me and said loudly, 'Cor, look at him, dear. He's had one over the eight, all right.' The other one said, 'One over the eighteen, you mean.'

It was all Hallam needed to locate me. I decided to get up right away and get close to the two old ladies. There was a crash and rip of a .45 bullet passing above my cranium. 'Oops,' said the old ladies. 'There's a loud one.' Hallam wanted me to stay right where I was until he came over to do his task and then leave me there. The two old ladies said, 'Aren't they terrible?'

I felt in my pocket for the fireworks I had brought and found a 'Tiny Demon'. I lit and carefully threw it at Hallam. The explosion had him leaping aside and a man who saw it said, 'Stop throwing those bangers, you hooligans. I'll have the law on you.'

I lit another and threw that at Hallam too. He was ready this time but the blast had him keeping his distance. A man passing by said, 'Are you all right down there?' and his friend said, 'It's just an excuse to get plastered for some of them,' and they hurried away.

Behind Hallam, the fireworks were bright green and yellow, popping and sending little showers of golden rain into the sky. It gave me a chance to range him in. I watched the fine red tip of the firework land near Hallam's feet and for a second or so he didn't see it and when he did he moved fast. There was a big blast but Hallam was merely a little shaken. I looked around for some way out of this fiasco. The whole site was crowded with people coming and going, blissfully unaware of Hallam trying to kill me.

A man was looking into the crater, saying, 'Have you slipped?'

'I'm not drunk,' I said. 'I've twisted my ankle.' The man reached down a large hard hand to help me. I came to my feet like a man with a twisted ankle and there was a stab of flame as Hallam fired again.

Someone from the darkness yelled, 'Bloke there is holding bangers in his hand – you don't want to do that, mate.' Hallam shuffled to one side a little self-consciously. 'I'll be OK now,' I said to my benefactor. Nearby there was a whirling buzz as a Catherine wheel tore a golden hole in the night.

As the man moved away there was another pistol shot and nearby someone laughed. Hallam had fired high for

fear of hitting the man, and I started to think that he had
decided to back me up against the bonfire, with the idea
of tipping me in. All sorts of ideas occurred to me such as
falling to the ground when I heard the next bullet in the
hope that Hallam would come within striking distance.
That plan assumed Hallam would be careless; there was no
reason to think that Hallam would be careless. To my right
there was the choking sound of a roman candle sending
livid balls of fire high above my head. Two red spots moved
towards me. One said, 'Where did you put it?' The other
one said, 'Under this bush, nearly half a bottle; Haig and
Haig.' They moved past. The other two men of a party of
four lit another roman candle.

I had lost sight of Hallam, which made me a little nervous. I knew that as soon as the second roman candle went
up Hallam would pinpoint me and he didn't have so many
rounds left in the pistol. The next shot might well prove
fatal.

I moved in among the men and their roman candles like
David among the Philistines. I put my foot on the roman
candle and ground it into the earth just as the ignition
began. 'Here, here,' shouted the biggest one of the men.
'What the —— hell you think you are on?'

'I'm doing a trick,' I said. 'Hold that.' I took the bottle
of rum out of my pocket and gave it to him. 'Suppose I
don't want to,' he said. 'Then me and my mates will smash
your head in,' I said in a surly voice. He backed away
hurriedly. I searched through their huge box of fireworks
and found a parachute flare. I put the stick of it into the
bottle and lit it. There was a great roar of sparks and it
took off to burst in a great white glow that momentarily
dimmed the bonfire. I stayed close to the tree. There was
a great 'Ooohh' and 'Aaahh' as the rocket burst, and I
picked out Hallam in his bowler hat standing near the old
Victorian perambulator. I had wedged three more rockets

into the crutch of the tree. Hallam looked around feverishly. I depressed the elevation of the first rocket and lined
it up with Hallam. I lit it.

'Steady on,' said one of the men.

'Come away, Charlie,' said his friend. 'He's going to do
someone an injury and I'm not going to be around.'

As I was lighting the second rocket, the first one began
to fire sparks, then it gained power and roared forward
like a bazooka shell. It passed about six feet over Hallam's
head and about four feet to the right side. I lit a firecracker
and let it burn its fuse well down before hurling it towards
Hallam's feet. By this time he was looking around and he
saw the fire of the second rocket begin. There was a flash
as he fired a pistol and a chunk of tree ripped a hole in
my sleeve. The second rocket roared towards Hallam. It's
easy to see a rocket. It leaves a trail like a tracer bullet.
He moved easily to one side and the rocket thudded harm-
lessly into the ground just beyond where he had been
standing. He fired again and there was a crunch of breaking
wood. I peeped over the crutch of the tree and saw a great
snowstorm of sparks, like it was raining golden sovereigns.
Beyond Hallam there was the asterisks of sparklers.

Nearer to me a man said, 'Well, I'll tackle him. I paid
for those rockets and I'm going to let them off.' His voice
was slurred with drink and I thought at first that it was
the men who had been looking for the Haig and Haig
coming back to remonstrate with me, but they walked past
the tree still talking. Hallam began to load the pistol. I
could just see his movements in the gloom. To his right
the bonfire was burning brightly; the wind had caught it,
and the side which had hitherto been hardly alight suddenly caught fire with a roar.

I groped around feverishly for more fireworks. There
was only one more rocket and some roman candles and
groups of tiny bangers with rubber bands round them. I

grabbed one bundle, lit them with my hand shaking so much I could hardly hold the match and tossed them in the direction of Hallam. I put the last rocket in the branch of the tree and lit it just as the bundle of bangers went off with a huge crash. It put Hallam off guard. My last rocket tore a yellow gash in the fabric of night. At first I thought it would hit him, but at the last minute he saw it coming and moved aside. It went into the soft earth a few feet behind him and expired softly. Two shots ripped notches into the tree. I shrank down behind it with the idea of running for the nearest cover. I looked at the brightly lit ground around me. There was no cover. Nothing between me and Hallam now.

I looked around the shadow side of the tree fairly low down, and as I did I saw what happened. The second or third rocket lying on the ground suddenly obediently discharged its flare. I saw Hallam's whole figure silhouetted in the great white light behind him. I could read the wrestling ad about Dr Death. Hallam half turned, probably thinking that he was being attacked from the rear and as he did I saw his scarf was alight. The scarf hung from his hand like a great flaming walking stick and he beat it against himself to put the flames out. Suddenly there was an enormous sheet of flame into which Hallam disappeared. It flickered for a moment and I saw Hallam's body twisted in the very centre of the flame. Then suddenly there was a roar like a jet motor, and where there had been flame there was nothing but a great white fireball, so bright that the bonfire looked dull and yellow. Some vintage, that Algerian wine. It was a Molotov cocktail to dispose of my mortal remains.

'Cor, what a beauty.'

'Hello, somebody's thrown a match into a box of fireworks; easy to do.'

'A few bobs' worth of whizzers gone up there, Mabel.'

'I bet my dog's going mad.'

'Mind how you go there, there's a hole there. One drunk feller has fallen into it already.'

'I wonder who clears it all up.'

'We've got some cold sausages in the fridge or we can stop off for some fried fish and chips.'

'Look at that green one.'

'Oooooohh, what a terrible smell of burning food. Look at that smoke.'

'Leave off, George.'

'Hello, there's a crowd gathering over there. I'll bet there's been an accident.'

49

If a player is not in check but can only make a move
that will place him in check; this is stalemate and is
scored as a draw.

Wednesday, November 6th

'Well, you had better not put any of that in the report,'
said Dawlish. 'The Cabinet will go dotty if you've been
mixed up with two nasty businesses in one week.'

'How many am I allowed per week?' I said.

Dawlish just sucked an empty pipe.

'How many?' I asked again.

'As one man who hates violence to another,' said Dawlish
patiently, 'you are developing an unfortunate habit of
being nearby when people commit suicide.'

'You are damn right,' I told him. 'I've spent my whole
adult life being nearby, watching half the human race com-
mitting suicide, and from where I'm sitting the other half
seem hell-bent on following suit.'

'Don't go on,' said Dawlish. 'You've made your point.'
There was a long silence with just the ticking of the clock.
It was 2.30 in the middle of the night. We always seemed
to be in Dawlish's office in the middle of the night.

Dawlish fiddled around with some papers in the tiny
light on his desk. Ouside I could hear lorries laden with
deliveries of milk roaring and clinking at breakneck speed
into the city. I sat in front of the tiny coal fire that no one

in the building except Dawlish could ever get to burn, sipped his best brandy and waited while Dawlish got ready to tell me something. By now I could recognize the signs. 'It's my fault,' said Dawlish. 'My fault that this happened.' I said nothing. Dawlish came across to the fire and sat down in the biggest armchair.

'You checked . . .' Dawlish spoke to the mantelpiece rather than to me. '. . . that Hallam was to leave the Civil Service next week?'

'Yes,' I said.

'You know why?' he asked.

I sipped my brandy and took my time about replying. I knew that Dawlish wouldn't hurry me. 'He was a bad security risk,' I said.

'My report said he was *not a good* security risk,' said Dawlish emphasizing the difference. '*My* report,' he repeated.

'Yes,' I said.

'You knew.'

'You kept telling me not to ill-treat him,' I said. Dawlish nodded. 'That's right, I did,' he agreed. We both stared into the fire for a long time, me sipping brandy, Dawlish with both palms pressed flat together and the two index fingers rubbing the tip of his nose.

'I don't like it,' said Dawlish. 'You know my views.'

'Yes,' I said.

'I sent in a long supplementary attached to his file, and three memos about him in particular and homosexuals in general. Do you know what happened?'

'What?' I said.

'A certain hooligan in the Cabinet' – I had never heard Dawlish describe his superiors in quite such terms – 'had Ross at the War Office check *me* to see whether *I* have homosexual tendencies.' He leaned forward and prodded the fire gently with the poker. 'Whether *I* have them.'

LEN DEIGHTON

'That's the way your mind works if you are a politician,'
I said. I suppose I smiled. Dawlish said sadly, 'It's not
funny.' He poured me another brandy and decided to have
one himself. 'That's what happens once you start moving
along these sort of lines. Look at the Americans. They
have invented some quality called un-Americanism just as
though Americanism were a concept of an individual
instead of a Government's concept. There are strong resem-
blances between Americanism, communism and Aryanism:
all are Government ideas and therefore will naturally
describe characteristics of the easily governed; other differences are minor.'

'Yes,' I said.

Dawlish wasn't talking to me, he was just thinking
aloud. I wanted to know what would happen about the
Hallam disaster but I would let Dawlish get to it in his
own way.

Dawlish said, 'That's what one doesn't like about this
homosexual business. We may as well say that all women
are a security risk because *they* can have illicit relations
with men. Or vice versa.'

'For those who like their vice versa,' I said.

Dawlish nodded. 'The only solution is to take the social
pressures off the homosexuals. These damned security
hunts just put more pressure on. If someone gets on to one
of these johnnies before we do he's got an extra threat for
him – losing his job; if they weren't going to lose their
job, they might ask to have "homosexual" entered on their
dossiers voluntarily. If they then had someone pressuring
them, they could report to their security people and we'd
have some sort of chance of dealing with it. This damned
system, all that happens is that we make enemies.' I
nodded.

'Don't even report to me,' said Dawlish, and I realized
that part of his mind had been thinking of the Hallam

296

situation all the time. 'Just act as if you knew nothing whatsoever.'

'That comes naturally to me,' I said.

'That's right,' said Dawlish. He sucked his pipe and said, 'Poor old Hallam, what a way to go,' two or three times and then finally, 'Are you happy, that's the main thing?'

'Sure,' I said. 'An all-laughing, all-dancing, all-singing, Technicolor wide-screen massacre. Why wouldn't I be happy?'

'Desperate diseases require desperate remedies,' said Dawlish.

'Says who?' I said.

'Guy Fawkes, I believe,' said Dawlish. He was just great at quoting people.

I said, 'Why don't you and me clear off to Zürich and claim the quarter of a million? We've got the proof.' I tapped the envelope full of Broum.

'For the department?' said Dawlish, walking back to his desk.

'Us,' I said.

'It would mean living with all those Swiss,' said Dawlish. 'They'd never let us grow weeds there.' He opened a drawer, dropped the documents into it and locked it, before coming back to the fireside.

'Shall we try and get that bastard Mohr?' I said.

'You are a callow youth,' said Dawlish. 'If we tell Bonn he is a war criminal, either they won't claim him at all or else they will give him some nice fat government job. You know what always happens.'

'You're right,' I said, and we both sat quietly staring into the fire. Every now and then Dawlish said how amazing it was that Vulkan never really existed, and poured me another drink. 'I'll tell Stok about Mohr,' I said.

'Do that,' said Dawlish, 'and we'll watch what happens.'

'If anything,' I said.

'So Vulkan never really existed?'

'Vulkan existed all right,' I said. 'He was a concentration-camp guard until a wealthy prisoner (who had been an assassin for the Communist Parties) arranged to have him killed. This man was Broum, and an SS medical officer named Mohr . . .'

'The one in Spain now. Our Mohr.'

I nodded. '. . . made a deal. The SS officer staged a death scene and made sure that Broum was believed dead by all the prisoners. Broum meanwhile dressed as a German soldier and disappeared. In 1945 even being a German soldier was better than being a murderer. What's more Broum (or Vulkan) got along very well financially even without the £250,000, but it was nice to think it was there waiting. Perhaps he intended to leave it to someone. Perhaps on his death-bed, beyond the reach of the guillotine, he was going to say who he really was. No. It was this new law about unclaimed property that made him suddenly start to move. What he needed was a way of proving he was Broum and then of not being Broum just as quickly.'

'It's astonishing,' said Dawlish, 'to think of a Jewish prisoner who had suffered so much going all through his life saying that he had been a Nazi guard in a concentration camp.'

'He didn't know whether he was up or down,' I said. 'He came to the conclusion that if you threw enough money around you don't have enemies. Vulkan, Broum, whatever you want to call him, his final allegiance was to cash.'

'Was it all worth it?' said Dawlish.

I said, 'We are talking about a quarter of a million pounds; it's a hell of a lot of money.'

'You misunderstand me,' said Dawlish. 'I meant, did he need to live in fear? After all, this was an old wartime political assassination . . .'

'Carried out by order of the Communist Party,' I finished.

'Would you like to enter present-day France with a tag like that?'

Dawlish gave a sour smile. 'Communist Party,' he repeated. 'Do you think that Stok knew everything all the time? Knew who Vulkan really was, and who he had been and whom he had killed? They could really have him in a cleft stick if they had all that on their war-time files, squeezing him until he cracked?'

'I thought about that,' I said.

'You are sure about all this?' said Dawlish anxiously. 'It's not just guesswork, the dead man was Broum?'

'Positive,' I said. 'It was the scars that settled it. Grenade confirmed it yesterday. I sent Albert six bottles of whisky on expenses.'

'Six bottles of whisky in exchange for losing one good operative doesn't seem a good way to do business.'

'No,' I said. Alice brought the coffee in Dawlish's one-and-sixpenny cups from Portobello Road. Alice never went home.

'I guessed in a way,' I said, 'when the old man said that a doctor in a concentration camp can even cure you. Cure, you see – to be released – or to die. It could be arranged by a doctor willing to fiddle a certificate of death. The extraordinary aspect of Broum's situation was the way he *must* impersonate his victim – Vulkan the guard – because in doing so Vulkan was still alive and his first victim assassinated by someone else.'

'And Hallam?'

'As soon as he was offered money he co-operated with Vulkan to the utmost. He was the only person authorized to issue documents of that sort. Without his connivance it wouldn't have been so easy for them.'

'Hallam didn't have much to lose, if he was getting the sack as a security risk.'

'That's it,' I said. 'It all depended upon me getting

LEN DEIGHTON

panicky when they made Semitsa persona non grata right at the last minute. Their theory was that I'd clear out and leave Vulkan holding the baby.'

'They trusted Stok to deliver Semitsa?'

'Hilarious, isn't it?' I said. 'They were so pleased with themselves that they couldn't bear to consider that Stok might be smarter than them. That he might be just kidding around to see what he could find out.'

'But it was obvious, you said.'

'Well,' I said, 'Stok and I are in the same business – we understand each other only too well.'

'There were people,' said Dawlish drily, 'who thought you might end up as his assistant.'

'You weren't one of them, I trust?'

'Gracious no,' said Dawlish. 'I said that *he* would end up as yours.'

50

Originally the piece we now call a queen was a
counsellor or Government adviser.

Thursday, November 7th

It was just like Hallam had said, there were so many accidents
on November 5th that the 'awful death of man on fireworks
night' didn't get into the national press at all and the local
paper only gave it a couple of paragraphs and that was
mostly devoted to a spokesman from the RSPCA.

November 7th was the anniversary of the Bolshevik Rev-
olution. Jean gave me four aspirins, which was her friendly
overture, and Alice a coffee made with milk, which was
her cure-all. I sent Colonel Stok an Eton tie from Bond
Street, which was my revolutionary gesture.

The Mother-in-law's Tongue was coming along nicely.
Jean said that on the window-sill over the radiator was
the best place for it and it certainly seemed to thrive there.
Dawlish had decided that he was going to spend a few
days busy in the country, which I suppose was to make
himself scarce. He had taken Chico with him so the office
was quiet enough for me to finish *It pays to increase your
word power*. My rating was 'fair'.

They wouldn't let us offer Harvey Newbegin a job partly
because he was foreign, and partly because I wore woollen
shirts and said 'like' instead of 'as though'. This left us
weaker in both Berlin and Prague.

'Going to the Home Office on Sunday?' Jean asked. 'You have an invitation. It's the Remembrance Service. I said I'd phone them back this morning. There are only twelve places in Hallam's room.'

'I promised to go,' I said.

'Is it true that Hallam is in hospital?' said Jean.

'Ask them,' I said.

'I heard . . .'

'Ask them,' I said.

'I did,' said Jean. 'They were very short and rude.'

'That's OK then,' I said. 'HO are like London theatres: if they answer politely, you can be sure the show is a little shaky.'

'Yes,' said Jean. She gave me a memo from Dawlish that said that some of the Broum documents had been damaged by grease and would I please submit a full explanation in writing. There was another document that authorized the cashier's department to pay me £1,000 subject to my signing that it could be deducted from my pay over a two-year period.

I said to Jean, 'How would you like a spin in the country this week-end in a new car?'

'Perhaps,' said Jean.

'I've got every kind of eyebrow pencil.'

'In that case,' said Jean, 'how can I refuse?'

'Friday then,' I said. 'Back Sunday morning.'

'Without fail,' said Jean. 'I'm looking after Hallam's cats.'

51

Repetition rule: it is a rule of chess that when the same sequence recurs three times the game can be terminated.

Sunday, November 10th

It is one of those misty London mornings when the British Travel and Holiday Association stock up with colour photos. Whitehall is a vast stadium of grey granite and thin white geometrical shapes have appeared on the black roadway overnight so that representatives of the whole nation can stand in their allotted places. Soldiers in black bearskins and grey overcoats are lined up to form three sides of a square and a cruel wind blows across the scene that so closely resembles a military execution. The pipes and drums are playing the Skye Boat Song. A general fidgets with a sword that the wind has wrapped into his greatcoat and the cocked hats flutter like frightened hens.

An aged civil servant beside me says, 'Here comes Her Majesty', as the Queen steps out of the front door below us. Dominating the whole scene is the gleaming stone pillar of the Cenotaph like the freshly built leg of a new overpass. Beyond the memorial the Chapel Royal choirboys in their bright scarlet Tudor costumes are blowing on their blue hands.

Mrs Meynard is laying rows of coffee cups across the desk behind us. I hear her say, 'Mr Hallam is not well, sir. He's having a few days off.' There is polite condolence.

'Nothing serious,' Mrs Meynard adds in a motherly voice. 'Just been overdoing it.' She didn't say what he'd been overdoing.

'Waaaaaahhhhhh.' The throaty cry of a drill sergeant bounces down the lines of bearskins and bayonets. Senile statesmen stand pierced by the chilly damp November air that has called so many predecessors away.

'Yip.' Fleshy palms smack artfully loosened metal as a few hundred rifles click into rows.

There is a sudden cannonade of artillery rumbling across the low cloud as Big Ben tolls eleven. Blancoed webbing and polished metal shine in the dull wintry light and there is a sudden flash of brandished trumpets. The notes of the Last Post crawl dolefully up the still thoroughfare as a thousand stand tensely silent.

Across the silent, wet street, a newspaper tumbles gently like an urban tumbleweed. It floats just buoyant on the wind, kisses a traffic sign, lightly dabs a slide trombone and plasters itself across army boots. The newspaper is rain-soaked to a dull yellow colour but the large headline is blunt and legible. 'Berlin – a new crisis?'

Poisonous Insecticides

In the late 'thirties a German scientist, Gerald Schrader, discovered a group of organic phosphorus insecticides from which Parathion[1] and Malathion were developed. The German Government immediately put a security blank over all this work, seeing the potential value of nerve gas as a weapon. They filmed the effect of them upon concentration-camp prisoners. The films and the research came into Allied hands during the war and the research was continued by UK, USSR and USA and still continues to be important as a military weapon.

There are many stories demonstrating the enormous potency of these poisons, like the crop-sprayer who reached his hand into a tank of it to retrieve a nozzle and was dead within twenty-four hours.

Dr Samuel Gershon and Dr F.H. Shaw (Departments of Pharmacology and Psychiatry, University of Melbourne, Australia) reported in the *Lancet* on sixteen cases of schizophrenic symptoms, depression, blackouts, impaired memories and inability to concentrate among horticultural workers where this group of insecticides was used.

Organo-phosphorus compounds although they break down quickly have a dangerous tendency to 'potentiate' one another. That is to say, two tiny harmless amounts get together and make a lethal combination.

[1] Parathion is a popular suicide drug.

Gehlen Organization

Gehlen came from an old Westphalian family but the family motto – *Laat vaaren niet* – was Flemish. The motto means, 'Never give up'. Gehlen entered the Reichswehr under General von Seeckt in 1921 and was seconded to military intelligence even before Hitler took power.

The Abwehr department he made his own was Group III F, directed against the USSR. By 1941 Major Gehlen was in charge of Abwehr Ost. His districts included the Ukraine and Byelorussia. He received many decorations including the Knight's Cross. When he compiled a report suggesting that the Germans formed a resistance based upon the Polish Resistance, it was suppressed by Himmler for being 'defeatist'.

In 1945 he was in a better position to summarize the world's position than Hitler was. Gehlen went to the Abwehr Archives at Zossen[1] and burned every document there – after microfilming it and locking the microfilms into steel canisters.

Gehlen allowed himself to be captured by the Americans and, after a little trouble, gained an interview with Brigadier-General Patterson, the US Army Intelligence chief.

The US Army gave Gehlen the 'Rudolf Hess Wohngemeinde'[2] – which was a large modern housing estate built for Waffen SS officers in 1938 – they put stars and stripes

---

[1] Now a Soviet Army Intelligence Unit.
[2] Pullach, Bavaria, not very far from Dachau.

on the roof, US Army sentries on the gates and lots and lots of dollars in the kitty. He was allowed to call upon old comrades of the Sicherheitsdienst and the Abwehr and some of his agents abroad scarcely had a break in their payments and communications.

The Abwehr

Nomenclature.

Group 1.   Intelligence.

Group 2.   Sabotage (a very small group consisting mostly of a structure without operatives).

Group 3.   Counter-Intelligence.

This group is sub-divided according to function and a suffix letter is added to indicate its activities as follows:

H = Army

M = Navy

L = Air Force

F = The detection and penetration of enemy intelligence.

Soviet Security Systems

One still hears Russian security men speak of Chekist opera-
tors. Originally these were an anti-sabotage, anti-
revolutionary force which became a battle gendarmerie
during the civil war and was empowered to hold courts
martial and execute Whites, or Reds who were getting a
little bleached. It remained as a part of the army although
nowadays has become merely a slang word. The actual
organization underwent many changes of structure, responsibility and name. It became GPU, OGPU, NKVD,
NKGB and in 1946 split into MVD and MGB. The latter
was renamed KGB in 1954; it is responsible for the most
vital part of security and intelligence at home and overseas.
(The MVD now handles police, prisons, immigration, highway police and fire services.) Stok's branch of KGB is the
counter-intelligence unit GUKR.

In 1937 Marshal Tukhachevsky tried to throw off Chekist control and was executed for plotting with Trotsky to
betray Russia to Hitler. Thousands of Red Army officials
were executed at the same period and the Red Army was
in bad repute. At the twentieth Party Congress in 1956
there was a movement towards proving the innocence of
the executed men.

Colonel Stok had had extensive political-military experience, starting from when he stormed the Winter Palace in
Leningrad in 1917. He worked with Antonov Ovseyenko
when the latter was military adviser in Barcelona. Some
say that he was responsible for Ovseyenko's removal. As

LEN DEIGHTON

a KGB officer, Stok's loyalty is to the Communist Party, but as an officer he must sometimes sympathize with the aims of the professional soldiers with whom he works. Stok is not a member of GRU (military intelligence) which is entirely separate.

APPENDIX 5

French Security System

A very complex arrangement of interlapping units which – like all intelligence units – tend to develop special allegiances.

The Secret Service as such is the top dog. I will not elaborate on that. Next in importance is the DST. (Direction de la Surveillance du Territoire) of which Grenade is a member. This unit combines the function of what is, in Britain, the Special Branch with MI5.

Thirdly, there is the General Intelligence which holds the files of politicians and trade union leaders. It is comprised of two parts; one part overlaps with the Sûreté Nationale and the other with the Paris Police Prefecture.

The Sûreté Nationale also leads a life of its own and has all sorts of specialized departments – from gambling to the huge phone-tapping department. The Ministry of the Interior controls General Intelligence as well as having its own private intelligence unit rather like WOOC(P) except that while Dawlish is responsible to the Cabinet via the Prime Minister, the French Minister gets access to his reports *before* the President.

The military have their own intelligence networks which co-operate with the above departments now and again.

The lowest echelon of agent consists of the so-called *barbouzes* or semi-official informers, who often speed up a slow season by fomenting anti-government plots in order to expose them.

APPENDIX 6

Official Secrets Act 1911

(as amended by the OS Acts of 1920 and 1939)

Section 6 provides that the police (or etc) may question someone suspected of having information in regard to a breach of Section 1 of the Act. Failure to answer such questions is punishable as a misdemeanour. It is under this section that results can be obtained from uncooperative persons. The law does not provide that Section 6 can be invoked to solve a breach of the less serious Section 2 of the Act. (The maximum penalty for misdemeanour is two years' imprisonment.) But until the information is gained by means of Section 6, it is not always clear whether Section 1 or Section 2 is the relevant one (if you see what I mean!).

Another interesting aspect of the application of the OS Acts is the use to which the prosecution puts the charge of 'conspiring to contravene the OS Acts', for a conspiracy charge automatically renders the Attorney-General's permission unnecessary and gives the Crown a catch-all way to plaster the sum of the charges across all the persons charged (some of whom might not have otherwise been liable for prosecution). This convenience is illustrated by the frequency with which the conspiracy charge arises in prosecutions under the Official Secrets Act.